CLOSER

CLOSER BOOK ONE

MARY ELIZABETH

Closer
(Closer #1)
MARY ELIZABETH
Copyright © Mary Elizabeth Literature

ISBN-13: 978-1540482037
ISBN-10: 1540482030

Cover Design: Hang Le
Model: Graham Nation with Love N. Books
Photographer: The Glass Camera
Editor: Paige Maroney Smith
Formatting: Champagne Formats

First Edition

NOVELS BY THE AUTHOR

For the fandom.

ellie ♡

CLOSER

Thank you for everything!

Melissa

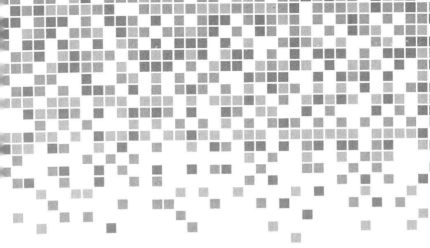

CHAPTER ONE

Before

Ella

Thick white smoke flows from his lips, stretching toward the sky in hazy ribbons. The bitter scent of tobacco burns my nose and cuts my throat, but the discomfort is minimal in comparison to the bricks stacked in the pit of my stomach. I stand beside this smoking human sculpture with a cigarette hanging between the tips of his fingers, careful not to brush against the bright red cherry. We make lingering eye contact for a moment, and then he flicks the butt ten feet in front of us and returns his look ahead.

"Is this your first year, too?" I ask.

"Third." He sticks another cigarette to his lips. Cupping a tattooed hand over the end, he squints against the orange flame and lights up. "I'm fucking terrified."

I laugh out. "That makes two of us."

Following his gaze toward the castle-like structure

made of red brick and the souls of undergraduates, I suddenly feel the need to fill my lungs with cancer-causing chemicals. Chain-smoker's a mind reader because he passes the Marlboro, exhaling another chest full of smoke.

"It takes the edge off," he says.

At the pass, our fingers brush together briefly. Cool excitement licks at scorching nervousness, but my hand still trembles as I lift nicotine and ash to my mouth and inhale. My head changes immediately—dizzy-like and how-am-I-supposed-to-make-it-through-the-next-four-years-like. My lungs burn, constricting against the intruding smoke. I hold it in for as long as I can, mean dogging the monstrosity that is ULCA and my foreseeable future, terrified to step into the next part of my life alone.

Cement stairs leading to the massive building blur as my eyes start to water, and with the sound of laughter from the cigarette giver beside me, I ugly cough poison out of my lungs. He exhaled ribbons, graceful and pretty; I spit out exhaust, suffocating and offensive.

"Take it easy," my companion says, chuckling and patting my back. "Don't die on your first day of college."

"It'd be a mercy," I say between hacks, doubling over, unashamed despite the hollow sound of him beating on my spine.

*H*e stops trying to save my life when I finally take a full breath and stand straight, wiping smeared mascara from under my lower lashes. The culprit of my near-demise hangs from the corner of his mouth, framed by the most arrogant smirk I've ever seen, belonging to the smuggest face I've ever laid eyes on. Even under the flat bill of his hat, his green eyes glimmer like jewels ... like emeralds.

This guy is cute, and he knows it.

"Teller Reddy. Pre-med," he introduces himself. The cigarette between his lips bounces with each syllable, and his smirk somehow becomes smirkier.

I accept his handshake. "Gabriella Mason, but everyone calls me Ella. And I don't know what I am yet."

Temporarily overlooked because of the choking and gasping for oxygen, fear slides back in, breakdancing on my nerves. I feel the color drain from my face as my palpitating heart sucks blood away from the rest of my body, greedy and gargling. Reaching out for another puff of nicotine isn't out of the question. Like I said, death would be a mercy.

Future M.D., Teller Reddy, takes one last drag from his habit before snubbing it beneath his shoe. The smile on his lips softens with his eyes as he witnesses my misery. He takes my hands in his—me, a total stranger on the brink of a panic attack—and rubs his thumbs over the tops of my knuckles before gently shaking my wrists.

"Where are you from, Ella?" he asks. His eyes don't waver from mine.

"St. Helena. Northern California," I answer.

"What brought you here?" His strong fingers knead my forearms, easing tension from my tight muscles better than tobacco.

"My dad died two years ago, so I was able to get all this money for college. I applied to a few different colleges, but this place seemed cool. So we moved here."

Teller laughs and asks, "Who's *we*?"

3

"My brother Emerson and I. He raised me after my dad passed, and my mom…" There's no need to spill the whole sob story. I pull my hands from his and run my fingers through my long hair. "I … I've never had to do anything alone."

"At least you want to be here," he replies.

"Pre-med? You better want to be here with a major like that." I scoff, shyly dropping my eyes to the cement under our feet.

The tattoos covering his hands continue up his forearms, in blacks and grays and reds. Whispers of more ink peek out from under the neck of his shirt, and I can only guess he has them on his back and chest. He's tall, lean, and long, and unlike any doctor I've ever seen in my life.

"Yeah, well, my dad's still alive, but he's a dick," Teller replies, patting his pockets to find his pack of smokes. He sticks another cig between his lips but doesn't light it. "This is his dream, not mine."

"Can you do something else?"

"No," he replies quickly.

"You don't like it a little?" I ask.

He drops the Zippo without lighting his smoke and smiles. "Maybe a little, but don't tell my pops. I need him to keep believing he's ruined my life."

I laugh out loud, dropping my head back. Bright sunlight shines in my eyes, turning everything red behind my closed lids. For the first time since Emerson dropped me off curbside to fend for myself, I feel the mid-September sun warm my face and bare arms, and a spark of hope flickers from deep within.

Diversity's everywhere. People in every shape and

color, as afraid as I am, here for the same reasons as me. Girls with pink hair, boys already showing signs of male pattern baldness ... short, tall, fat, skinny; black-skinned, white-skinned, brown-skinned.

Smoking future doctors covered in tattoos.

I needed out of the small town I came from, away from the ghosts of my parents and the shit I've been through since they've been gone. A clean slate is exactly what I asked for, and exactly what I've been given.

A new beginning in a new place will be the answer to all my problems.

That's how life works.

"No smoking on campus, asshole," a guy with oily black hair, dressed in dark clothing, mumbles as he passes, surly on his way to class.

Teller throws his hands up, cigarette narrowly hanging from his lips. "It's not lit."

"Fuck you." Guy liner turns around and flips us the bird before continuing on his way.

Sticking the Marlboro behind his ear for later, Teller tightens his black backpack over his shoulders and turns to me. "Where are you headed?"

"Biology," I say, pulling the printout of my schedule from my back pocket and handing it over.

"That's on my way. I'll walk you." He hands my schedule back and waits expectantly, smirking and patient while I ready myself.

I straighten my hair and take a deep breath before stepping forward, taking the plunge.

MARY ELIZABETH

*H*e's standing against the wall with his hands in his pockets after class, face shadowed by his hat, with the same cigarette still at his ear. I hesitate just inside the door, afraid he's not waiting for me, but I'm the last one to leave because I dropped my pencil box from my desk and fifty unsharpened, yellow number twos scattered everywhere.

I only recovered forty-three.

"Everything okay?" Teller asks, straightening up as I appear before him.

"I'll eventually get the hang of it." My cheeks still burn with embarrassment.

"Where to next?" he asks with a grin. Not the jerky smirk he showed me before, but a real smile that lightens his face and animates his already glowing eyes.

"Economics." I blow my bangs out of my face.

My chaperone steps to the side and allows me to pass first, bowing his head as I do. With my very first class of my very first year of college officially complete, anxiety that's overwhelmed since my brother and I moved away from home six weeks ago settles to a low hum. I take a deep breath as Teller's hand rests on my lower back, guiding me through a sea of students. He smells like a kaleidoscope of nicotine, Irish Spring soap, and ginger—a scent so comforting the hum of unease diminishes to an afterthought.

At the pitter-patter of my heart, I inhale once more and ask, "Don't you have friends?"

He laughs lightly, moving beside me as the walkway clears, and answers in a joking tone, "I have so many friends."

"I only meant, why are you with me and not your

people?"

"My sister and her boyfriend don't have classes today, and I don't care about anyone else enough to keep tabs on their whereabouts." Teller takes his hat off, revealing a head full of flattened hair before pushing it back on. "Besides, you came up to me first."

Playfully, I shove him. He stumbles onto the lawn. "Jerk."

"Besides," he says, speed walking back to my side, "we're friends now."

"We don't even know each other," I say, not sure where I'm going, but following the sidewalk with sway in my hips and my head held high, not to look like a lost idiot. Campus is bigger than my hometown.

"Sure we do."

"How old am I?" I ask.

"Nineteen," he answers quickly.

"Wrong," I say. "Eighteen."

"I'm twenty, so we're practically the same age." Teller emphasizes his point with a lazy shrug.

"What if I don't want to be friends?" I glance at him through dark stands of my hair that are blown across my face.

"You picked me! I was minding my own business when you intruded on my pondering self-doubt. You need me. I'm your *only* friend."

"Everyone in my biology class wanted to know me," I say confidently but not truthfully. I was nothing more than another face in the room. Our instructor didn't even look in my direction.

"Was that before or after you dropped your stuff and

everyone stole your pencils?" He laughs.

"You *saw* that?" My cheeks redden, and the tips of my ears burn.

"Yeah, I saw that." Teller loosely drapes his arm across my shoulders, keeping enough space between us to make me feel comfortable. He turns us around, back in the direction we came from.

"Were you not taught about personal space as a child?" I ask, grateful he seems to know where we're going.

"Nope."

"I'm not fucking you," I say, turning my head toward him purposely to inhale his delicious scent. It softens my heart and invites him totally into my life. Everything about Teller Reddy—the curve of his lips, the glow in his eyes, the rumble of his laugh deep within his chest—soothes me.

"You'd be so lucky, new girl."

The boy is a charmer, and he waits on me after class for the rest of the day, greeting me with his sly smile and a promise of direction until I get to know my way around. The next day he comes bearing gifts—a campus map, pencils, and new friends.

"Ella, this is my sister Maby and her boyfriend Husher," Teller introduces me to a short blonde girl with eyes the same shade as his, and her shy-guy, who addresses me with a shrug and a wave. Charmer then points to an extremely beautiful sandy-haired, bronze-skinned stunner standing behind Maby. "And that's Nicolette, but ignore her. She's a bitch."

"Go fuck yourself, Tell." Nicolette pushes past Teller to stop in front of me before she continues by.

"Do yourself a favor and run as far away from him as you can. He will eat you alive."

"Come on, Nic. Don't scare the poor girl off," Maby pleads as she storms by. "He didn't mean it. "

"The fuck I didn't," smugness replies, standing so close the heat from his body warms mine. "She's just mad I *wouldn't* eat her."

"You're foul." His sister scoffs, and her boyfriend chuckles.

Nicolette keeps walking, and I don't see her again until the next day when my brother arrives to pick me up from school. A head taller and twenty pounds heavier than my tattooed escort, Emerson only has eyes for her and apprehension for Teller. Future physician Reddy is calm under Em's cynical father-like glare, pre-warned about his protective manner beforehand.

But it turns out Nicolette isn't the only one capable of casting a spell on my brother. After Em and Teller share hard looks of understanding, complete with arched eyebrows, curt nods, and a fist bump, conversation appropriately switches to the red 1965 Fastback my brother inherited after our father passed.

"It needs some work but runs like a beast," Emerson says, lifting the rickety hood. Dust-like rust sprinkles over the engine, layering it in an orange-red powder.

"I know a guy who can hook you up with a deal," Teller says, officially winning Emerson over. By the end of the discussion, they've exchanged phone numbers and made plans to get together sometime during the weekend for brews and car talk.

And this is how Teller ends up at our apartment Saturday night with a six-pack and Nicolette. I answer the door with the bowl of cereal I just poured, ice-cold milk dripping over the sides as I rock back, surprised by our guests' arrival. My three-days-dirty hair is tied in a knot on top of my head, shampoo thirsty and tangled. For my brother's sake, I'm wearing a bra under an old band tee, threadbare and stretched around the neck.

"Nice to see you dressed for the occasion." The intruder cracks a half-smile, taking a step toward me … coming closer.

He's gorgeous magnified, killing me as he steps by, brushing his warm lips across my cheek. I smell alcohol on his breath, warm and stinging, mixing with the overwhelming scent of soap and ginger that's naturally Teller. His cheeks are flushed and his eyes glossy, drunk but steady on his feet and confident.

"Don't worry," Nicolette utters. She steps past me, flipping her hair in my face, and unknowingly, into my bowl. "I drove."

"I wasn't worried," I reply, kicking the door closed. "I'm not his mommy."

"Not yet," Teller says, cracking open a beer and handing it to me as I drop wasted marshmallow charms into the kitchen sink. He winks and pulls out of reach when I motion for it. "You live in Venice Beach, and it's only nine o'clock. Why the fuck are you in pajamas?"

"We live in Venice because the rent's cheap." I cross my arms over my chest. Not because I'm angry, but because I think my shirt might be see-through.

"The rent is not cheap!" Teller laughs, giving me the beer. Our fingers touch again, and again, I'm a little out of breath.

"It's not Beverly Hills expensive," I say accusingly. "We all don't have millionaire parents who can afford to live in gated communities next to famous actors and pop stars."

"My parents live in Beverly Hills. I just stay there." He narrows his eyes, but the smirk curving his lips gives his arrogance away.

"Whatever." I scoff, taking a swig of the bitter golden liquid. "Richie Rich."

While Teller and I bicker about outrageous rent in Los Angeles and money that doesn't belong to him, but only to his pharmaceutical bigwig father, my brother emerges from his room, having been the one to invite the pain in my ass over.

Nicolette pushes him back in and slams the cheap hollow wood door closed, leaving nothing but the scent of floral perfume and glitter in her wake.

"When did that happen?" I ask, pointing the neck of my bottle in the direction of Emerson's room. "They met two days ago."

"The fuck if I know, but it's why I brought her over." Teller pulls a fifth of whiskey from his back pocket and places it on the counter between us.

My throat catches fire looking at it.

"Get dressed," handsome and lush says. "I want to take you somewhere."

Twenty minutes later, my hair is powdery with dry shampoo, and I manage to get a curl on the ends and braid

11

my bangs out of my eyes. Teller stops me before I bother to put any makeup on.

"You don't need that shit," he says, leaning against the doorframe of the bathroom. A beer bottle dripping with condensation hangs from between his pointer and middle finger at his side.

"We're going to be in public. With other people." I make clear as I pour my makeup bag onto the small counter. Concealer and tubes of lipstick clutter the tiled surface.

"It's dark, and everyone's high in Venice, anyway. You'll blend in."

I breathe flames after every sip from the small bottle of peppery liquor. The tips of my fingers go numb, and my skin tingles wonderfully as the warm liquid sits in my stomach. A sense of weightlessness has me light on my feet and cheerful beyond control as Teller leads me toward the beach by my hand, past boys on long boards, girls with temporary tattoos, and cops on bicycles.

The sticky salty air smells like marijuana and shoddy cigarettes. A thin cloud of smoke hovers above the orange-lit boardwalk. Street performers earn dollar bills by hammering drumbeats on the bottoms of buckets and juggling fire. Another man walks on broken glass, and a young homeless girl plays a harmonica.

"Give her some money," I say, tugging on Teller's plain white T-shirt when I make eye contact with the music maker.

He drops a few bucks into her guitar case lined with purple velvet and guides me swiftly past the other entertainers before I give away his fortune. We run past masterpieces painted on the sides of buildings, through the palm trees and grass, onto the sand where the ocean sings a calming lullaby as small whitecaps crash onto the shore. Teller kicks off his shoes and helps me with mine as it becomes very apparent he handles booze better than I do.

"Are you drunk?" he asks, folding the hem of my jeans up toward my knees.

I stumble back, grabbing his shoulders to keep from falling on my bottom. "No."

Barefoot and ankle deep in the cold sand, Teller unscrews the bottle of whiskey and tilts the brim of smooth glass to my lips. Moonlight reflects off his eyes, and I can't look away as thick liquid pools in my mouth. It doesn't burn as much as it did the first, second, and third time. I swallow without flinching, but not without a drop trickling down my chin.

Teller licks it off.

He takes a swig from the bottle, drinking more in one gulp than I have since he cracked the seal. With liquor-wet lips and booze-brave sureness, bad intentions holds me against his body and lowers his face close to mine. The woodsy aroma of malt from our mingled breath has me spinning, and the awareness of our hearts beating so close together fades the rest of the world to black.

"Are you going to kiss me?" I ask, turning my gaze to his lips.

"Yeah," he breathes.

Heavy eyelids slowly shut as he leans in, holding me tighter, causing a blast of warmth to explode through my body, returning sensation to my unfeeling fingertips and balance to my unsteady legs.

But numbness and unsteadiness return with a

vengeance as Teller's eyes suddenly shoot wide open and he jumps back, kicking sand, scaring me, and angering our party crasher. The black and white pest crawls between our feet with its tail up, already emitting the stomach-turning scent of garlic and sulfur.

"Don't make any sudden movements," Teller says as he takes a tentative step away. His hands are up in surrender, like the skunk gives a shit about compliance.

"Since when are there skunks on the beach?" I hiss through gritted teeth. The animal's tail brushes along my bare ankle.

I'm a statue. I'm marble. I'm titanium.

Teller chuckles, steadily putting distance between us. "Since the beginning of time."

"This is why I don't leave my apartment." My heartbeat slows as the beast wobbles by. I don't move a muscle until it's a foot away. "All I wanted to do tonight is watch a movie and—"

"Ella, stay still!" Teller yells, but it's too late for me.

The skunk showers me in spray, and I fracture the night with my anguish.

"Just … stay there." Teller covers his nose in the bend of his elbow while hovering outside the bathroom door.

"Should I turn the water on?" I ask, standing in the middle of the empty bathtub. Alligator tears leave my face tacky, and my teeth chatter. "It'll wash off, right?"

Teller does his best to stand straight, resting his hands on his hips like the odor staining my skin doesn't burn his sinuses. I watch his green eyes turn glassy and his face go red from lack of oxygen. Left with no other choice but to inhale, he loses all composure and gags, doubling over.

"No, we need something stronger." He coughs, concealing his nose and mouth again before darting away. "I'll be right back."

"Where are you going?" I call out. My voice echoes off the shower walls.

I can hear him as he opens and closes cabinets and drawers in the kitchen while I strip off contaminated clothes, throwing them on the floor with every intention of sacrificing them to the fire gods later. After the skunk showered my feet and ankles in spray, I ran to the ocean looking for relief between the waves. But polluted saltwater only intensified the dank smell, leaving me wet, reeking, and with sand in my underwear.

"There's a reason no one goes in that water," Teller said as he maintained at least six feet between us on the walk back to my place.

Under the dim yellow light from an exposed light bulb above the bathroom mirror, I avoid my reflection and weep in a pair of black underwear and mismatching white bra. Goose bumps kiss my exposed flesh, and I stink so badly, my own stomach begins to turn.

"What is that smell, Gabriella?" Emerson appears in the doorway, falling back and pulling the neck of his shirt over his nose after he's taken a whiff of me.

"Oh my God," Nicolette mimics my brother.

"Don't worry," Teller says, pushing past them. "Husher got sprayed by a skunk when we were in high school. I know what to do."

"Oh, thank God," I rejoice.

"You'll thank me for this later," he says, stepping into the bathroom with one hand behind his back.

"What are you going to do?" I know by the curve of his lips I'm going to be sorry I wanted to know.

I'm right.

Only when Teller finally shows me what he's hiding, there's no time to be sorry. There's no time to scream, or run, or duck for cover. There's nothing more I can do but stand in the tub as thick red tomato sauce sails from the tin can in Teller's hand through the three feet of space between us. I lift my arms up to protect my face, but it splatters across my chest, neck, and face, and seeps into my mouth.

"What the hell!" I shriek, coated in sauciness.

"Calm down, Smella." Teller laughs at the clever name he's given me.

"The skunk didn't spray me in the face, asshole." I spit the bitterness out of my mouth.

"You're right." He turns toward my brother and Nicolette. "We're going to need more tomato sauce."

CHAPTER TWO

Now

Ella

"Come on. I don't want to fight with Joe tonight," I whisper with a smile, attempting to push Teller back with no such luck. "You know how he gets."

Caged between his arms on this sultry summer night in Echo Park, under city-dim stars and a full moon, white light gleams off his licked wet lips and drunk-hooded green eyes. Teller's cool breath smells like brew and peppermint as it drifts across my face, competing with the woodsy smell of his cologne lingering on his shirt, deepened by the humidity in the air, for my undivided attention.

"My house. My girl. My way. Joe can fuck off," drunk and disorderly says. He dips down and brushes his nose along my jaw. "We need to talk tonight."

I surrender to the pleasant tightness in my chest for a moment and lean against the brown stucco, inhaling until my lungs object. Like a drug, I'm weightless. Like a drug,

I'm riddled with guilt. "I'm not your girl, Tell."

He groans against the pulse point at my throat and pushes himself away from the house, away from me. My heart reaches for him with grabby hands and desperation to beat that heavy drum it only thumps for Teller Reddy, but I keep my feet planted and my back against the wall. Seven years have passed since the day we met—eighty-four months of breaking boundaries; two thousand five hundred fifty-five days of trying to crisp blurred lines; eight thousand seven hundred sixty hours of disorderly conduct to finally realize we're better as friends—but the blaze between us remains the same.

This spark.

This live wire.

This slow burn.

"Not my girl," Teller repeats the words unbelievably. He steps to the right and reaches into the ice bucket that sits beside the massive sliding glass window and retrieves a cold beer. He offers it to me, but I've had enough. After shaking the excess water from the bottle, he pops the top and takes a long swig. "You'll never not be mine, Ella."

Behind him, inside the house Teller bought a year ago, draped by pale yellow light from the kitchen and safe from this midsummer's heat, are our family and friends on each side of the long wooden table playing beer pong. It's Friday night, and like most Fridays after a long week, we come together to decompress, get drunk, and catch up. Most of the time it's uneventful and predictable, but some of the time the situation between the homeowner and me gets ... complicated.

With a drink in his hand and an arm slung over

Nicolette's shoulders, my brother narrows his eyes, searching for me past the glare the kitchen lights reflect off the glass. I turn away before he can see me and realize this evening might turn out like those complex ones. Emerson's witnessed countless complexes between Teller and me. Now he can tell by the look on our faces when things are about to go bad. They all can.

"Can we not do this? Joe and Kristy are in there…"

"Kristy wants to move in," Teller says before I can finish.

Bent over the table, ready to jet a ping-pong ball toward the beer-filled cups at the opposite end, is his girlfriend, Kristi Reinhart. Her sand-colored hair sweeps along her exposed lower back, and when she makes her shot, she jumps up and down in delight.

He met the big-busted, tall blonde a year ago while he pumped gas in my G-Wagen. She was at the pump beside ours and couldn't figure out how to get the gas cap open, helpless as she was. While I sat in the passenger seat of my Mercedes, stirring over whatever we were fighting about that day, Teller introduced himself to the next girl he'd fall in love with.

There was nothing I could do. I was already with Joseph.

"What did you say?" Anger stiffens my tone, intensified by alcohol thinning my blood.

"I told her I needed to think about it."

"Really?" I push away from the house, unsteady on my feet after drinking three beers on an empty stomach. "That's something you need to think about?"

Tall palm trees rustle in the slight California breeze, and water spilling from the hot tub to the pool trickles above the sound of crickets in the bushes bordering the backyard. Echoes of exhilaration flourish from the house; Maby's voice is an octave higher than everyone else's when the song changes to one she loves. She dances alone, drunk in love with the hypnotizing beat and blues-like lyrics.

Her happiness means nothing to me as I zero in on Teller. A temper only this person and our history can rouse simmers beneath my skin, roasting to a boil. I shove his arm, and the beer bottle falls from his grip, shattering on the slate flooring.

"Are you ready to do this now?" He turns to me. The loaded question thickens the air between us until I choke on his words and look away. "I didn't fucking think so, because anytime I want to talk about us, Gabriella, you shut down. It's been this way for the last seven years."

"That's not true," I argue, tasting the bitter lie in my mouth.

Teller closes the distance between us and cradles my face between his hands. Our bodies press together, leaving no space for more than erratic heartbeats and unsure exhales. His thumbs caress the curve of my cheekbones, and his eyes are absorbed on my lips. I lick them, hoping the intensity of his stare has a taste.

"Tell me not to let her move in. Say the words and we'll figure out the rest later. Say it, Ella." He rests his forehead against mine and blinks slowly.

I grip his wrists and lift onto my toes, forever trying to get through the barriers of skin and bones and gravity and relativity, hoping to find answers by crawling inside of him and mending our everythings. Teller pushes back until I'm against the wall once more and all it would take is the tilt of my head for our lips to touch.

"Come on, Smella," he says playfully, breathlessly. "Say it."

Releasing my hold on his wrists, I take the front of his shirt in my fist, like I've done so many times before in both rage and fascination, and urge him closer. Everything tingles, from the very tips of my ears to my bare feet, and the world melts away when the scent of ginger and nicotine is this near. A blanket of warmth envelops me, moving through my body like a slow wave, and pressure that should not belong to him builds between my legs. It makes it easy to forget how bad we are together. It makes it easy to wish for history to repeat itself.

The words he wants teeter on the tip of my tongue when the back door suddenly slides open and Teller's sister clears her throat, propelling us back into the real world.

"Why is there glass everywhere?" She bends down to pick up the biggest pieces, placing them carefully in the cup of her hand. "You guys might want to get inside before someone comes out here and sees this."

Teller doesn't move right away, but when I let go of his shirt and drop my hands to my sides, he pushes himself back and winks condescendingly before turning toward the house.

"Leave it, Maby," he says, crushing glass beneath his shoes as he walks by.

With a handful of dark-colored shards, turmoil's sister motions for me to step around unseen splinters of glass to come inside. She follows behind. "Is everything okay?"

"I need a drink," I reply.

A direct contrast from the temperature outside,

ice-cold processed air bites my hot skin, giving me goose bumps and cooling sweat that's dampened my hairline. I can smell the heat on my skin and on my clothes, a mixture of chlorine and sweat and day old dry shampoo. Walking directly to the kitchen bar, I pour myself a shot of tequila and shoot it, not bothering with a chaser. I'm pouring a second, cutting Teller's throat with my sharp glare as Kristi hugs him from behind, kissing his neck, when Joe takes the golden liquid from my hand.

"Are you ready to go?" The Brooklyn born boy drops my shot glass into the sink, so I pick up the bottle and bring it to my lips.

Joe.

Joseph.

Dr. West.

Stumbling in love with him was an accident, but not completely unwelcome. Teller introduced me to his reserved, curly-haired classmate during a time when my life and relationships were whirling completely out of control. Everything felt like pandemonium, but Joe was harmony. When I thought I was going to lose my mind between school and the *are-we, aren't-we* with Teller, the New York kid with the New York swagger offered solace. Being around him quieted the chaos to a low hum. It was so addicting, I found myself seeking him out when I needed a break from the noise.

Teller must have felt the same way, because an unlikely friendship formed between the two and survived the hit it suffered when we started dating. They went through medical school together, and now they're doing their residency at the same hospital I work at. Joe wants to break into oncology, while Teller sticks with emergency medicine.

"Joe, it's not even midnight." I attempt to take another drink, but he confiscates the bottle.

"Don't you have to be at the hospital tomorrow, Nurse Mason?" he teases, leading me away from the bar. He sits on a chair and pulls me onto his lap.

"Please, don't remind me." I drop my head back to his shoulder and close my eyes as fiery liquid spreads from my stomach to my limbs. I've given him a hundred reasons to leave me in the two years since we've made it official, but kindness continues to stand by me for some reason, writing love letters and surprising me with flowers. I don't hate him for it.

The rise and fall of his chest against my back is spellbinding. Searching for enchantment's pulse, I turn my head into his neck until my lips find what they're searching for at the base of his throat. The steady rhythm of his heart pumping blood to the rest of his body calms my erratic beat, and slowly, one muscle at a time, I relax in his arms as the bare tips of my toes brush across the tile floor.

Lazily blinking, I look at Joe from under my long lashes and smile when I find him looking back with eyes that I've always thought were a little too big for his face. His curly hair is a mop on top of his head and overgrown around his ears. And his lips, perfectly proportioned above a small chin, have done wonders on every inch of my body.

"Let's go," I whisper. The thought of crawling in bed beside him sounds better than tequila.

The sudden rush of conversation, laughter, and music hits me as I sit up. Husher somehow lost the last ping-pong ball, so now no one can play, to my brother's and Nicolette's dismay. Maby's still dancing in the corner with a red cup in her hand and the lyrics on her lips, and Teller pops open what he announces is the last beer.

"What do we have left?" my brother asks, approaching the bar.

Teller lifts the half bottle of tequila I drank from and says, "This is it."

Emerson searches his pockets for car keys, turning around to search counter and tabletops when he comes up empty. "I can go for a beer run, but does anyone know where my keys are?"

"You're not going anywhere," Nicolette says, swinging the keys to his Jeep from her pointer finger before capturing them in her hand and shoving them into her back pocket. "You've had way too much to drink."

My brother's about to protest when Husher presents his set of keys. "I've only had a couple. I can go."

"I don't think so," Maby says, lifting the black fedora from Husher's head and placing it over her short textured haircut. She stands beside her guy, only as tall as his shoulders. "You lost too many beer pong games to go behind the wheel."

We've been friends long enough to know Teller's never sober if he doesn't need to be. No one bothers to ask him if he's okay to drive, and he doesn't offer. Instead, he swallows the last swig from his beer and tosses it. The bottle smashes against the bottom of the empty trashcan, shattering glass for the second time tonight.

"We should leave, anyway." I stand and take Joseph's hand. "I have to be at the hospital tomorrow afternoon for a twelve-hour shift."

The entire first year of college went by before I decided what I wanted to do with my future. Teller had tons of influence on my decision to earn a degree in science and becoming a registered nurse. The classes he took intrigued me, and how hard he worked to get through medical school. A doctorate was out of the question for myself, but the medical field was my calling. I've worked pediatrics for the last two years and can't imagine doing anything different.

"It's not even midnight," Teller protests. Kristi hangs from his arm like a fucking ornament. She's not fooling anyone with that head of blonde hair and those dark eyebrows, or that fake beauty mark she wears on her face like a knock-off Marilyn Monroe.

I see you, bitch.

"Do you want a ride back to the apartment?" I ask Emerson, slipping my feet into a beat-up pair of Vans. We moved from Venice to Hollywood as soon as we started making better money. The place we share with Nicolette is a short drive to the hospital, but well worth the couple of hours I sit in traffic each week. Nothing beats the hustle and bustle of Los Angeles.

"No," Joe says quickly.

My head snaps in his direction defensively. "Why?"

Joe's cheeks burn with embarrassment. Everyone looks to him, and he shrugs. "There's something at my place I want to show you."

"You're not leaving, Ella," Teller says, rounding the bar. Kristi's a half step behind him, not bothering with pretenses and chopping me up with her eyes-like-knives. Unlike Teller and Joe, Kristi and I have never gotten along. It's for Teller's sake that I don't backhand her on a regular basis.

"We're outta of here, Tell. See you tomorrow, man." Joseph's accent slips as it does sometimes, causing *here* to sound like *hea*, and *man* to sound like *mahn*. He hooks his arm around my neck and pulls me close, kissing my temple.

"Gabriella, I don't want you driving. Call a cab or something," Emerson says. "Or we can stay here tonight. There are more than enough rooms."

"Sleepover!" Maby calls out. Husher's hat falls from her head.

Joe has a tight grip around me, and Kristi pulls on Teller's arm, begging, "Let's go to bed. Let's watch a movie. Let's—"

Teller and I make eye contact from across the kitchen, and my stomach tightens with longing that never completely goes away. Collapsing into his arms would be thoughtless, and breaking Kristi's fingers for touching him would be a dream come true. But there's a reason why Teller and I don't sleep in the same bed anymore, despite what his piercing green eyes do to the part of my aching heart that will only ever belong to him.

"We're good, Em," Joe says. He hugs me tighter, stingy for my affection, like he can feel my body wants to stray. "I didn't drink at all."

"Pussy," Emerson whispers jokingly, but smiles, satisfied I'll be escorted home safely. My brother squeezes my hand. "Call me tomorrow, sissy."

"Wait," Teller calls out as we head toward the front door. Kristi follows right behind him. "You can go get beer."

Joseph shakes his head. His arm's still around my shoulders, and I find myself swallowing panic as claustrophobia creeps up my esophagus with legs of a spider. Bowing from under his hold, needing some breathing space, I take a step back. He looks to me with furrowed eyebrows and his extended hand, to which I don't accept right away.

"I have to get her home," Joe says, opening the oversized door once I slip my hand into his.

"Let them go," Kristi whispers, gluing herself to Teller's side. She runs her hand up his chest and kisses his sharp jawline. "Come on, baby. I want to go to bed."

"Then go to bed." Teller shakes himself free from his girl.

"Wait a second." Emerson's loud voice booms from the kitchen. He appears in the hallway a second later, alleviating the tension that was about to strangle us all to death. "I've had a long week, Joe, and I'm not ready to call it a night. There's a liquor store right around the corner. Do us a solid and get some beer before you go."

"I'll go with you for the ride," Husher says. Maby, the only one left enjoying the music, dances in front of him.

"But who will dance with me?" high on life whines. Her short hair sticks out every which way, and her light skin is tinted pink from exhilaration.

Joe releases the door handle with a heavy sign. He considers me with polite frustration, straight lips, and a heavy exhale through his nose. "Do you want to come with me while I run to the store?"

"If you want me—"

"Kristi can go with you," Teller offers, meeting Joe with a stare so bold it dares him to object. He produces a money clip full of cash from the front pocket of his dark denim jeans and flips through his funds, passing Kristi three twenty-dollar bills. "Get me a pack of cigarettes, too."

Her jaw drops, and she blinks, once, twice, three times before accepting the money. She turns her face toward Joe, and her cheeks redden before she looks away. "Fine, but when I get back, can we please call it a night?"

"Whatever you want," Teller agrees with a smile that doesn't reach his eyes.

Joe leads me outside, down the long driveway toward his car parked curbside. Teller and Kristi are a few paces back, arguing in clipped tones and quiet aggravation. The sticky night only amplifies their unease, and the quiet neighborhood carries Teller's voice when he stops halfway down the drive and says, "Then I'll go. They're my cigarettes. I'll fucking go."

I look over my shoulder to find Kristi tugging on Teller's hand while she whispers apologies and promises, "I'm just tired. I'm sorry. I want to go. I don't mind going for you, Tell."

Moonlight washes yellow hues from her hair, leaving it silvery-white. Her long lashes leave an exaggerated shadow across the curve of her cheekbones, and her pale-pink lips seem blood red as she smiles at my first friend. Teller's shoulders drop, and he directs his body and consideration fully on the girl I secretly fear he might love more than me one day. He runs his tattooed hand through her long hair and presses his lips to the corner of her mouth.

"Don't get too comfortable. I'll be right back," Joe says, disengaging the car alarm. The headlights illuminate the street.

"I'll come with you," I say, following him to the driver's side of the dark blue Acura. "Just let me run back in and say goodbye."

He leans against the vehicle and pulls me between his parted legs, circling his arms around my lower back. Joe's calming effect is immediate, and I rest against his chest to listen to the solid drum of his heart's lullaby.

"Say your goodbyes when I'm gone." He kisses the top of my head. "I'll be back in fifteen minutes."

"Okay." I sigh, wishing I felt as regretful as I sound.

Backdropped by the inky black sky, I could drown in the depths of his eyes and the amount of devotion they hold for me. He studies my blank expression with irises the color of the bluest oceans, and I compel my lips to curve before he detects some of my attention isn't his. If there were ever a time he could truly *see* me, it would be now, while his soul is exposed under the fullest moon.

"I have something for you when we get back to my place," he says, sweeping his thumb across my bottom lip. "Something I've wanted to give to you for a while."

"Chocolate?" I ask.

Over Joe's shoulder, I'm tethered to Teller's shadowy figure. Much like the first time I met him, he's a statue of tribulation, unmoved by Kristi's demand for attention. She crosses her arms over her chest, and then uncrosses them to pull on his hand. Teller shakes her off, whispering something I can't hear, but it's enough to get Kristi to stop her temper tantrum.

I can't look away.

"Better than chocolate," Joe says.

"Sex?" I ask, driving my gaze away from Teller. Constant electricity that links me to him sizzles and pops, urging me to return my stare where it doesn't belong. Fighting instinct is exhausting, but I return commitment with determination

29

despite the toll it takes on my nerves. "Because if you're offering orgasms, we can leave right now."

"That will come after," Joe whispers, lowering his head to kiss me. His lips fall short when Teller clears his throat and closes the car door with Kristi inside.

"Hurry back." I move out of his arms, pushing away the small ease of relief that sneaks down my spine.

"You're killing me with this shit, Tell," my guy teases as Teller comes around the back of the car and tucks me under his arm for safekeeping. "Get your hands off my girlfriend, would ya?"

I roll my eyes, but the devil at my side pulls me closer and says in a dark tone, "Keep your hands off mine."

"Be ready to go when I get back," Joe replies, breaking his eyes from Teller's face. The engine starts, dimming the dome light from inside the Acura. Brilliance from the gages glows vibrantly, illuminating Joe's face with neon blue. In the seat beside him, Kristi connects her phone to the Bluetooth and searches for music, like she's purposely avoiding us.

"Drive safe," I offer as he shifts the car into drive.

"Fifteen minutes," Joe repeats.

We wait until red taillights disappear around the corner before we exhale and walk back toward the house. Tension between us does all the talking, and our body language gets the point across better than words ever could. We're small smiles and slighter touches, sweeping fingertips and brushing elbows. Every inhale, exhale, step, and movement is noticed, and it's been this way since we met.

He's a second skin, and my counterpart.

"Ella, don't leave with him tonight," Teller says right

before I walk back through the front door. "Stay with me."

The only thing that beats the hustle of the city is Teller's two-story house in Echo Park. If it were not for the impressive view of downtown from the front yard, it would be easy to believe this place was in the hills somewhere far from here, away from traffic, smog, and crushed Hollywood delusions. A slice of heaven hidden amid madness, the lake, the trees, and the crisp summertime air isn't what I thought I wanted when Emerson and I moved to LA all those years ago, but it's definitely where I can see myself ending up.

"What's going on with you?" I ask, turning around to face him. "Are you and Kristi in a fight or something?"

Teller's on the edge of the lawn, stripped of aggression and pride, offering me easy posture and an honest expression. He holds his hands out, palms up, like a prayer. Careful, like I would ever be afraid of him.

"I can be better than before," he says, turning his gaze toward the end of the street. Teller presses his lips together and looks back, wild-eyed, like time is running out. "We were fucked up before, but don't leave with him. I can't pretend like there's nothing here, Ella. Do not leave with him."

We've never pretended. Obsession dug its claws in us, and damn anyone who told us we were wrong. Passion is a fickle bitch, up and down, up and down; passive one moment and roaring the next. It makes for a turbulent relationship that forces the people in our lives to accept it or choose sides. Because it is possible to lose yourself to desperation and not realize it until you don't recognize your own reflection in the mirror.

"I want to be with him," I say. I lie.

"It's not the same thing," Teller replies. His lips curve

into a smirk.

He closes the distance between us and captures me in his arms, instantly washing away traces of calm Joe left behind, trading it with fever. Dopamine rushes my system, flooding my veins with burning pleasure and deliverance. Blood reddens my cheeks, and heat blasts through the palms of my hands.

Wanting Joe is *not* the same.

Absolutely nothing compares to the dope-like feeling Teller inflicts on my senses, like a shot of adrenaline directly to my heart. I hold on to him, burying my face between his neck and shoulder, accepting that his proximity is dangerous and deadly and axis tilting. Inhaling against his skin to breathe him into me, my lips brush the sensitive skin under his unsteady pulse and he groans.

"Don't leave me again," he whispers in a ragged tone. Teller turns his face, pressing his lips to my temple, gripping the back of my shirt in his fingers. "They'll understand, Ella. They'll know. I've been trying to tell you all night."

"Why does this feel different?" I ask through a new level of need.

Teller pushes my hair away from my face before placing one hand on the back of my neck and the other one against my cheek. His green eyes are glassy under the porch light, and his eyebrows come together right before he says, "Because Joe's going to ask—"

Before he can finish, Teller and I look to the street as an oversized pickup comes flying down the long road, playing music so loud I can feel the bass beneath my feet. The white 4x4 barrels past the house, easily driving eighty miles an hour, blowing a gust of wind so powerful it ruffles tree branches and blows my hair from my shoulders. The driver swerves to the left and to the right, narrowly missing cars parked along the curb, showing no attempt to lower his speed.

"Stay here," he says, walking to the middle of the lawn, looking toward the right.

I follow a few paces behind, stepping onto the damp grass in time to see Joe's blue car come around the corner as the white truck gains control but doesn't slow down. Teller runs, but only makes it as far as the sidewalk before the vehicles collide in an explosion of metal hitting metal and destruction, followed by deafening silence.

CHAPTER THREE

Now

Teller

Time comes to a complete stop, and all I can do is stare at the wreckage. White smoke stretches for the night sky, seeping from the truck's engine, now tipped on its side. The headlights are on, illuminating the small intersection, casting jagged shadows across the surface of the street. Joe's two-door car is flipped on its hood in someone's front yard—a neighbor I never bothered to introduce myself to. The back tires spin, and the horn honks in one continuous sound.

All at once, house lights flip on and front doors open. People in carelessly tied bathrobes and bedhead emerge from their homes, stopping like statues when they see what I see. It isn't until Ella runs past me, checking my shoulder as she passes, that I get ahold of myself and chase her.

"Don't," I say, catching her in my arms and spinning around. I hold her against my chest. "Don't go over there."

34

"Oh my God!" she screams, fighting me with pointed elbows and sharp fingernails. We drop to the road on our knees, and I arc over her body to keep her from running. "Oh my God."

Emerson suddenly appears and lifts his sister to her feet, carrying her to the house where Maby and Nicolette stand at the end of the driveway, motionless. Husher sprints past me with his cell phone to his ear, calling off the address and stopping beside the crumbled Acura. The phone drops from his hand and breaks at his feet.

"We need some help over here!" an older man with gray hair and bare feet shouts. He's climbed atop the truck on his hands and knees, looking into the cab through the shattered window. "I think he's breathing."

Husbands hold their wives; mothers shoo their children back inside before their innocent eyes see something that will haunt their dreams for years to come. Car alarms trigger, and every neighborhood dog howls and barks, scratching against fences to get free. When all I want to do is cover my ears to stop the cry from approaching sirens, I move forward and announce, "I'm a doctor."

Obligation corrects my state of mind, and I block distraction and concentrate on what needs to be done to help anyone involved in the accident. Instead of climbing onto the truck and attempting to lift the heavy door, I break the windshield and crawl through rubble on my hands and knees. Broken bits of glass cut my palms and slice between my fingers, but it doesn't stop me from searching for a pulse from the man trapped inside the pickup.

The cutting scent of alcohol mixed with vomit burns my nose and stings my eyes, causing them to water. Empty beer cans that were tossed during the collision have collectively landed around the driver's body. A glass handle of vodka broke open, soaking his hair and mixing with blood trickling from his wounds.

"Can you hear me?" I ask, observing his visible injuries. "Open your eyes if you can hear my voice."

Blood seeps from a laceration at his hairline, and he's suffered extensive road rash on his left arm from skidding across pavement once the truck flipped. Despite minor bruising, small cuts and scrapes, and a broken nose from striking the steering wheel at one point, his wounds are superficial and the motherfucker will survive.

"Help is on its way," I say. Passed out from booze, or knocked unconscious from the collision, he's unresponsive. There's nothing I can do for him as long as he's in the truck, restrained by the seatbelt. If I stay any longer, I won't be able to stop myself from killing him with my own bare hands.

I crawl away from the truck to find a collection of people standing in a semicircle around the crash site. Some are on their phones with the police; others linger with their hands over their mouths, but most just stare. On the brink of losing myself to rage, a woman approaches and places her steady hand on my shoulder and stares at me directly in my eyes.

"I'm a paramedic. How can I help?" she says, bending at the knees. In a pair of slippers and a silk nightgown, her hair is damp like she just washed it, and I can smell mint on her breath.

"You don't look like one," I respond with the first words that come to mind.

"I'm off duty." The EMT pulls shards of glass from my

hand. She nods toward the crowd. "And you don't exactly look like a doctor, but that's what they're saying."

"I need to get over there. Those are my friends." I scramble to my feet. "He's drunk, but stable. Stay with him until the ambulance arrives."

Pushing myself through the mass of onlookers, nothing I've witnessed in the hospital prepared me for what it feels like to see the people I love so helpless. Terror lifts the hair on the back of my neck, and utter panic turns my blood ice-cold. My feet are cement-block heavy, and no matter how hard I try, the mangled vehicle feels out of reach.

Emerson stands ten feet back with both hands in his hair, gasping for air like he can't get a decent lungful. He paces with tears streaming down his face.

"Go to the house with the girls," I order, pushing him away. "You don't need to be here."

"What the fuck happened, Teller?" he asks. His tone staggers on the rim of hysteria. "How did this happen?"

"Go!" I say, leaving him behind.

If I hadn't witnessed the accident myself, I wouldn't believe this disaster is Joe's car. It's an unrecognizable wreck of twisted steel and broken metal, upside down to expose the undercarriage. The passenger side took the initial impact, crushing the entire section of the vehicle, creating a concave void where Kristi sat. The Acura was tossed like it weighed nothing, and the car landed on the hood, nearly flattening the sedan.

A wail of sirens splits my head open as the entire block brightens with red, blue, and white lights from police cruisers and emergency vehicles. Massive diesel engines roar when fire trucks arrive on the scene, rattling and hissing to a noisy stop. Ambulance doors open, and stretchers collapse to the pavement. In minutes, the scene will be controlled and no one will let me near Joe and Kristi.

Husher's on all fours beside the wreckage with his head dropped between his shoulders, dry heaving after he empties his stomach onto the grass.

I fall to my knees beside him … beside the car.

"Don't, Teller," Husher cries out, pulling me back by the arm of my shirt.

Shaking free from his grip, I lower myself onto my stomach to inspect what's left of the car. At first glance, it's impossible to make anything out. What I'm confronted with doesn't resemble a car anymore; it's a maze of battered metal, broken plastic, and exposed wires. The back seat has been pushed to the front, propelling the driver's seat where the dashboard once was. It's as if the whole thing has been turned inside out.

"We need everyone to please take a step back," a deep male voice announces. "Make room for the paramedics. Feel free to return home. Someone will be by to take statements soon."

My eyes adjust to the low light, and I finally see Joe, blanketed by a deflated airbag. His head's bent at an unnatural angle against the compressed hood, trapped between the seat and engine of the car, barely visible beneath the debris. His face is coated in a thick layer of dark blood, veiling any exposed skin. It drips from his chest, where the steering wheel's embedded, and his legs are complexly crushed and not within sight.

"Joseph," I say, extending my arm toward him. "Joe, say something to me."

I'm met with silence.

No cries for help. No gasps for breath. Nothing.

I cry louder, grasping the airbag and tugging. "Joe—"

It pulls free in my hand, unattached to anything, protecting no one. I shove the airbag to the side and motion for Joe again, when Kristi's arm falls across his face. White skin laced with blood—it's a beautiful disaster amongst utter waste, and the only visible part of her body.

"Baby," I choke out, stretching to reach her.

The muscles in my arm extend to their full ability, tearing and splitting and raw, but it's nowhere as excruciating as the pain caused from this scene being burned to memory. I dig my feet into the ruined lawn and exhaust all the strength I have to give to lunge forward, but my body doesn't fit between the remains of the car.

"Kristi," I sob through clenched teeth, squeezing the very tips of her fingers. "Answer me."

Her skin's warm and her blood's sticky, but she's lifeless and unresponsive. Unable to tighten my grip and incapable of crawling any closer, I push away from their metal prison and run to the other side of the car. I claw at warped steel and razor-sharp slivers of glass, and kick the frame, jarring the vehicle.

"Somebody help me!" I shout, cutting chunks of skin from my hands and jamming my foot. "They're still inside. They're trapped."

I fall in front of the wreckage, where the windshield once was, to find some of Kristi's sandy blonde hair visible between the lawn and front end of the car.

"I'm so sorry, baby. I'm so sorry," I say through thick tears, weaving blood-caked strands between my fingers. My girl's crushed under the weight of the vehicle, out of reach and voiceless. I yell, losing all composure, "Somebody help them!"

"Sir, you need to step away from the vehicle." A large hand bears down on my shoulder. "We can't help them until you've cleared the site."

Dropping my head to the palms of my hands, I press my face into Kristi's hair and breathe in. Under the heavy copper scent of blood are traces of the floral perfume she wears mixed with cigarette smoke from being with me all night. Soft blonde tresses caress my lips and sweep across my cheeks, and I cry against what's left of the girl who hated it when I smoked around her.

People move in a frenzy, barking orders to gain control of the situation, readying for a rescue mission. Ambulances, hospitals, and surgery rooms are on standby, firefighters dressed in full gear gather around the wreckage, and my neighbors are thirty feet back. Too shocked to go home, they stand around, stunned silent.

But no one will be rescued tonight.

"Let go of me, you son of a bitch!" Ella screams. The panic in her voice rattles my bones. "Teller!"

I stand to find her struggling with an officer behind barriers set up to keep people from getting too close. Ella pounds into the man's chest with mighty fists and screams until her voice gives out.

"That's my family," she cries. Her eyes are wild, and her long dark hair is crazed.

"Let her go," I say, rushing past the officer trying to get me to leave. "Get your fucking hands off her."

"Teller, please!" Misery lunges for me, confined by

law's arms.

Grabbing the cop by the front of his uniform, I shove the motherfucker away and take a step forward to make sure he doesn't lay another finger on her again. Ella throws herself into my arms before the patrolman corrects his footing, preventing me from doing something I'll regret later.

Her embrace is a vise, and her sorrow is a living nightmare, pledging to haunt me for as long as I live. We cling to each other, searching for ease but succeeding in only shattering the night with our grief, murdering starlight and damning the moon.

"Tell me this isn't happening," she cries, climbing onto my body until she's wrapped around me.

Close is not close enough.

I turn my face into her neck and shut my eyes, unable to bring myself to utter the truth. We melt into the crowd of wordless bystanders swallowed by a sea of faces as the car is broken apart piece by piece. A firefighter shakes his head and the coroner van arrives, confirming what I already knew.

There's no one to save, only bodies to recover.

*S*ubtle blue peeks over the horizon when the last patrol car packs up and drives away. Huddled together on the curb, Ella and I watch it slowly pass, crushing broken pieces of bumper and glass under its tires. Both bodies, both vehicles, and the drunk driver are gone, leaving behind a street corner with a broken stop sign and rubber marks on the pavement.

"It's like nothing happened," Ella says, wiping tears

away on the sleeve of her black hoodie.

Ruptures of orange, reds, and yellows lighten the sky, silhouetting palm trees and kissing contrail clouds with a touch of sun. The temperature rises, and exhaustion settles deep within my bones as my skin warms. Heavy eyelids fall over dry eyes, stinging with every blink. As morning air fills my lungs, it becomes harder and harder to stay awake.

"Come on, you two," Maby says softly. She has a blanket draped over her shoulders and a mug between her hands. "Come inside now."

Walking hand in hand, we follow her across the damp lawn into the dark house. All the curtains are closed, and the air conditioner already blows cool air from the vents, intensifying my fatigue. The rich, comforting aroma of coffee loiters from the kitchen to the living room, where Husher's fallen asleep on the couch.

"Want some?" my sister asks, sitting at his feet. She offers her mug.

I shake my head, standing in front of the doorway. The rest of the house is silent. "Where are Em and Nic?"

Maby settles into the oversized sofa, nearly disappearing under the large blanket and cushions. Her eyes are red, and her hands tremble. "They took one of the guest rooms upstairs a few hours ago. I was going to head home, but Husher fell asleep and I didn't want to wake him."

"Stay as long as you want, Maby," I utter, guiding Ella toward the stairs. "I'm going to put her to bed."

Shock wears off, returning sensation to my sore muscles and the gashes in my hands and arms. Each step feels more impossible than the last. The stairs are never-ending, as if we're walking up the same step over and over again.

Panic crushes my insides, and dread robs oxygen from my lungs, strangling me.

"Teller," my sister calls before we reach the second floor.

Ella continues to my room, but I pause. "What?"

"I am so sorry."

My heart pounds hard enough to rattle my teeth. It thuds under my fingernails, in the bend of my arms and behind my eyes, chopping at the small amount of composure I maintain for sanity's sake.

Unlike the rest of the house, my room's sharp with Saturday morning sunshine streaming through the open shutters. It glimmers past messy brown hair and pours over Ella's shoulders, pooling on her lap. She's on the edge of my bed, clutching on to the comforter, wrapped in golden light that trembles around her unsteady frame.

"How am I supposed to fall asleep?" she asks. The tip of her nose is red, and her full lips are swollen.

"I'll help you." I close the bedroom door and walk over to the window, pushing out the light and forcing it to shine somewhere else.

"How the hell am I supposed to do anything, Teller? They're dead, and we're going to what, go on living our lives like it never happened? Tell me how I'm supposed to do that."

I kneel and untie Ella's left shoe, and then her right. I set them to the side and slip my fingers under the hem of her hoodie and tug it over her head, dropping it to the carpet. The neck of her shirt is stretched out, and her knees are scraped. She's helpless, hopeless, and beautiful.

"Let me help you," I whisper, easing her fingers from the heavy blanket.

She circles her arms around my neck and lets me lift her to pull the bedding back. The tips of her bare toes brush the carpet before I carry her across the mattress. We face each other against the pillows, silent in the blank space, accompanied by nothing but dread—the breath that we breathe.

"Stay here," I say, pressing my lips to her forehead. "I'll go in one of the other rooms."

"No," she answers immediately, clutching on to the front of my shirt. "Don't leave me, too."

Her hair breaks as I brush my fingers through knotted strands, pushing them away from her face. Ella lifts a shaky hand and wipes my own heartbreak from under my eyes, brushing salty tears across my lips. She scoots closer, tucking her head under my jaw, against my throat. I take her hand and place it against my chest, where my heart beats the truth.

I'm glad it wasn't her.

"This is how we sleep," I say, pulling the sheets over our bodies and holding her tight. I listen to her steady breathing beside me; it's a song that finally pulls me under.

There's a gap between sleep and consciousness where nothing exists. The void brought on by the end of a dream and the beginning of awareness, where commitment, stress, and obligation melt away. It's a mercy, a sip of bliss, a miracle—dark around the edges and cozy. If death's anything like this weightless space, Joe and Kristi are the lucky ones.

Somewhere in the house a door opens and closes, and my eyes flicker behind thin lids. I squeeze them shut, striving for that last second of reprieve, but it's pinched from me as reality sinks in, hammering against temporary ease. An onslaught of images from the night before fill me with dense anxiety and piercing pain, pushing air from my lungs.

I sit up, sweat soaked and gasping, clawing at my chest, because I'm still here … I am.

"Teller." Maby knocks on the door and peeks her head in. "Can I come in?"

Swinging my legs over the side of the bed, I search my nightstand for my pack of cigarettes and mumble, "Yeah."

"You've been asleep all day," my sister whispers, looking past me toward Ella. She's curled up, dead to the world. "Do you need anything? Do you need me to make any calls for you?"

I slip a smoke between my lips and shake my head. "No, I'll take care of it later."

"A detective came by asking questions. I asked him to come back later. He left his card."

Rummaging for a lighter, I knock my wallet and a two-day-old glass of water to the floor. Ella stirs beside me, stretching her arms above her head and turning over to her back, but she doesn't wake up.

"Is everyone still here?" I ask, standing to sore feet.

"We are. Come downstairs." Maby takes a step forward, but stops when I move toward the balcony that extends from my bedroom.

"Later, Maby. I'll wait until Ella's up." I open the set of French doors to the warm summer evening. The sky's streaked with pinks and purples, and the sun, deep orange and yellow, hangs low. Time passed outside my dark space, moving despite my life sliding to a standstill.

"Mom and Dad called three times." She follows me outside, careful to keep distance between us. "They're going to come over if you don't reach out, Tell. They're worried. It was in the newspaper this morning. The accident's being covered everywhere."

Leaning against the railing that overlooks my backyard, I light a cigarette and take a deep drag, filling my lungs with toxic smoke that immediately takes the edge off. Green leaves float on the surface of my pool, gathering around the edges. Twenty-four hours ago, before anyone showed up, I watched Kristi dive into the deep end. Her long legs moved with grace through the blue water, and her long blonde hair stuck to her back and shoulders when faithlessness came up for air, unaware I knew the truth.

The red towel she used to dry herself hangs over the back of a chair.

"I'm not dealing with this shit right now," I say, flicking ash and inhaling another hit.

"Okay," she replies in a soft tone. My younger sister closes the doors and disappears behind them.

The sun sets before I've smoked my second cigarette, and I'm not ruling out a third when I hear Ella move around the room. Exhaling gray smoke into the night sky, I flick the butt into the neighbor's yard and go inside. The sheets and blankets are tossed completely to the floor around the bed, but the mattress is empty. Yellow light seeps from under the bathroom door, and the overhead fan is on.

"Are you okay?" I ask with my hand on the door handle.

The toilet flushes, but not before the sound of Ella emptying her stomach straightens the hair on the back of my neck. Ready to break the fucking door down, it pushes open and slams against the wall, swinging back at me. Gabriella doesn't flinch at my intrusion. Her arms rest across the white porcelain, and her head leans against the inside of her elbow. Agony's on her knees, and her pink painted toes curl as she turns her head and heaves.

I stand behind her, gathering her spit-damp hair in one hand and rubbing her back with the other. She's nothing more than noises and pleas, white-knuckling the side of the toilet. Yesterday's mascara runs down her light freckles, and her lashes clump together.

Once her stomach settles and she gasps for air, I sit alongside the bathtub and pull her between my legs, against my chest. I reach over my shoulder, blindly searching for the faucet and start the water.

"Come on, Smella," I say lightheartedly, stepping into the bathtub. The water's freezing, so I adjust the temperature and close the drain before I lift her in after me.

"Our clothes are still on," she whispers, sitting between my knees. Hot water warms her bones, and the trembling stops. She lets me help her out of her ruined shirt, leaving Ella in a pair of olive green shorts and a black bra.

"It's okay." I pull off my own shirt, then rest her against my bare chest. Our skin touches, dosing me with a taste of rapture that licks my veins and detains my heart. "We're going to be okay."

CHAPTER FOUR

Before

Ella

"**S**nap out of it, girl." Maby takes my shoulders and shakes me, loosening tense muscle and all over edginess. "She's been dating your brother for six months. You can't miss her birthday party."

I roll my eyes. "Nicolette won't notice if I'm here or not. She's said three words to me the entire time I've known her."

The small blonde takes my hand, lacing our fingers together before she leads me toward the Hadden residence. Nicolette's parents' house is a Spanish villa inspired mansion tucked in the corner of the Hollywood Hills. Week after week, more of her things show up at the apartment, to the point where I brandished her toothbrush, asking Emerson if she moved in. She'd taken mine out of the holder and replaced it with her own. The countertop's cluttered with face creams and curling irons, and she leaves her clothes everywhere.

But she apparently still lives at home.

"Where's your brother?" I ask, trotting to keep up with her little, but mighty legs.

"Don't know," she says, opening the massive front door to a party spread wall-to-wall. "He and my dad got into an argument earlier, and he took off. I'm surprised he didn't go to your place."

"I haven't heard from him." Anxiety instantly ups my heartbeat. The last time Teller took off, no one saw him for two days. He returned with a black eye and broken ribs. "Maybe I should call him."

"Ella, no." Maby takes my wrist in both of her hands. She walks backward to face me, bouncing with bone-jarring beats and persuasive treble. "For one night, forget him. Let the boy make his mistakes, and tonight, we'll make our own."

"You better get me drunk then," I say as she guides us toward the kitchen.

My only girlfriend grabs a bottle of cinnamon rum from the countertop and passes it to me first. We swallow throat-searing swigs, using beer to chase the burn to our stomachs. The prickle in my limbs is immediate, and the touch of apprehension that could have ruined my night disappears. My face warms, and my entire body only gets hotter when Maby forces me to dance. Surrounded by bodies, lyrics, and carelessness, I toss my hands up and move, throwing caution to the late winter wind.

The floor beneath my feet vibrates, and my hair sticks to heat on the back of my neck. Husher and Emerson eventually find us, bidding more liquor and dance partners.

MARY ELIZABETH

My brother twirls and dips me, like our father used to do with our mom before she took off, until Nicolette comes around.

Her cheeks are a shade lighter than the deep red lipstick on her kiss, and her slender body is coated in a sheen that shimmers under the dim light. She's in a short black dress, and her tousled, sandy-colored hair is in a high bun that's fallen to the left.

"You came!" she says, opening her arms for me. The sweet smell of champagne is on her breath, but her tacky skin smells like lavender and honey. "I'm so glad you're here, babe."

"Happy birthday," I reply, returning the gesture. It's the first time she's ever touched me, let alone greeted me with an entire sentence.

We dance until our legs are gutless and tender, and the heat in the house becomes overwhelming. At midnight, Nicolette opens a wall made of glass doors, and the bitter night gusts overhead. She blows twenty-one gold sparkling candles out on a three tier cake, and the cops show up, puffy-chested and superior.

"Who hired strippers?" Nic laughs in the doorway. The bottom of her bare feet are dirty, and her bra straps show from under her dress. Candle smoke idles in the air.

"There was a noise complaint." Three of them shine their flashlights past the host and Emerson, only to see a hundred or so red-faced college kids waiting for them to leave so we can turn the music back up.

"It's my birthday," sloppy like the rest of us says. She straightens her dress. "These are my friends."

"I don't want to see any of you on the road tonight,"

one of the police officers warns. He leans forward to study our faces, as if he can memorize them all.

"No, sir," Nicolette says. "Never, sir."

She's the first to jump into the pool with her clothes on, and the first to be cut off from alcohol—something she doesn't handle well. It's past two in the morning and the party's half the size it was when I arrived, and the people who linger settle on couches and chairs, taking it easy. We're aware Nicolette's losing her shit in the kitchen, but only my brother acknowledges it.

"You can get the fuck out of my house," she cries, shoving her fists into Emerson's chest. "It's my party."

He holds a bottle of vodka above her head. "You've had enough, babe."

"You don't know my life!" she shrieks.

I push myself from the edge of the heated pool and float onto my back. The floral printed dress I'm dressed in sticks to the shape of my body, and water whooshes in and out of my ears. Steam rises from my exposed skin as the early morning gets cooler by the minute. I'm counting stars when my feet graze against someone and I straighten myself to apologize.

"I'm sorry," I say to the blond boy who took my foot to the ribs. I've drifted to the deep end of the pool, so my toes don't touch the bottom like I expect them to. Unprepared for nothingness, I go under without air in my lungs.

"Careful." The guy I kicked yanks me to the surface and holds me against his body.

Blinking water from my eyes, I smile once I get a clear view of my savior.

He's cute.

He's cuter than cute.

He's almost worth drowning for.

I think of Teller for a moment, but stop myself before guilt creeps in and crashes the party. We're not official, and he wasn't here to save me from a watery grave. We haven't even kissed. And after six months of riddles and a halfway commitment from Tell, I can use a confusion-free moment with a good-looking guy.

"What's your name?" I ask, swimming toward the end of the pool. My back faces the house, and Nicolette's breakdown comes to an end, leaving only the sound of water hiccupping in and out of the filter to accompany us.

"Max." Bright blue lights glow beneath the water to his face, illuminating his soft smile and softer eyes. "You?"

"I'm Ella. Nicolette is my brother's girlfriend." I lift myself out of the pool and sit on the tile edge with my feet in the water.

"Who's Nicolette?" Max sits beside me. Water cascades from his tanned skin and drips from his sun-bleached hair, like some kind of beach bum. He smells like chlorine and beer and salty ocean.

"We're at her party," I say with a smirk. "This is her house."

"Oh, well, I came for the brews."

I wring moisture from my hair and laugh at his honesty. "That makes two of us."

Comfortable stillness falls upon us. Partygoers, here and there, stumble out to the backyard but turn back to the house when they feel how cold it is. Ankle deep in heated water, my feet are warm, but the rest of my body freezes. Thin wet cotton does nothing to hide how hard my nipples are, and my teeth chatter.

"Have my eyebrows turned to icicles yet?" I ask Max, wiggling my brows.

He leans in to take a better look, dramatic and funny, leaving mere inches between our faces. His breath blazes against my chilled skin, and his fingers brush against mine, shooting the wrong kind of chills down my backbone. As tight pressure fills my chest, regret tap, tap, taps on my shoulder, making it impossible for me to disregard my affection for Teller.

"I should go inside." I scramble to my feet and turn toward the house only to come face-to-face with the object of my loathing.

"Did you just kiss him?" Teller asks, staring over my shoulder at Max.

Regret dissipates to yearning, letting go of tight pressure, topping me with warmth like sunlight instead. As my body defrosts from the inside out, a smile bends my lips and my heart's beat charges adrenaline through my just-frozen veins. He's a shot of intensity I take straight to the head, and I've missed him.

"Where have you been all night?" I step forward, but stop in a shallow puddle because of the dark look in Teller's eyes.

"Did you just fucking kiss her?" he asks Max, disregarding me.

Standing between innocence and misplaced anger, I've witnessed enough of Teller's lack of self-control to know that blond boy needs to leave. I hold my arms out to keep them apart, but it doesn't stop either from coming closer. Teller pushes his chest to my hand, and his heart-beat pounds against my palm. Up close, his eyelids are rimmed red and his pupils are ink black and expanded.

"Max, you should leave," I say, pressing my palms to Teller's chest. He hasn't even looked at me.

"I didn't kiss your girl, bro." Max walks by, grinning. "But I should have for all the fucking trouble she's causing."

There's nothing I can do once Teller shoves away from me.

"Idiots!" I scream, smacking water as I stomp my foot. My voice carries over the fistfight breaking patio furniture, through the still night wrecked by violence, and into the house for everyone to hear.

But there's nothing anyone can do to stop him.

"Wake up, you stupid son of a bitch." I kick the bed frame. The headboard bashes against the wall, shaking windows and both nightstands; a bottle of water tips over. "Teller, wake up."

He's on his stomach, dressed in nothing but a pair of plaid boxers and black socks, sleeping on top of the covers. The bastard's right foot hangs from the edge of the mattress, and he still has a hat on his head. Bloody knuckled and bruised, the fight he got in the night before is evident on his body and in the condition of his room.

Dirty clothes mound in the corner, full ashtrays and empty booze bottles are littered across every surface, and schoolbooks sit piled, open-faced on the corner desk. The air smells like grass stains, stale beer, and rust from the blood.

"Get the fuck out of here, Ella."

"Max needed ten stitches thanks to you." I rest my hands on my hips. "You're lucky he didn't have a concussion."

"Ten? That's it?" Teller lifts his head and smirks. Sleep lines crease the side of his swollen face. There's a small bump bulging from the bridge of his nose, and his right eye is black and blue.

"What was that about, Tell?"

He covers his head with a pillow and mumbles, "Get out."

"Something's up." I open his curtains, scattering particles of dust. The late afternoon sun stings my eyes, and I squint against the sharp light before I turn toward the source of my frustration. "I don't hear from you for almost a week, and then you show up out of nowhere and beat the shit out of some guy who didn't do anything wrong."

"Leave." Teller flips me off. The ten feet between us is the only thing that stops me from breaking his tattooed finger off at the knuckle.

"No."

Anger stacks on top of annoyance, draped with a thick layer of regret, glued together by disappointment. Emotion twists my insides dry, leaving brittle bones for my heart to beat on, scattering powder into my blood. Undigested alcohol stirs in the pit of my stomach, and sleeplessness reddens the white in my eyes. I came here hanging by a thread, but Teller's indifference severed the cord.

I grab the glass bottle by the neck from the windowsill and send it across the bedroom. It sails through empty space, end over end, dripping sour beer before the brown glass collides with the wall and shatters. Teller sits up, wide-eyed and confused, as I throw a second over his bed. We watch it hit the wall and splinter, spraying day-old liquid across the gloss finish, sprinkling razor-sharp shards to the floor.

"Ella, don't fucking do it." Teller approaches, palms up in surrender.

The third bottle narrowly misses his head and clips the bedpost, breaking but not shattering like the other two. Without another bottle near me to throw, I improvise, chucking a shoe, a pair of jeans, and then a bottle of cologne at his body.

"Knock it off," target practice groans, taking cologne to the chest.

My temper chases air from my lungs, but fury has me scattering for more things to throw. Determined to beat him down one textbook at a time, I sprint to Teller's desk before he can grab me and fling seven hundred pages of anatomy across the room.

"Do I have your attention now, asshole?" I shriek, tossing his notebook next. Spiraled lined paper flaps before landing on his bed.

"Dammit, Gabriella. That's enough." Teller takes a scientific calculator to the jaw before he's able to wrap his arms around me. "Are you fucking crazy?"

"Let go of me," I kick and scream.

His bare chest presses against my back, exposed through my scoop-necked sweater, and his lips brush across my neck as he whispers, "I'm sorry, okay. I'm sorry."

Teller's low tone drives a shiver down my arms, and I

drop the pencil I considered stabbing him with.

"Is anyone here?" he asks, turning me to face him.

"No." I knock the hat from his head, showcasing a head full of dirty dark hair.

Green eyes outlined with bruises are bright with desire, and his large hands rest on each side of my neck. My hair's in a messy bun, and it took effort to wash my body and brush my teeth this morning, so I don't know why I feel beautiful under his stare. But I do.

"Why do you even care if he kissed me?" I ask, inhaling a shaky breath.

His thumb sweeps across my collarbone, and Teller licks his busted lip, pulling me closer until our bodies are flush. "How can I not?"

"What are we doing?" I give no protest as he pushes me toward the bed and gladly open my legs for him once my back hits the soft mattress. "What is this, Tell?"

Broken lips leave bloody kisses on my skin, starting from the soft spot under my ear to the hollow part of my throat. He holds himself up on his hands, indenting in the pillow under my head, and strokes deeply against my softest place.

Teller's big, and hard, and barely sober, but with only my leggings and his boxers separating us, I don't mind getting drunk on his breath, his skin, his one hundred proof lust. Sliding my hands up his sides, my fingers tremble over muscles that flex each time he thrusts against me.

"Tell me what this isn't," Teller whispers, lowering himself to his elbows. "Try to tell me this isn't everything."

I inhale his words, tasting their sweetness on my tongue, and part my lips for more when the bedroom door opens.

"Where are your keys? You parked your car on the grass again—oh my God!" Mili Reddy, Teller's beautiful, sophisticated, stunned-stupid mother, closes the door as quickly as she opened it. "I'm sorry. I didn't know Ella was here. Shit, sorry. The car can stay on the lawn."

Her son drops his forehead to my shoulder and groans, and I hide my blazing face in his neck and laugh. I've met Teller and Maby's parents, Theo and Mili, a dozen times in the last six months, but our encounters up to this point have been nothing less than polite. I may be fully dressed, but the woman of the house saw me utterly exposed.

"I didn't think anyone was here," I say. "No one came to the door when I rang the doorbell, so I walked in."

"If she didn't come in when you were throwing shit against the walls, she wasn't here." Teller sits on his knees between my thighs. "This isn't your fault. She should have knocked."

Hiding my face under my hands, I say, "Kill me now."

Teller gets off the bed and adjusts himself in his boxers. Despite bruises and wounds from a match that wasn't his to fight, this guy is drop-dead gorgeous. Vivid pigments mixed with shades of gray decorate his skin in elaborate art and teenage rebellion, and I have no doubt that any unmarked spaces will be covered eventually.

He's a masterpiece.

"I'm not going to kill you, but I am going to take a shower before my dick snaps off."

Five minutes go by before I crawl out of bed and head toward the bathroom to splash cool water onto my burning cheeks.

"It's only me," I say, pushing open the door.

Steam envelops me, thickening the air, rushing out to the bigger, colder bedroom. My bare feet step onto the lush rug in front of the sink, and I'm glad I can't see my reflection in the mirror. Frigid water pools in my cupped hands, and I take a small sip before wetting my face, instantly chilling my temperature.

"I'm still in here," I say when his water shuts off, patting my face dry.

Before I can escape, Teller opens the glass door and steps out with a white towel around his waist. His dark hair drips to his shoulders, and his feet leave footprints on the mat outside the shower. Embarrassed all over again, I turn away from him and squeeze my eyes closed, as if I wasn't willing to let him inside of me ten minutes ago.

"Forgive me," he says, standing right behind me. I can smell soap on his skin. "I fucked up last night. I was fucked up."

"It's okay," I reply like a whisper.

He reaches past me with his chest once again pressed to my back, and I look when he tells me to.

Written on the foggy mirror, dripping condensation where his fingertips touched, returning our reflections in his words says *we're going to be okay*.

CHAPTER FIVE

Now

Ella

I watch the battery die each time my phone rings, wielding a New York area code. For the last two hours, while Teller sleeps on the bed beside me, I've done nothing but sit in the dark until the next time Joe's family calls, blessing me with moments of light. My finger hovers over the *Accept* button, but twenty-three attempts later, I've yet to answer. My battery clings to life at two percent, and the voicemail box is full.

"You can't ignore them forever," I whisper, telling myself I'll pick up the next one.

It comes a few minutes later, vibrating in my hand but not ringing out loud. The battery life plummets to one percent, and it's now or never. They deserve answers. The Wests should know what happened to their son. Joe's parents, although I only met them twice, deserve to hear it from the person their only child spent his life with.

I press the green *Accept* button as the screen turns black, and I'm not mad at it.

Tossing my cell to the end of the bed, I lie back and appreciate darkness so bleak I can't tell if my eyes are open or closed. Oblivion takes the edge off, and I can breathe for the first time since the accident, sinking into nothingness.

"Are you awake?" Teller's voice smashes silence to pieces, dragging me to the surface of awareness.

"Yes."

"What time is it?" He sits up and exhales heavily.

"After two in the morning," I say. My traitorous eyes adjust to the obscure, and I can see Tell's shape at the edge of the bed. "Are you okay?"

His bare shoulders bend, and his head falls forward. We're alone with our inner struggles, but when Teller cries out for the first time since he led me upstairs after the crash, I don't hesitate to inch across the bed and wrap my arms around him.

"I'm right here," I say softly, pressing my lips to the back of his neck. Teller's body heat seeps through the shirt he lent me after our bath, and I mend myself to his form, wanting every part of me to touch every part of him. "I'm not going anywhere."

The sound of his grief demolishes my heart, but it's not a burden I let him bear alone. I sit against the headboard and guide his head to my lap, where I cradle him gently to rake my fingers through his hair and catch his tears in the palm of my hand. Sadness streams steadily down my cheeks, but I don't take this moment from him, and give it entirely to Teller.

"We have to leave this room eventually," Teller says

sometime later.

My head's back and my eyes are shut, unafraid of the images that come to life behind my closed lids with him in my arms. I replay the accident from beginning to end over and over again with perfect clarity, able to point out things I missed while it happened and I was in shock. The trace of gasoline mixed with burnt rubber is so strong, it's as if I'm standing wreck side. Transported back to the scene of the crime nearly two days later, I can count broken glass on the street and look into the faces of every person circled around the debris.

And then there's Teller, trying to save everyone.

"We can stay a little longer," I reply, pulling his hair between my fingers.

"Are you hungry? Do you want me to go downstairs and get you anything?"

I open my eyes and smile, even if he can't see it. "The only thing I need is for you to stay with me, just like this. Let me take care of you for a little while."

"*E*lla, what are you doing?" Teller groans. "Stop shaking the fucking bed."

"I thought that was you," I say in a sleep-thick tone. We've completely shifted positions, wrapped in heavy blankets and in each other. He's underneath me on his stomach, and I'm lying across his back with one foot hanging off the side of the bed. I drooled on his shoulder.

"How can I do anything pinned beneath you? When did you get so heavy, anyway?"

"Eat shit," I say, doing nothing to move my heaviness

from his cozy body. "I'm lovely."

"Seriously, Smella, stay still or go sleep in another room."

"Does it feel like it's getting worse?" I ask, lifting my head to look around. The ceiling fan above the bed trembles, and the shutters over the windows tremble against the glass. All our things on the nightstands shake, shake, shake to the floor. "It sounds like a fleet of diesels are about to drive down the street."

My heartbeat accelerates when the bedroom door is kicked open and Emerson rushes in. He's naked, holding parts no sister should see in his hands. "Earthquake, motherfuckers!"

Teller and I dash to correct ourselves, kicking off blankets and straightening the clothes we slept in. He jumps from the bed first, quick to reach for my hand and pull me out the door and down the stairs. Nicolette bolts from the guest bedroom across from Teller's, tying her robe and cursing her boyfriend.

Frames fall from the walls, books fall from shelves, and cupboards in the kitchen slam open and closed. Husher, Maby, and Emerson are outside, so Teller follows them to the front lawn. The six of us stand in the grass and watch the entire house sway from side to side as the ground rolls under our feet.

"It's never going to end," Emerson whines. "The world is ending."

Like us, a few of our neighbors find safety on their lawns to avoid the roof collapsing on their heads or being injured by a flying plate. Thankfully, Teller's shirt hangs to my knees, and he's not entirely inappropriate in a pair of boxers that hangs low on his hips. Everyone else is in pajamas with no indecent body parts exposed.

Except my brother.

"Did you seriously ditch me to save the TV?" Nicolette asks. She crosses her arms over her chest.

"Emerson!" I scold, trying my hardest not to laugh.

"What? I couldn't leave it to get destroyed. Teller just got it, and there's a game on later." He looks to his girlfriend, sympathetic but unapologetic.

Standing with his bare ass facing the street, naked and afraid saves us from a full-frontal experience by covering his man parts with Teller's brand new sixty-inch television he ripped from the wall. Morning sunlight reflects from the surface right into Nic's eyes, tipping her over the edge of madness and making it impossible for me not to laugh.

"Find a way to fuck that TV, because you're not touching me anytime soon."

"Babe, don't be like that." The television slips from his fingers, but his grip tightens.

Emerson's linebacker big—at the gym seven days a week muscular. My brother sacrificed a lot after our father died and he took me on full time, including his aspiration in law enforcement. He couldn't think about the police academy when his little sister needed to be taken care of, and after a while, obligations and a steady paycheck forced his dream further out of reach.

Not long after our move to LA, his large physique was noticed and appreciated. He got involved in personal security and works for a celebrity bodyguard service. Which only makes this situation more ridiculous.

The only thing Emerson guarded today was the high

definition flat screen.

"Do you think it's safe to go inside?" Maby asks when the ground stops shaking.

"I'll probably chill out here for a while. There's going to be an aftershock after an earthquake like that." My brother turns from the house to us, blinding our eyes with the reflection of the all mighty sun. "But can someone throw me some sweats? Babe, will you make coffee?"

Nicolette shakes her head in disbelief. "You are an absolute idiot."

He doesn't rally for her attention when she heads toward the house and turns to me instead. "Sissy, you'll make me coffee, right?"

I throw my hands up and back away. "I'm staying out of this one."

"And I'm going to need this," Teller says, taking his TV from Em.

Emerson's hands immediately cover his private parts, but I rush after Maby and Husher to stay on the side of caution. The damage caused by shifting fault lines is superficial and broken glass is an easy fix. Teller hooks the TV up so we watch the local news, and I run upstairs to put on a pair of shorts and some shoes. I'm tying my laces when I see a pair of Kristi's nude heels peeking from under the bed.

My heart drops to my stomach.

The entire city just shook, and they're dead.

Tectonic plates moved, and they are not here.

The Earth could tip on its axis, and they would still be gone.

I kick Kristi's shoes under the bed and run down the stairs before grief I won't win a war against invades, ending this brief cease-fire. Teller catches the shirt I toss to him, and I go to the kitchen to sweep broken coffee mugs from the floor. My hands tremble, so I grip the broom harder and concentrate on what I'm doing.

I won't think about Joe. I won't think about him in a morgue. I won't think about never hearing the sound of his voice again.

"Let me do that." Teller hijacks the broom, but instead of taking over, he draws me against his body and holds me close. The broom crashes to the tile, scattering the small pile of glass I swept.

"It's been two days since the accident, Tell. We can't pretend this didn't happen. Neither one of us has made a single phone call, I haven't talked to anyone from the hospital, and we've disregarded their families." Grief blooms to panic, and I push myself away from Teller, needing space to breathe. "Does anyone even know where they are? Someone has to make funeral arrangements, right?"

"Stop," Teller says, grasping my face in his hands. My tears spill over his fingers. "Everything will be taken care of, Ella. After we clean this mess, we'll figure out what needs to be done. I promise to handle it."

It's a blurry line between grief and logic, but I manage to keep myself in one piece while we put the house back together. Husher threw Emerson a blanket to cover himself, and he eventually joined us once enough time passed without an aftershock. The news reported the tremor as a 4.0, centered ten miles away.

I try not to pay too close attention to the television in case something's reported about the wreck that killed our friends, but forty-eight hours later, we're the only people in the city who care.

"When was the last time either one of you ate?" Maby asks, opening the built-in refrigerator. She grabs ingredients to make her brother and me a turkey sandwich, dropping an armful of vegetables, deli meat, and condiments to the counter.

Teller and I sit beside each other at the bar, and I didn't think I was hungry until she mentioned food and my stomach roared. The younger Reddy kid has dark circles under her jade eyes, and her skin is as pale as porcelain. She's a natural caretaker with the best interest intentions, so I'm not surprised she's made herself at home while Teller and I locked ourselves in his bedroom.

"There's not an easy way to start this conversation, but we should probably hash out details while I have you in front of me." Maby spreads mustard and mayonnaise onto four pieces of bread with a butter knife. Her chin quivers, but she maintains a straight face. "I've been in touch with the coroner. Autopsies were performed on Joe and Kristi, and their families requested death certificates and burial forms."

"Joe's not going to be buried in California, is he?" I attempt to mimic Maby's strength but crack at the edges, unable to keep my face from falling.

She doesn't meet my eyes and slices a steak knife into an overripe tomato. "I don't think so, Ella."

"And Kristi?" Teller asks.

The tomato splits apart, oozing seeds onto the cutting board. Maby tosses the blade into the sink on top of other dirty dishes. "Mom actually spoke to Mrs. Reinhart, Tell. Her body's going to be transported to Anchorage tomorrow.

The funeral's in a week."

Teller scrubs his hands down his face. "I don't know why I expected them to wait."

"The flight's booked," Husher says, pulling out a chair for him and Nicolette at the kitchen table. Just like Maby, sleeplessness bruises their eyes and washes color from their complexion. We're echoes of the people we were days ago. "We'll go together."

This house contains the sorrow of six people, and its claws are sunk deep into our hearts. We tried to ignore it, but avoidance did nothing to help our loss hurt less, and taking it head-on is killing us. Sadness spills freely from my eyes, dripping onto my untouched sandwich, and I can't bring myself to take a bite despite the growl in my stomach.

Maby leans against the counter, noticing how closer Teller and I sit near each other, and continues. "Ella, we know this is tough, but if you can get in touch with Joe's family, maybe they'll work around the date of Kristi's funeral. It's a shitty thing to ask, but I would hate for them to fall on the same day. Especially since they're on opposite sides of the country. If you give me their phone number, I—"

"No, I'll do it. I'll call them right now."

"Eat first," Teller says as I slip from my seat. He hasn't touched his food.

"Can someone wrap that up for me? I'm not really hungry."

"Gabriella, don't go back into that room, please," my brother bids. I recognize the concern in his eyes. "I can take you home, sissy. I'll look after you there."

I walk past him and climb the stairs to Teller's room

where my phone's on the charger with the ringer still off. There's comfort in this lightless sanctuary. Familiarity and the sense of affection, which comes with Teller, make me feel safe. The walls smell like ginger and nicotine, and the pillows still hold the shape of my head from the night before.

Sitting on the edge of the bed with my phone in hand, I don't give myself a chance to back out and dial the number. It rings once before a somber gentleman's voice answers, and an explosion of nervous heat ruptures through my body.

"Hello, is someone there?" he asks when I don't respond right away.

My heart beats me. It hammers at me. It swings and punches. "Umm … yes, this is Gabriella Mason. We've met before. I'm Joe's girl—"

"Do you know how many times I've tried to get ahold of you?" Subdued shifts to barefaced wrath.

I bite my bottom lip before replying, "I know. I'm—"

"You know?" He stops me, raising his voice even louder than before. His thick New York accent distorts his words. "Then you must know that my wife and I learned from a stranger that our only son was killed. It was something like, five in the morning, and I wasn't going to answer my phone because I didn't recognize the number, but thank God I did, Gabriella. Would we even know Joe passed otherwise? Would we know if it was left up to you? If it wasn't for the coroner finding my number in Joe's phone, would I still think my son is alive right now?"

"I'm so sorry," I choke out.

"You're sorry?" he questions, scoffing. "That's what you

have to say to me? You're sorry?"

"It … it was an accident," I say, slipping from the mattress to the floor.

"The wreck that killed Joseph or your negligence since it happened?"

I cover my mouth with my hand and swallow anguish deep into my belly. There's nothing to say to this man—to the person who gave life to Joe—to a grieving father. His anger is warranted, and I'm a coward. I deserve this.

"Are you there?" Mr. West asks.

I nod my head as if he can see me and whisper, "Yes."

"Assuming you have a key to Joseph's house, you should take this time to retrieve your belongings. I'll be in LA after the funeral to manage his assets and other effects. It would be easier for us if your side of things is taken care of before I arrive."

"I have a key," I say softly.

"Leave it there once your possessions are collected," he replies harshly.

"David," I speak, using his first name. My vocal cords tremble. My bones quiver. My nerve endings shake. "Please forgive my carelessness. Joe is so important to me. What happened to him has really messed me up. I should have contacted you right away, but please understand that it's not because I don't care for him."

"I never wanted him to move to California," he replies stoically.

"Can you give me any information about the funeral?" Dropping my head between my knees, I clench my teeth together to keep from crying out.

"The service is in Brooklyn. Joe's going to be buried on

a plot with my parents—where his mother and I will some-day be buried as well." His voice cracks.

"If it's okay, I'd like to be there."

"Of course. A private viewing is scheduled Friday evening, and the memorial and burial service are the following morning at All Saints Catholic Church. Feel free to attend Saturday."

"Saturday?" I ask hesitantly.

"Is that a problem, Gabriella?" Any trace of vulnerability he showed a moment ago is overcome by sudden suspicion.

"A friend of mine was in the car with Joe." I run my hands through my shampoo-needy hair and pull at the roots. "She also passed in the accident."

"I'm aware of Joseph's passenger."

"Her funeral's on Thursday. In Alaska, David, and I don't know if we can travel to both states with only one day between services."

His voice is even when he replies, and he knowingly or unknowingly goes straight for my jugular. "Then maybe you should have picked up the first time I called you."

Teller, carrying my sandwich and a bag of chips, finds me on the floor with my face in my hands and the phone in pieces across the room. Thoughtfulness after the devastating conversation I suffered through officially kicks me over the point of sensibility, and I come apart.

I pulverize into one billion pieces.

He closes the door with his foot and sets the plate down before squatting in front of me to patch my shattered parts. His eyes are beautiful, my light at the end of a dark, never-ending tunnel.

"We'll make it work, Smella," my heart mender says. He listens with sweet consideration as I retell the details of my talk with Joe's father. "I'll get us there. We won't miss it."

When I get to the point in the conversation when David requested I get my things from Joe's and leave the key, Teller's jaw tightens and he stands straight. Easily frustrated and totally overprotective, he steps onto the balcony and lights a cigarette, drenched in sunlight. I watch smoke leave his lungs and reach for the blue sky, and I'm envious as it disappears into thin air.

"Get up and get dressed. I'll take you to pick up your shit." Teller's eyes squint as he takes a long drag. He holds nicotine in his lungs as he adds, "I need to get the fuck out of this house, anyway."

CHAPTER SIX

Now

Teller

"**I** should go home with Emerson after we get back." Ella's black bra shows through the thin white cotton T-shirt I lent her. She ties it in a knot at her waist and rolls the sleeves for a better fit. "He's ready to get out of here, and I need my own clothes. Besides, you probably want your space."

"Your clothes are fine," I say, spitting suds into the sink. After slipping my toothbrush into the holder, my eyes fall on Kristi's pink Oral-B. Without thinking, I open a drawer and drop it inside before I face absurdity. "And why would you say some shit like that?"

She shrugs, purposefully avoiding my eyes. Ella walks out of the bathroom, and I follow the scent of just-scrubbed skin and vanilla shampoo. Her long brown hair sweeps across her back, air-drying to a natural wave. She slips her bare feet into a pair of shoes and challenges me.

"This isn't a good look." Ella points from herself to me. "I shouldn't sleep in your bed, Teller. Joe and Kristi aren't even buried yet, and we're acting like they didn't exist."

"Don't be fucking ridiculous." I pull a flat-billed hat over my head and pocket my wallet and keys. "We don't need space from each other. That's not what we're about."

"They don't like it," she replies in a less aggressive tone. "And don't act like you didn't notice the way they looked at us earlier."

I stop with my hand on the doorknob and turn to the only person who has ever truly understood and accepted me. The only person who can handle me. "Who? Your brother and my sister? When have I ever given a shit about what they or anyone else thinks about us? Why the fuck would I start now?"

"What are we doing?" Her dark eyes drop to the carpet, and my heart falls with them. "Tell me what this is."

The right side of my mouth lifts at the question she's asked me over and over in the time we've known each other. Never once have I given her a straight answer, because never once have I had one to give. We are a conundrum of fucked up. A disappointment bomb. Ella and I are wrecked and damaged. But we own it.

So, I say what I always say.

"Tell me what this isn't."

I quietly follow her downstairs to an empty living room and whispers coming from the kitchen where we last left everybody. They're sitting around the table with cold coffee poured in untouched cups, speaking in hushed tones with troubled looks on their faces. Maby's the first to notice they're no longer alone, and she sits straight and forces a smile. The others fall into formation soon after.

"Are we already back to this shit?" I ask, smirking at their predictability. How many times have Ella and I walked into this spectacle? "We haven't done anything wrong."

Ella opens the refrigerator door and grabs a couple bottles of water, snubbing Emerson's death gaze. Her pale face is indifferent, and she doesn't utter a word before she opens the door leading to the garage, allowing it to slam closed behind her.

"We're concerned," Maby speaks for everyone. She always does. My sister's the smallest in our group, but she demands the most respect.

"Don't be," I answer with a shrug. "It's none of your fucking business, anyway."

"It's one hundred percent our business, asshole," Nicolette speaks up. Her hands are flat on the table, and her hazel eyes catch fire. "If you start this up again, it's only a matter of time before you're trying to murder each other. Don't forget that we're the ones who have to break it up."

I snatch an apple from the counter and smile. "Stay out of it, Nic."

Before I get the opportunity to follow Ella to the car, Emerson pushes his chair back and stands. He's dressed himself since the earthquake, but there's no sign of the comic relief he usually delivers when the mood's tense. He's nothing more than an older brother turned father figure, concerned for his little girl.

"You guys are bad for each other, Teller. I won't stand by and watch my sister go through that again," he warns.

Sinking my teeth into the red apple, bitter then sweet juice pools in my mouth and dribbles down my chin. I wipe it away on the top of my wrist before taking a second bite. Four pairs of eyes zero in on me so intensely that if animosity had a color it would be green-brown-hazel-hazel.

"Oh, was I supposed to respond to that?" I ask Emerson. His jaw clenches. "Because I thought you were talking about something you have no fucking idea about again. Ella and I are fine. Back off."

"Teller," Husher interjects. He turns in his chair to face me. "I'm not judging or telling you how to live your lives. It makes sense you'd turn to each other after the accident, but things got really intense right before Ella met Joe. The mindset you guys fall into isn't healthy. The way you talk, move, and think, it's almost like you become one person. It was just starting to get better."

I toss my half-eaten apple into the trash and leave, doing my best to ignore the sinking feeling in my stomach that comes with knowing they're right.

"Told you so," my co-disappointer chimes in. She leans against the driver's side door with a smile curving her red lips.

"Shut up and get in," I say playfully, unlocking my black on black Range Rover.

I reverse out of the garage and stop at the end of the driveway. With sunlight brightening the coppers and reds in Ella's hair, she adjusts the seat forward to a comfortable position. She doesn't know the last person to sit there was Kristi, whose legs were longer than hers, and I don't tell her.

I won't ever tell her, because it won't ever matter again.

Avoiding the corner where the accident happened— where the stop sign is still down and my neighbor's lawn is still destroyed—I open the moon roof to drench us in vitamin D and drive away, watching my house in the rear-view mirror until I turn the corner and it disappears.

"Where are we going?" my passenger asks. She sits back in the red leather seat as her hair swirls with the breeze.

"Let's find somewhere to sit before we head to Joe's. I want to talk to you about something."

*E*lla and I end up at a small café not far from the lake. We ask for a table on the patio and order orange wheat beer and appetizers. Our chairs are unsteady, and we pick at our food, but fresh air gives me new perspective, and Ella has color in her cheeks. She sits on the opposite side from me with her legs crossed and questions on her lips. It kills me not to know what she's thinking, but I'm content with the easy silence between us.

I finish my beer and don't order a second. She orders a third and finally asks, "What's on your mind, troublemaker?"

"When you were on the phone with Joe's dad, I called the hospital," I say, smiling at the waitress as she places a glass of water in front of me. "I got us some time off."

Ella's cheeks burn red, and her long eyelashes lazily sweep across the tops of her cheekbones. "It's funny how I didn't think to do that myself. No one needed to talk to me?"

I shake my head. "They know what's up, Smella. The papers we need to sign will come in the mail."

"When do we go back, next week?"

"Thirty days," I reply. She stops before the glass touches her lips and sets it down in front of the breadsticks. "Don't argue. We deserve the time."

"I don't know, Tell. Won't it be easier if we return to our normal routine?" She exhales heavily and sits back. The chair rocks from side to side. "We're needed at the hospital, and I have bills."

"It'll be easier if we're together." My heart beat, beat, beats inside my chest. "And I have an idea about your bills."

Ella rolls her eyes and laughs out loud. "An idea? Like when you would take care of my car payment and I had to threaten your life to get you to stop?"

"Something like that," I say, clearing my throat nervously.

Her eyes search mine, and she replies, "No. You're not paying my bills. I'll move stuff around if I need to. I'll figure something out, but I won't take your money."

"Move in with me." Words I've kept locked behind my lips bolt without abandon, shocking both Ella and me. But they feel like the truest things I've said in a while.

"No. Hell no," she responds immediately, leaning forward. "You cannot ask me to move in with you, Teller."

"Why not?" I say, meeting her head-on. Bravado trumps nervousness, and I love a challenge.

"Are you being serious right now, because if you're messing with me, that's mean." Frustration takes a drink from her beer, blinking over the top of the glass. Late afternoon light glistens from her nail polish and the rings on her fingers, and I can still smell the scent of vanilla in her hair.

Excitement fills me all the way up, lessening leftover guilt that plagued me after the shame squad cornered me. There are a million and one reasons why Ella and I shouldn't be within thirty feet of each other. God help us if history re-peats itself—we won't survive—but she's my girl, and that's a solid enough reason for me to follow this through.

"I'm not messing with you," I assure her.

She presses her lips together and taps her fingertips on the table. "You can't ask me to move in with you because Kristi isn't here. It's not fair to me, and it's not fair to her."

Dodging the reality of our situation, I scrub my hands down my face and push the accident from my mind. If I try hard enough, it's almost possible to forget the person I spent the last year of my life with is dead. Then I don't have to feel guilty about *not* feeling that guilty, because I can pretend it didn't happen. I don't feel anything.

Avoidance is bliss.

"We didn't finish our conversation the other night … before the crash," I manage to say, rubbing my hand across the back of my neck.

"When you told me Kristi was moving in with you? That conversation, Dr. Reddy?" Ella wipes her mouth on a white paper napkin and throws it on her plate. She looks away from me, straight-lipped and shaking her foot. "Can we go now?"

"It wasn't like that, Gabriella. I said she wanted to move in, not that I wanted her to." I pat my pockets for my cigarettes. "I didn't have a chance to say everything—"

She scoffs, shaking her head. "Can we not do this right now? As flattered as I am to be your second choice, I need to go to my dead boyfriend's house and pick up my things before his dad tosses them out on the street. If you can't handle that, take me home so I can get my car."

I slip a smoke between my lips, about to light it when

our waitress—a blonde twenty-something aspiring actress, who looks identical to every other twenty-something aspiring actress in LA—rushes over, blinking too fast and gaping like a fish.

"You can't smoke in a restaurant, sir. That hasn't been allowed in California since, like, forever." She sets the check in front of me and walks away, muttering something about cancer and premature wrinkles.

With the unlit Marlboro between my teeth, I drop cash to the table and head for the exit. Ella swallows the last swig from her glass and follows me out, hooking her finger in my belt loop. Fifty feet from the café entrance, I light my cig and take a drag, filling my lungs with toxic chemicals that talk me off the ledge.

I exhale a dense cloud of smoke over my head and flick ash to the sidewalk. A lady jogging with her black Great Dane runs between Ella and me, clipping me with her elbow and muttering, "You can't smoke here, asshole."

"Maybe you should quit, Prick," my partner in crime teases, turning her head to watch the woman pass.

Draping my arm across her shoulders, I tuck Ella into my side and inhale another hit. "Maybe everyone needs to get off my dick."

She tosses her head back and laughs, lacing her unmarked fingers with my tattooed ones. We stay this way the entire walk back to my car, untroubled for a few priceless minutes. To be with her in this way feels like the most natural thing in the word.

She's your best friend, I remind myself. *It didn't work out for a reason.*

I'm going to hell, and Joe's going to kick my ass the

entire way there.

As distance closes between us and Joe's house, trauma tightens around our throats, choking the sense of sensibility we got into the car with. Ella shuts off, lifting her feet to the seat and circling her arms around her knees. She turns her body and stares out the window, watching the world pass. Tears run from her eyes and down her cheeks. When she smacks them away, I pretend not to notice, giving this moment to her.

We're all ticking time bombs.

I pull onto the brick driveway in front of Joseph's storybook home and kill the engine. Neither one of us moves. We don't breathe or blink or exist outside of my Range Rover. Ella stares at the house, and I look at her, waiting for sorrow to tell me what to do.

I would walk to the ends of the Earth for her. Die for her. All she has to do is ask.

She asks for my company, not for my life. "Will you go in with me?"

"Yeah, of course," I reply, unbuckling my seatbelt.

The porch light's lit because Joe didn't get the chance to come home and turn it off, and the sprinklers turn on, watering grass he'll never mow. His girlfriend's here, but he'll never invite her in again. I walk around the front of my vehicle, kicking three editions of the *LA Times* out of my way, to the passenger side where big brown eyes brimming with sadness swing from the house to me.

"It feels haunted," she says. Ella's eyelashes clump together with tears, and her chin quivers. She's bitten her nails so low they're bleeding.

"That's not the house," I respond, undoing her grip

around her knees and capturing her trembling hands in my own. "It's us."

When she can't steady her hands long enough to unlock the deadbolt, she passes me the key and takes a step back with no intention of going in first. The red painted door sticks to the frame but cracks open to a dark, humid room. When you're in the medical field, coming home in the middle of the day after a twenty-four-hour shift, you need to trick your mind into thinking it's dark. We all have blackout curtains over most of our windows.

"Let me find the lamp," I say when the pastel evening light following us inside isn't enough to brighten the room.

Ella shuts the door and stands in the entryway while I walk over to the coffee table beside the couch, remembering where it is from memory. Nearly knocking it over, I pull the chain and illuminate the family room with dim yellow-orange light. A split second passes before my brain catches up with my eyes, interpreting the scene we walked in on.

I turn the light off.

"Teller, turn it back on."

"No way," I reply. My heart pounds hard enough to chatter my teeth.

"Please, turn the lamp on," she repeats in an even tone, void of the panic I feel. "Now."

There's no delay between my eyes and intellect the second time around. I know exactly what I'm looking at when I see it. I know because Joe told me he was going to ask Ella to marry him a month ago. I knew, and this is part of what I was trying to tell her before the wreck.

It *was* now or never.

Now it's just never.

But I didn't know it was going to be like this.

On every flat surface from the bookshelves, the entertainment center, and the hardwood floors, sits bouquet after bouquet of red roses in murky glass vases. Some tipped over during the earthquake, and it's a jungle in here. After three days in a stuffy house with no one to take care of them, the water on the bottom of the vases is cloudy, releasing a heavy mildew scent. Petals darkened around the edges and wilted, decaying from their normal shade to a burnt orange color. Flower buds droop over dry stems, and leaves fall to the floor.

"What the hell is—" Her eyes find it when I do, and we both chew on our words.

On the center of the coffee table is a small blue box holding a diamond ring.

It shines in the low light, waving a future Ella won't ever live in front of her face. My first instinct is to flip the fucking table over, because Joe was going to marry my person and because the look on her face tells me she might have wanted to, but Gabriella walks over and snaps the lid shut, enclosing the rock.

"What did he think I was going to do with these roses?" she asks in a still-calm voice. Color has drained from her face again, and her expression shifts from regretful to indifferent. "It's wasteful."

Ella doesn't give the flowers or the ring any more consideration and walks to the back of the house to Joe's room. While she's gathering her things, I take it upon myself to make sure the windows and doors are locked, and I turn on a few more lights so it won't look like the house is empty from outside. There's a dirty plate in the kitchen sink and a photo of Ella stuck on the fridge by a magnet. The trash needs to be taken out, and his answering machine light blinks. Time's stopped, and everything is so utterly normal, Joe could walk in the door and I would believe he never left.

"Will you help me with the flowers? I don't know when his dad plans on coming by, but I can't leave it like this for him to find." Ella places a small suitcase by the door and faces the room.

The roses, dead or alive, look absurd next to her.

"You already packed your stuff?" I ask.

She nods, looking to me with brittle determination. "I don't have much here."

For the next half hour, we leave the front door open as evening turns to night, and cool air carries away the scent of decay. I toss the wilted flowers and dry leaves into the garbage can, and Ella washes the vases, towel drying and setting them on the kitchen table. Before we take off, she goes through the refrigerator, throwing away anything that can go bad, and I check the mail, dropping bills that won't be paid and fast food coupons Joe will never use beside the house phone.

Ella sweeps crushed leaves and stray rose petals from the floor, and I replace the trash bag, even though there won't be anyone here to fill it again. We both avoid the ring, walking around it and looking everywhere but at the coffee table. While I push the couch back against the wall, she goes down the hallway, straightening picture frames.

I wait by the front door with an unlit cigarette between my lips and my hands in my pockets, still contemplating flipping the table over when Ella reappears with a small fish tank between her palms. An orange goldfish swims in circles as its water sloshes back and forth, trickling over Ella's fingers.

"What the fuck is that?" I ask. My cigarette bobs up and down.

"Joe's pet," she answers, holding it out for me to see. The fish keeps swimming, and more water dribbles to the floor. "It was in his office."

"That's not a pet, Smella. Put it back where you found it."

"We can't leave it here," she says, tucking it under her arm. The ends of her hair dip into the tank. "Do you think there's a goldfish rescue or something we can take it to?"

My laugh echoes off the walls. "I doubt it."

"Then I have to take it home." Without looking around one more time, she walks past me toward the car. "Leave the key after you lock the door."

"What about the ring?" I call out, sticking my cigarette behind my ear.

"Leave it." She slips into the front seat. Her eyes meet mine through glass and distance. "It's not mine."

Fish water sloshes around the tank on the drive home, and I have teeth marks on my tongue from biting it so hard. If it were up to me, I'd leave Joe's animal on someone's porch, ring the doorbell, and run. But Ella's gripping the tank like her life depends on it, and I can't bring myself to tell her she has to give one more thing up today.

"What's its name?" I ask instead, ignoring the water dripping onto the leather.

"Phish with a P," she answers, looking into the tank. "It

was a patient's, and no one claimed the fish after he … died. So Joe brought him home. Maybe I can take him back to the hospital. The kids would like it."

That do-good motherfucker was always acting selflessly, making the rest of us look like chumps. I'm too busy saving lives to rescue unclaimed goldfish.

"Did you know?" Ella asks softly.

I slow the car down to a stop at a red light. Headlights from vehicles crossing traffic in front us shine in my eye, and music too low to hear plays faintly from the speakers. Pink and blue rocks on the bottom of the tank swish, and it's not the fish's fault its rescuer was killed.

"No, I didn't know Joe was the fucking fish whisperer," I say, tapping my fingers on the steering wheel.

Ella laughs lightly, and I look up to find her watching me.

"Did you know he was going to propose to me?" she clarifies.

The light turns green, but I don't drive forward. "Yes."

It's as if air has been sucked from the car and we're left to breathe remorse. For seven years, she's been everything to me. For the last seven years, I've taken what I can get from her and stolen what I could not. No matter the consequences, Gabriella Mason is who I have always wanted—*needed*—most. At one point, that meant giving her up. But now…

Traffic honks once, twice, three, and four times. Ella stares at me like there's hope, and I can't move because I'm hopeless.

"I could never have said yes to him, Teller," she whispers. Tears she must have an unlimited supply of fall from her tired eyes.

I lift her hand to my lips and kiss her knuckles, letting my own sadness drop to her skin. "It killed me."

"You knew," she replies, resting her hand on the side of my face. "You've always known."

As the light turns from green to yellow, the line of cars behind me maneuvers around us, screeching their tires and their drivers shouting expletives. I accelerate right before the signal changes red and slam on my brakes in the cross-walk to keep from colliding with oncoming traffic.

The tank slides from Ella's lap and hits the dashboard, splashing goldfish water everywhere and tumbling to her feet. Like this isn't a one hundred-thousand-dollar car, she scoops it up, flinging tiny colored pebbles and plastic sea plants across the red interior.

"Oh my gosh. Phish is still in there," she says, lifting the tank. Swimming in an inch of water, the tiny fish gapes at me.

"You have got to be fucking kidding," I say, white-knuck-le gripping the steering wheel. "I told you to put that thing back where you found it, and now look at my car."

She cradles the fish tank against her chest. "It's water, Teller. It'll dry."

We pull into my garage twenty minutes later, soaked in fish water and pissed off. She's a thoughtless disaster, I'm a condescending ass, and neither one of us is going to apolo-gize first. Thus, ending this night like any normal Tuesday.

Ella runs into the house to save the fish from its un-timely death, and I lower the windows to air out my Rover. Tiny rocks fall from my lap and tap, tap, tap against the ce-ment floor, rolling under my shoes as I step over them. The fish ambassador is placing the tank on the bookshelf when I walk into the living room, ignoring my dirty looks and general presence. Maby, Husher, Nicolette, and Emerson ignore me, too—still here, still watching my TV, still sitting on my couch.

"That thing isn't staying," I say, pointing to Phish. "I don't have time to take care of it, Ella. Take it home with you."

She faces me with a sly grin on her pouty lips. The front of her shirt is wet and sticking to her skin. "Don't I live here now? Isn't this *our* fish?"

"What?" my sister and Emerson question concurrently.

"Here we go," Nicolette mumbles under her breath. She turns off the television.

"You're moving in?" I ask. Anger melts away, leaving me lighthearted and unable to hold back a smile.

"Only if my fish can move in, too."

"I love Phish," I say.

And the ground shakes.

Literally.

An aftershock from today's earthquake rocks the entire house back and forth.

Emerson dashes across the living room and nosedives under the kitchen table, and the fucking fish tanks falls over again, dumping a two-inch goldfish onto the floor. They both flop around like idiots, and I couldn't care less because Ella's going to stay.

CHAPTER SEVEN

Before

Teller

"**Y**ou got another tattoo?" my dad asks, pouring himself a cup of coffee. Steam rises from the freshly brewed caffeine, but he takes a drink without flinching. Judging by the bags under his eyes, it was another late night at the hospital. "On your neck of all places. Are you purposely trying to destroy your future?"

Mid-bite, I lower my spoon into my cereal bowl. It hits the glass with an audible clink, and milk splashes onto the table. "I don't know, Pops. I was kind of banking on my patients being more concerned with my ability to save their lives than what I look like."

America's most respected cardiac surgeon turned multi-millionaire after his investment in a groundbreaking heart medication took off licks coffee from his mustache and laughs. "Do you realize how stupid you sound?"

"Thanks for the vote of confidence," I utter, carrying

my uneaten breakfast to the sink.

Dad's glasses slide down the bridge of his nose as he studies my ink. "At least it's quality work. I don't like giving you a hard time, Teller, but you're making your life harder than it needs to be. There might be a day when your patients won't judge you by the way you look, but your professors and your colleagues will. You need to be smarter and work harder than everyone in your class to be taken seriously now."

"I've always been smarter than those motherfuckers," I say, smirking. "And can I get through college before I think about medical school?"

"You're going to medical school, Teller. We're not having that argument again." My dad gulps liquid adrenaline, assessing me over his blue mug. Green eyes the same shade as mine harden. "Have you started applying yet?"

Leaning against the counter across from my father, I lift my backpack over my shoulder and scrutinize the man who gave me life. Sometime during high school, I grew a few inches taller than him, but no one has ever wondered what I'll look like when I'm older. Minus the mustache—I'm a spitting image of this guy.

"Applications aren't due until this summer, and I'm only applying to one school," I remind him. Smirks fall from our faces.

"You can at least attempt to get into Stanford, Teller. Appease me," he says. The veins in his neck expand with his rise in blood pressure. "We made a deal when you decided to stay in LA and go to UCLA. You said when it came time to apply for medical school, you'd apply to Stanford. And to be honest, at this point, you'll need all the help you can get. I have connections there."

"Sorry to disappoint you." I cross my arms over my chest, unwilling to budge.

I've spent my entire life accepting the fact that my family expects me to follow in my father's precise footsteps. There's no shame in our career choice, so I've never put up much of a fight.

But things have changed.

My dad reaches past me and drops his mug into the sink with my bowl. "Does this have anything to do with Gabriella Mason?"

Heat rushes to my face, and I can't bring myself to look at him.

"Are you dating her?" He continues. His tone of voice softens. "I've never seen you get this serious with anyone. Maby says the two of you are close."

Pushing myself away from the counter, I grab my keys and head toward the front door. Class starts in an hour, and I'm as interested in discussing my relationship with Ella as I am in applying to medical school at Stanford. This is one part of my life I'm in control of, and I'm not willing to give it up.

"I won't be home tonight," I call out before I leave.

"Think about Stan—" Dad replies before the door slams closed, crushing his last word.

Summer arrived early this year, dropping a record-breaking hot spell over Southern California. Barely tipping nine in the morning, heat waves hover over the street, stretching to the end of the block. Leather interior burns my bare arms, and the air conditioner doesn't cool fast enough. I drive the gun metal gray BMW M2 my

91

parents bought me when I graduated high school down the road, with every intention of going to school until my phone rings.

"Can we ditch today?" Ella asks in her just-woke-up voice. "We won't have another chance before finals. Take me somewhere before I melt."

When I get to her apartment, Nicolette answers the door with oversized curlers in her hair and makeup dotted under her eyelids. She's barefoot, dressed in shorts that are too short and a shirt that exposes her navel.

"What do you want?" she asks, annoyed.

"Do you ever go home?" I take two steps forward and one step back.

Nic stands in the doorway and presses her hand to my chest, blocking the way. She smells like hairspray, and her hazel eyes are more brown than green without fake eyelashes framing them. Her expression is regretful, but I pretend not to notice.

"Emerson said it's probably not a good idea for you to come around for a while, Teller."

I lean against the doorframe and smirk, letting cool air from the apartment chill my heated skin. I've watched this girl grow from a dirty-faced kid, to a teenager with a crush on her best friend's older brother, to this *Real Housewives of Beverly Hills* wannabe. And it's the latest reinvention I despise the most.

"Ella and I are fine," I say, poking one of her pink rollers.

She ducks and swats my touch away, fixing the wayward curl. "She tried to scratch your eyes out, and her brother had to lift her over his shoulder because she wouldn't leave the bar."

Dragging my hands down my face, I hold back a laugh at the memory from last weekend's mess. Too much booze and a simple misunderstanding turned our night upside down; Ella, drunk and overreacting, was carried out kicking and screaming, and I, drunk and defensive, wasn't allowed to follow. Which was unacceptable, and resulted in a near-physical altercation with Em.

"We had too much to drink." I shrug. "It's not a huge deal."

Nic arches an eyebrow. "And the weekend before that when you threw her phone out of a moving car?"

"You forgot to mention that she threw mine first," I reply, but it knocks me down a level. Nicolette doesn't need to remind me that my relationship with Ella is ... volatile. But it's *my* relationship.

I also don't need her to stand in my way, because one way or another, I'll find my way in.

"Fine." She exhales heavily and steps aside, allowing me to walk by. "Please don't make me regret this. I have class today, and Emerson's already at work. There won't be anyone here to referee."

The small television in front of a mint-colored sofa broadcasts the morning news with the volume on low. Mid-morning sun filters through the mini blinds above the kitchen sink, and two slices of burnt toast pop up from the toaster, filling the air with the scent of dough and smoke.

"Don't judge me, fucker," Nicolette says with a small smile on her lips. She drops the charcoal-like bread onto a napkin and uses a knife to scrape grape jelly across the seared surface.

"Have some soot with your bread, Nic," I joke, heading toward Ella's room.

"Asshole," she mumbles under her breath.

Gabriella's door is cracked open, giving me a small glimpse inside her space before I step inside. An untouched glass of orange juice sits on the nightstand beside her bed, and yesterday's clothes are thrown across the top of her laundry hamper. Ella's sleeping on her stomach under pink sheets with her hair fanned across the pillow. Sunlight shines through thin violet curtains, painting the walls lavender.

Walking around to the side of her queen-sized bed, I lift the corner of the sheet and slide in, pressing my body against her sleep-warm form. I slide my hand under her tank top, up her backbone and down her side, brushing the tips of my fingers along Ella's bare breast. Her breath hitches.

"I thought you were awake," I whisper into her hair.

Sleepy in Venice curves to her side, rubbing her bottom against my shorts. She beats my composure half to death, deliberately rolling her hips, inciting a riot. I feel myself harden, and a rush of effervescence spreads through my limbs and numbs my face, waving a white flag.

"My bed missed me." Ella turns in my arms and shoves me against the mattress, straddling my legs. She slowly creeps closer to my cock, pushing her hands under the hem of my shirt and along my abs. "My bed was lonely."

Saccharine torment strokes her softest part over my hardest, trailing her nails down my chest. I cover my eyes in the bend of my elbow and pull my bottom lip between my teeth.

"I thought you didn't want to melt today?" I ask, keeping my hands to myself before Ella gets fucked hard enough for the entire complex to hear.

She grips my wrists and forces my hands to the bed, slowing the sway in her hips. Peppermint sweetens her breath, and freckles across her nose and cheeks are close enough to count. Ella's full chest is barely contained by her low-neck tank, and I can see her nipples through the thin fabric.

"Don't worry," she says, lowering her face to mine. Pretty lips hover over my own. "I brushed my teeth."

Her kiss comes close enough to taste, but a knock on the door stops it from getting deeper. Ella sits straight and rolls her eyes, bringing my hand to her chest so I can feel how hard her heart pumps.

"What?" she calls out, pressing her hand to my heartbeat.

They're flying.

"I'm out of here, girl. Em and I are meeting my parents for dinner tonight, so we'll be home late," Nicolette says. Her voice is muffled through the door.

"Sounds good," Smella replies, meeting my eyes as our beats palpitate. "See you later, Nic."

"Do I even want to know what you guys are doing in there?" she asks.

"Get the fuck out of here, Nicolette," I say, throwing a pillow at the door.

"You're such a jerk," she grumbles, walking away. A minute later, the front door opens and closes, leaving us alone in the apartment.

Carefully lifting Ella from my lap, I position her beside

me and roll out of bed, turning to adjust my shorts out of her line of sight. My face is hot, my fingertips tingle, and my dick is hard. We never get past the over-the-clothes shit, and it leaves me aching and thoughtless. But if one of us doesn't stop, we can do this all day.

We *have* done this all day.

Heavy touches, harsh rubbing, and pushing each other so close to coming our skin catches fire. We stop before the world burns, because it's never the right time. We stop because we're not official, and I won't fuck her until we are, no matter how hard she begs or how badly I want to know what she tastes like between her legs.

"Where are you going?" Ella stretches across the bed and clutches onto the hem of my shorts. "Get back in bed with me."

"Fuck no." I step away from her reach and head toward the bathroom to splash cold water onto my face, not ruling out a shower if my dick doesn't soften. "Get dressed. I can't be in this apartment with you all day. You're insane."

She follows me into the living room, dressed in nothing but a pair of black cotton underwear and a see-through top, sipping orange juice. Her hair's tangled, and she still has sleep lines embedded on the side of her face, but she's easily the sexiest woman alive.

"Stay away, Smella," I warn her, hurrying my pace.

Setting the glass onto the coffee table, she tiptoes after me with the right amount of sway in her hips, tousling bedhead between her fingers. Perfectly round, pink nipples peek through slight fabric, hacking at my tenacity, and I know what her breasts feel like cupped in the palms of my hands. It's too good to deny.

CLOSER

"What if I promise to keep my hands to myself?" she asks, closing the space between us. "What if I'm a good girl?"

"You're a shitty liar, Gabriella." I slam the bathroom door in her face and lock it, immediately turning to the sink for deliverance. "And you're the fucking Antichrist. Leave me alone, witch, and go put some clothes on."

An hour later, we arrive at the Roosevelt Hotel in Hollywood. It's noon on a Thursday, and the pool's packed with hipsters wearing fedoras and girls in small bikinis searching for celebrities. In a city full of dreamers, where everyone's a star, nothing slows down—not for a job, another person, or a breath.

While the rest of LA whirls around us, Ella and I take it slow.

"Should we get a room and stay for the weekend?" I kiss the top of Ella's bare shoulder, licking banana-scented sunscreen off my lips.

Eyes hidden under a pair of Aviators, she looks back and smiles, reflecting my image in her sunglasses, sharp with palm trees and the Roosevelt Tower in the distance. "Will there be sex involved?"

I lie against the chaise lounge with persistence between my knees and stretch my arms over my head. The sun's out, drinks flow, and the water's cool. UVAs and UVBs warm my bones and redden my skin, and sipping stars in the middle of the day makes it feel like Friday.

"Depends." I smirk. My cock twitches, and I'm glad

97

there's a cold pool to dive in if needed.

Ella reclines against my bare chest, resting her head under my chin and reaching for my arms to wrap around her stomach. Her legs run parallel with mine, parading the difference between her untouched skin alongside my tattooed thighs.

"On what?" she asks, sweeping her fingers across the top of my hand.

"If you're ready to call me boyfriend."

"You're already my best boyfriend, Tell," she replies in a guarded tone.

Disappointment shady enough to block the sun hovers over my head, but I'm in no mood to dwell on this crap today. My manhood can only handle so many hits, and I've reached my limit of shits to give this week. I'm going to bask in this motherfucking sunshine, but not with her.

"I need a drink." I urge her shoulders forward until she sits up. Space is essential before bad blood turns the pool crimson. "Want something?"

"Teller, don't overreact."

Pulling a red V-neck over my head, I drop a pair of Ray-Bans over my eyes and slide an unlit cigarette behind my ear. I scratch the back of my neck, hardly containing my temper and ask, "Are you sure you don't want anything? Water, beer, a beating heart?"

Lightheaded from the champagne Ella ordered when we got here, I approach a cocktail waitress on my way to the bar, but I don't need someone to take my drink order. The redheaded server touches my elbow as she passes, as if there wasn't enough room for her to get by without doing so. I return her smile, but can't see past the heartbreaker who was drinking straight from the Korbel bottle, flipping me off as I walked away.

"Corona, please," I mumble to the bartender.

Cold beer strokes my tongue and cools my body from the inside out, giving me exactly what I need to clear my mind for a moment. I order a second and spin my stool around to face the pool and lean back, dulling anxiety with booze. Ella hasn't moved from the chaise I left her on, sunbathing on her stomach with the champagne bottle dangling from her hand over the edge of the lounge chair. Judging by the steady rise and fall of her back, she's asleep.

"How's it going?" redhead asks as she walks by for the tenth time. She loads her tray with napkins and straws she doesn't need more of, sucking in an already thin stomach, flaunting her fake chest.

"Good, thanks," I say into the neck of my brew, tasting lime and salt on my lips.

Jessica Rabbit's lipstick looks black under my dark lenses, accentuating her abnormally plump mouth. "Are you from around here?"

"Beverly Hills," I say vaguely, turning toward the bar.

"Nice," she replies, sliding a white paper napkin in front of me with her name and number written in pink marker across the top. "I'm off in a few hours. We should hang out."

The E in Everly bleeds into the V, and it's so fucking basic, I pocket the napkin to show Husher later. She mistakes this for an invitation and squeezes herself between my stool and the fella's beside me, pressing her tits against my arm. The bartender smirks as he walks by, and I lift my empty Corona, indicating that I need a new one.

"I have plans later, but maybe another time." I let her down easy, offering a casual smile.

The other men can't take their eyes off of her rack, but I can't get over how much makeup she has on her face. Nothing about this girl is authentic, and the hand drawn arch in her eyebrows has left her expression permanently surprised.

"What's your name, sweetheart?" she asks, circling her finger around the lip of my beer bottle. Because I didn't want to drink it anyway.

"Prick," a voice I know by heart answers. Ella, barefoot and sun-kissed, saunters over and shoos the waitress away. "His name is Prick. Motherfucker for short."

The entire bar laughs at my expense, and I laugh with them, known to go by motherfucker from time to time. Jessica Rabbit takes one look at my favorite smartass and rolls her eyes, stomping away to find another idiot to fool.

"I called Emerson. He's coming to get me." Ella shoves my towel into my chest and stalks off, uttering, "Feel free to leave with your girlfriend, Prick."

"Shit," I say under my breath, tossing a few twenty-dollar bills onto the bar. I chase Ella into the hotel lobby and run between crowds of people trying to check-in, tripping over a suitcase. "Gabriella, wait a second."

Capturing her by the elbow right before she disappears, I guide Ella toward the hall of elevators, away from rubbernecked hotel guests too fucking nosy to mind their own business. She shakes free from my grip, but doesn't put up a fight when I force her into an empty elevator car and press the button for the top floor.

"Nice. You've kidnapped me," she says, pressing every other button on the control panel. "Are you going to sleep with that girl since you won't sleep with me?"

"Don't be ridiculous," I reply. "I don't even know who she is."

"Save it." She stands directly in front of the double doors, waiting for them to open. "I can't stomach your bullshit today."

Resentment barrels through me, crushing my patience and splitting my heart. I spin her around and push her against the gold-plated wall, caging defiance between my arms. She slashes my throat with the sharpness in her eyes, and I use my dying breath to say, "Fuck you."

The elevator suddenly dings and the doors open on the second floor, where an older couple in matching fitover sunglasses and Velcro shoes hesitates outside the entrance. The man attempts to smile, but the woman scowls.

I slam the palm of my hand against the *Door Close* button.

Ella pushes against my chest, breaks stitches in the neck of my shirt, and digs her fingernails into my arm until small beads of blood paint her nails red. I inhale deeply, surviving off her rage, taking it to my vein like a junkie.

"You're all I want," I say, pressing her against the wall with my body. "You're the only person I want to be with."

The elevator doors open on the third floor, and this time she closes them. Ella wraps her legs around my waist, grips my hair between her fingers, and slowly rocks her hips along my hardening cock. Her head drops and she cries out, arching her back. I kiss mouthfuls of her chest, pulling down her yellow bikini straps to lick the curve of her breast. We slide into the corner of the elevator, barely breathing and indecent when we arrive on the fourth floor.

"Teller, stop," Ella whispers breathlessly, looking over my shoulder. Her lips are swollen, and she hurries to correct her top.

"We can catch the next ride," someone says gladly.

I look over my shoulder to find a middle-aged man grinning from ear-to-ear, covering his son's eyes. He gives me a thumbs-up, but I don't return his enthusiasm and help Ella cover herself. She steps unsteadily to her feet, straightening her hair and lifting her bag from the floor.

"This is our stop," she lies, walking past me. Ella waits for our company to leave before she asks, "Do you honestly think this will work between us?"

"Are you joking?" I ask. My heart races. "I'm not your mom, Ella. I'm not your dad. You don't have to worry about me leaving you."

"Why would you bring them up?" Her entire body stiffens, defensive and small. "What do my parents have to do with how insane you are? Think about it, Teller. Really think about this. When have we ever spent an entire day together without it turning into a fight?"

"It doesn't stop you from rubbing all over my dick," I reply.

She scoffs. "You're a joke."

I smile, despite the ache in my chest. "And your nipple is showing."

Ella straightens her bikini, slaps me across the face, and takes the stairs down to her brother.

CHAPTER EIGHT

Now

Teller

"**W**e should head in."

Early morning Alaskan weather turns Ella's breath white and the tip of her nose red. Her eyes shine like glass, and she stands close to me for warmth, but not too close under the microscope of Kristi's family.

The sky's gray, and the scent of rain hangs in the air—something we don't experience much of in California. Bound by snowcapped mountains and green forests, summertime in Anchorage is nothing like summer in Los Angeles. I could use a cigarette, but secondhand smoke might kill the trees.

"In a minute." Licking my lips, I taste nicotine from the last cigarette I smoked before we left the hotel. I suffocate in my suit, trapped by wool and cashmere, choking on the necktie. Panic closes my veins and claws at my chest, and I need the fuck out of here.

I unbutton my jacket and loosen my tie, searching for an escape.

"Hey." Emerson clamps his hand over my shoulder and turns me away from the church. He discreetly presses a silver flask into my chest. "You doing, okay? We need you to hold it together until the service is over. We're going to get through this, Tell."

Jack Daniel's tastes like avoidance, peppery and woodsy as it numbs my tongue and leaves a trace of fire from my esophagus to my stomach. I swig mouthfuls, preferring bourbon's burn to guilt's emptiness.

"Is that better?" Ella fixes my tie. There's no judgment in her expression, only undiluted understanding. "Maby and Husher ran inside to save us a seat, but we can't stay out here much longer. The funeral's about to start."

My head swims in liquor-based comfort, and my heartbeat settles to a low rhythm. I can't take my eyes off her, long-legged in a black dress made of lace. Ella's nails are painted bright red, and her long brown hair is curled and pulled half up away from her face. Black heels still don't make her as tall as I am, but I can look into her eyes without bending my knees.

"We'll meet you inside," Emerson says. He takes Nicolette's hand and leads her toward the red brick church with a green roof, small enough to be a single family home.

"I don't want to do this, Smella," I admit. Pressure builds behind my eyes, and my jaw aches.

"Neither do I." She takes the flask from my hand and takes a swallow, handling her liquor as well as I can.

Running a hand through my hair, I exhale and say, "I never met Kristi's parents, and the one time her sister came to visit, I took them to dinner and she talked shit about my tattoos the entire time. It got weird, so I left."

Ella smiles, sipping another swig and coughing. She passes the flask back to me. "I remember that. You didn't see Kristi again until she left town."

Scoping out the church, backdropped by boulders, brush, and hundred-year-old trees, I can't place the girl I know here. Kristi's a star-struck leaf eater who thinks every song is about her. She loves sun, sand, and shitty reality television. Kristi once stood in line overnight for a cell phone and spent entire paychecks at the boutique she works at.

There's no trace of her amongst the great outdoors, flannel jackets, and sixty-degree weather in August. It feels like I'm here to honor a complete stranger.

"Come on, Teller. It's time to go in." Ella takes my hand and squeezes my fingers.

I follow her up the cobblestone path, impressed with her ability to walk on this shit in stilettos. The scent of wet wood and myrrh welcomes us at the door, followed by a gray-haired gentleman in rubber rain boots, offering us a memorial pamphlet.

"Since when is Kristi Catholic?" Ella whispers, nodding toward the life-sized crucifix suspended above the altar.

"She might have mentioned it once or twice," I say, putting my sunglasses on. "But she didn't actively practice or anything."

Ella takes one more opportunity to flatten my tie and run her fingers through my hair, correcting the mess I made of it. Heads turn when we step onto the green carpet between pews, but confidence leads me to our seats with her shoulders back and chin held high, and it's impossible not to mimic.

Our family greets us with half-smiles and tears in their eyes. My parents, who flew in this morning, saved Ella and me a place beside them. I've managed to avoid their phone calls in the week since Kristi and Joe passed, but the sight of my mother and the comfort she comes with nearly drops me to my knees.

I slip Emerson the flask, and Ella accepts a Bible from Maby before we sit. There's no space between our bodies, from our legs to our shoulders, but I want more. I want to fall onto her lap and squeeze my eyes shut while she holds her hands over my ears, until this thing is over.

"How are you holding up, baby?" Mom asks, patting my leg affectionately.

I don't answer, because there are no words to offer once my eyes fall on the casket. Covered by a white pall, resting at the front of the church, it's surrounded by boring flower arrangements she wouldn't have chosen for herself. An unrecognizable photo of Kristi with dark hair and a round face rests on a three-stand easel beside the spectacle, and it's so fucking disturbing, I want to knock it down.

The feeling doesn't go away once the service begins. We stand, sit, kneel, and chant prayers until the priest proclaims the word of God, promising that Kristy Reinhart is in the Kingdom of Heaven, cloaked by holy light, looking down upon us until the day she's resurrected.

"Her physical body has perished," he says from the altar, behind thick glasses, "but the human soul never dies."

Two rows in front of us, Mrs. Reinhart crumbles into her husband's side and breaks down, inconsolable by the loss of their daughter. She covers her face with both hands, but it doesn't help hide the strangled sound of agony rupturing from her lips. The man with the same nose as Kristi rocks his wife with his expression turned up, eyes closed. Amy, their only remaining child, sits frozen beside them, blank-faced and unemotional.

Father Regis Fortuna declares Kristi based her short life on the love and teaching of Jesus Christ. He dashes her casket with holy water, a token from her baptism and the day she gave her life to the Lord, followed by incense, a sign that our prayers are carried to Heaven.

I cough.

Holding on to the bench in front of me, I drop my head and stare at my shoes while Kristi's aunt approaches the altar. She begins the eulogy by remembering the life of her niece—her sister's daughter who loved the snow and lived for hunting season.

Hunting.

She was a fucking vegan.

I couldn't order a steak without a lecture on animal mistreatment and my environmental footprint.

"Have you ever watched an animal being slaughtered?" she asked me once, forking her tofu and kale. *"You'd change your mind about that steak if you saw how barbaric it is."*

"Who the fuck is she talking about?" I turn my head toward Ella and ask. She looks as confused by the eulogy as me. "This isn't real, right? Please tell me this is a fucking nightmare."

"Maybe they don't know her like we do," she whispers, like it's the only explanation. Her expression changes to something confident.

And my gut tells me she's right.

An hour later, I stare at the mahogany casket lowered six feet into the ground, covered with pink roses and handfuls of dirt, wondering how well Kristi and I knew one another. Twelve months doesn't compare to a lifetime, but the version of her I know is an illusion compared to the girl we paid tribute to today.

There are no dots to connect or strings to follow—the facts line up: we're opportunists.

We walked into each other's lives when we needed distraction the most. She's everything Ella's not, and what better way to say *fuck you* to an old life than fucking a tatted hooligan she meets at a gas station?

We weren't in love with each other. We loved what our relationship represented.

Distraction.

Realization doesn't keep my spirit from breaking. Kristi did more than warm my empty bed until she didn't—she gave me perspective and taught me patience. I can have a connection with someone that isn't volatile, and I have the ability to show affection without jealousy and anger.

Maybe.

And the most important thing I learned because of Kristi is no one has my heart like Gabriella Mason.

"What the hell do you think you're doing?" I whisper to keep other passengers from hearing.

"Are you blind or just dumb?" Ella asks, sipping whiskey straight from the bottle she snuck onboard. She waves her arm around her, showcasing the luxury of first class. "I had a long day, and tomorrow will be longer. I'm going to enjoy this, if that's okay with you, Prick."

"I was just asking." I fidget with my neck pillow, cross my arms over my chest, and settle for takeoff. It's nearly midnight with a seven-hour flight to New York ahead of us, and we'll only have a few hours to check into our hotel and change before Joe's service. We need to sleep now, but Ella's ready to party.

With the exception of a few cell phone screens illuminating faces and casting shadows across the ceiling, the first class cabin is dark. As the pilot prepares for takeoff, flight attendants grab their seats and the *Seatbelt* sign flashes. Luggage shifts in overhead compartments, and Emerson's already snoring. Jet engines run on high, and I close my eyes, surrendering to exhaustion.

We're not three feet off the runway when Ella starts to laugh, holding her stomach. "Oh my gosh, I forgot how much this tickles."

I lunge for the bottle, but she pulls it out of reach.

"Keep your claws to yourself, Reddy." She clutches it to her chest like it's her firstborn child and not a bottle of Jim Beam.

"Calm down." I stretch for the bottle a second time, but she lifts it like she's going to hit me over the head with the damn thing. "Floozy."

"Fall into a coma, asshole."

Her liquor-heavy eyes widen as her jaw drops dramatically. Ella pats the bottle, still holding it like a newborn, and shakes her head in mock disbelief. With today's mascara smeared under her eyes, she's thrown her hair up and taken her bra off, jumping headfirst into not giving a fuck.

I hold my hands up and face forward, situating myself

again. Altitude and booze don't play well together, but if she wants to learn the hard way, who am I to stop her?

"Don't try to wake me up when you get sick, Smella. I'll be in a coma, minding my own business. You're on your own." I close my eyes, instantly feeling the lull of sleep pulling me to unconsciousness. My limbs become heavy, and slowly, slowly, slowly my breathing steadies and my heart rate eases.

As I give in to oblivion, Ella whispers, "Quit acting like a little bitch."

An hour hasn't gone by when my father wakes me up, shaking me by the shoulder. My body's stiff, and in spite of the stupid fucking neck pillow, my head still fell forward and my neck hates me for it. I blink fatigue from my eyes until I see Dad's mustache and grimace clearly.

"What's going on?" I ask, rubbing the back of my neck. My elbow pops, and my eyes want to close again.

"Gabriella's locked herself in the restroom and she won't come out. She only wants you."

Waving him off, I yawn and say, "Tell her I'm still comatose."

"Teller, get her back into her seat before she scares the other passengers on this plane and the captain is alerted." He steps back so I have room to stand. Dad holds up Ella's half-finished bottle of whiskey. "The flight attendant already confiscated this from her. Why are you letting her drink, Teller?"

Ella drank less than half of what she snuck onboard, but for a one hundred forty-five-pound girl, no doubt it's enough to knock her on her ass.

"Have I ever been able to stop her from doing anything?"

I ask, stepping past my dad toward the small restroom up front. Maby's awake, watching a movie on her tablet. She gazes at me as I pass, her face illuminated in color from the small screen.

"Need some help?" she asks.

"No," I reply. "I got it."

"I should have listened to you," Ella cries after I knock on the door to let her know I'm here. "But, I'm just so sick of being sad, you know."

"It's okay, baby. Open the door and come back to your seat." It would be easier to break the motherfucking door down and drag her out by the back of her shirt, but we're on an airplane, and there are rules about that kind of thing.

"Are you mad at me?" Ella asks in a small voice. She hiccups.

Scanning the cabin over my shoulder, I confront my father, two flight attendants, and a blonde woman with an impatient expression, obviously waiting to use the restroom. Mom stands from her seat, stretching to look over heads, and Nicolette shakes Emerson awake.

"I'm not mad, but you need to come out now."

The latch switches from red to green—*Occupied* to *Vacant*—and my pale-faced lush peeks at me from under her long eyelashes, unsteady on her feet. I open my arms, and she throws up on my shirt. The line of people behind me scatters, and I'm glad my mouth wasn't open.

Eight hours later, Ella sits on the edge of the hotel bed, wet hair dripping down her back and towel covered chest. She falls to the mattress and groans; her bare feet drift right above the carpet. I tuck my shirt into my black slacks and walk past suffering toward the window with the view of

Central Park.

"Tell me it's going to be okay, Tell."

"It's a hangover, Ella, not Ebola. You're going to be fine," I answer, knowing it's not what she meant.

Heaviness fell on our shoulders when we landed in Alaska two days ago, but it's unbearable here, where we should be untouchable fifty stories high. There were no signs of Kristi in Anchorage, but even I can see Joseph in the New York City swagger—an untouchable momentum that only New Yorkers own.

The person who checked us into the hotel spoke with the same accent as Joe, and I watched Ella's poise capsize. It happened again with the man who handled our luggage, and again with a couple in the elevator. He's in the way the locals dress, and stand, and walk—seamless, to the point, and in a hurry. It's never been more obvious to me that Joe was out of place in LA, and I've never felt more envious of him than I am today.

"The hangover's going to be a problem," Ella says with a small smile. She stands and walks toward the bathroom. "But David made it more than apparent that I'm not welcome. I don't think he ever liked me."

A flash of anger blasts through me, filling my chest with heat and tightening my jaw, but I swallow resentment for her sake. Unwilling to make this day any harder than it needs to be, I put on my watch, burying what I really feel about David West and say, "We're not here for him, Ella. This is about Joe."

My truth: I'll kill that motherfucker if he so much as dares to look at her wrong.

"You missed the viewing." Mr. West pulls on the lapels of his black sports jacket, straightening it over his shirt. Hair as dark as his clothes is slicked back, and he has rings on every finger.

Gabriella's speechless, her damp hair frizzes in the humid air and her makeup-free complexion whitens. I smirk and knuckle up, stepping forward between innocence and arrogance.

"Allow me to introduce myself." Dad pushes me back a pace and offers his hand. "Dr. Theodore Reddy. I knew your son personally. We've all suffered a great loss with his passing."

David glances at his outstretched hand, unimpressed with my father's title or condolences. His wife, a short woman with thin blonde hair is gracious, thanking us for our attendance with tears in her eyes and the massive stone cathedral behind her.

The service proceeds like Kristi's, with the crucifix, holy water, and the affirmation that Joseph West is in the Kingdom of Heaven. With only standing room available, the temperature quickly rises and anguish is tangible and brash. Moments pass when mass is inaudible over the volume of sadness, and the outpouring of emotion is downright overwhelming.

These people—hundreds of them—some with the same mouth, eye color, and head of hair as Joe, fall over each other and open their arms to the sky, praying for mercy, praying for peace, praying to bring him back. It's an honest display of affection, and I feel proud because I knew him, too.

"I didn't love him like these people do," Ella whispers. She grasps my arm and closes her eyes, holding so tight my fingers chill.

He wasn't perfect.

Understanding, I kiss the top of her head and place my cold hand on her thigh, protective and insecure all at once. Toward the end of the service, I notice people whispering and glancing in our direction with suspicious eyes. Apprehension is as touchable as anguish, and the two don't mix well.

"Stay behind me," I say, leading Ella out of the church after Joe's casket is wheeled to the awaiting hearse. With tear-stained cheeks, she clutches onto my hand with trembling fingers and uncertainty.

I squint against the morning sunlight as we walk down the granite steps to the sidewalk where Joe is being lifted into the last car ride he'll ever take. The church is in the middle of a thriving neighborhood. Kids throw water balloons from rooftops, and an old ice cream truck drives by playing scratching music from a blown speaker.

The hair on the back of my neck stands when I notice glances shift into shameless glares and whispers rise loud enough for us to hear.

"Did she really bring her new boyfriend to the funeral?" someone spits.

"Joe's not even buried yet and she's already fucking someone else," another says.

"Why the fuck is she even here?" A group of girls dressed in black stands shoulder-to-shoulder as we walk by.

Ella keeps her head down as I lead us through the crowd of people, feeding off their animosity, hoping one of them tries to touch her so I can break their neck. They don't know shit about Ella, but she's an outsider—the girl Joe found and fell for in California—and that's reason enough to blame her for his choice to live and die there.

But she isn't the reason he left, and after being around these people for the last hour, I can see why he did.

I was wrong. Joe's not here.

There's not a trace of him in this group.

"Where's the car?" I ask my dad, who walks beside me.

"I just called the driver. He's around the block." He holds my mother's hand harder, seeing what I see. "Keep walking. We'll meet him at the corner."

Emerson steps up front, using his large body and expertise to make a path for us to get by. We nearly clear the church when some guy shoulder checks Ella, knocking her back. I grab the son of a bitch by the front of his shirt and shove him against the stone structure, smirking in his smug face.

"Apologize to her," I say.

Gabriella puts a hand on my shoulder. "Let's go, Tell."

"Not until he apologizes for pushing you," I say between gritted teeth.

Sounds of scuffling, Emerson pushing people back, and my father trying to calm the situation before a riot ensues do nothing to deter me. I see red, redder, reddest. Joe's cousin, or friend, or whatever-the-fuck turns his head and spits on the sidewalk beside Ella's feet, and it's the only excuse I need to pull him from the wall and slam him to the concrete sidewalk.

Noise and movement detonate around me, but I see nothing outside of my fist colliding with this man's face. Blood bursts from his nose, and the smile's beaten from his face. It's a week's worth of rage, pent-up and ignored, exploding from strength and muscle.

I spit on him once Husher manages to get his arms around my torso, pulling me from the sorry piece of shit. He doesn't get up right away.

"Come on, motherfuckers," I say, urging the rest of them to step to me, bloodied knuckled and mindless.

"That's enough, Teller. It would be helpful if you didn't get yourself arrested today." My dad hurries me along when I break free from Husher's grip, mumbling, "I've never been so embarrassed in my life. Who gets into a fight at a funeral?"

Shaking my arm free from his hold, I search for Ella and find her staring at the hearse. Her black heels hang from the tips of her fingers. No one so much as speaks to her.

"Let's get out of here, baby," I whisper, pressing my lips to the top of her head. "It's over."

CHAPTER NINE

Now

Ella

"**H**ear me out, okay. I'm serious." Maby refills her wine glass and takes a seat at the dinner table with the rest of us. "I have an idea. A really, really good idea, and we need this, so just listen to me."

We've been back from New York for a week, and with the help of my brother, I officially moved the rest of my things into Teller's guest bedroom today. The sun's setting, the temperature's falling, and now that the heavy lifting's done, we're picking right back up where we left off before the car accident turned our lives upside down: Friday night at Teller's.

Well, it's my house now, too.

Overworked, a little bit drunk, and with a stomach full of pizza, this is the closest to normal I've felt since Joe died. I smile. I can't help it.

"If this is about those stupid leggings you were trying

to get me to buy, the answer is no. Ella," Nicolette looks to me, "tell Maby she can't have a leggings party here either. I refuse to buy a pair. They're hideous."

I laugh into the neck of my beer bottle before taking a sip. My bare feet lounge on Teller's lap, and he's rubbing his hand up and down my shin. The look I'm given when he realizes I haven't shaved in a couple of days is great. He's beautiful in low sunlight, unshaven and dressed in paint-speckled clothes and unlaced work boots. His hair is overgrown, and the top is long and curly.

Maby shakes her head. "No, this is better than leggings."

"Did you hear that?" Emerson says sarcastically. "This is better than leggings!"

"I don't want to buy candles, or costume jewelry, or oils either," Nic clarifies in a teasing tone. "I always get conned into buying shit I'll never use. I'm over it."

"Don't worry, babe. She'll buy whatever you sell," Husher says, resting his arm across Maby's chair.

"This is why I said to listen." Teller's sister swallows the contents of her glass and continues. "We're out of work for the next couple of weeks. Let's take a road trip."

"That sounds awful." Nicolette rolls her eyes. Maby's excitement is contagious, but the idea goes in one ear and out the other.

"We don't have to go anywhere far. Vegas is five hours away, and from there we can go to the Grand Canyon…"

"Can we fly?" I ask, entertaining her since no one else will.

"You heard me say *road trip*, right? No, we can't fly, because then it won't be a road trip. We're going to drive. In a car. On the road." Maby tilts her wine glass upside down above her open mouth and wine drops onto her tongue.

"Sitting in the back seat with these two—" Emerson jabs his thumb in my and Teller's direction. "Doesn't sound like a good time. No offense, sissy."

I stick my tongue out at him.

"We'll take separate cars," Maby replies, exasperated. "Come on, guys. Think about how amazing it will be to drive to San Francisco for a few days."

"They do have stellar clam chowder," Nic ponders. "Are you sure we can't fly?"

Emerson's tone softens when he says, "We haven't been by the house in a while, Ella. San Francisco is only an hour away…"

"I know how far it is, Em." After we moved from St. Helena, I'd take the trip home a few times a year with my brother to check on the house we grew up in and inherited after our father passed. The windows are boarded up and the door padlocked, but we haven't come to a point where we can sell it yet. Not even after all this time.

My mom is there, somewhere. Keeping the house makes me feel like I haven't given up on her.

"Sounds like a good time, babe," Husher says, forcing regret into his tone. He stretches his arms over his head. "Maybe another time."

"No." Maby elbows his side, narrowing her eyes at him. "We won't go another time, because we're going this time. I already booked our rooms, so everyone should probably pack, because the Skylofts don't offer refunds.

Teller chuckles. "You booked the fucking Skylofts without asking if we even wanted to go first? Those rooms run a grand a night."

She rolls her green-like-his eyes. "I had to reserve the rooms while they were available. Don't act like you don't want to go to Las Vegas."

Nicolette holds her hand out, pausing the conversation between brother and sister. "What exactly do you mean *we better pack*? When are we leaving?"

Maby's cheeks burn and she sits straight, eyebrows up. "Tomorrow."

"We don't have to go," Teller says from my bedroom floor with pieces of my dresser in front of him. He looks at the pile of screws, second pile of unassembled wood, and frowns. "Why didn't you buy a dresser that was already built?"

I shake a new yellow comforter over my queen-sized mattress and say, "Because I'm obsessed with Ikea, and there are worse places to visit than Vegas. We'll go."

After midnight, a shadeless lamp casts his misshapen shadow across the freshly painted walls. The smell of wet paint, the touch of new sheets, and the look of concentration on Teller's face as he reads directions he doesn't understand lifts the right side of my mouth into a smile.

In less than a day, he's managed to turn this unused space into home. Champagne we poured in celebration after everyone left fizzles and pops in plastic cups on top of an unopened moving box with my name on the side. I straighten my bedding before jumping onto it. Reaching for sparkling liberation, I cross my legs and sip bitter stars and watch the muscles and bones in Teller's hands move as he builds my furniture.

"We're taking our own car," he says.

My heart picks up with his inclusion of me—*our.* "Fine."

"And I'm not sharing a room with those motherfuckers."

I smile into my cup, parting my lips when the cool liquid touches them. Carbonation pops on my tongue and warms my belly, and with each swallow, heaviness I carry on my shoulders drifts away.

"We'll get separate rooms, Tell." Lightness captures me, and this feels like floating.

My roommate—heartmate—drops the screwdriver and scowls. "You and I won't have separate rooms, Smella. We'll be separate from them, but not from each other. We stay together."

"That's what I meant," I say, pouring myself a second cup of champagne. "But we'll go on Maby's road trip. Emerson's right. I haven't been home in a while, and I should go check on the place. There's no one there to visit my dad's grave but us."

Teller takes the bottle from my hands, disregarding his cup, and drinks straight from the source. I sip when he does, secretly loving that for just a moment, I know what his mouth tastes like. He licks Korbel from his lips, and I mimic the gesture, savoring the flavor of his kiss.

"I've listed my demands. We'll go as long as they're met. But, Ella—" he replies playfully. Teller's pout shimmers in the yellow light. "—your home is with me now."

An hour later, my dresser is assembled—sturdy and level despite the piece of wood my builder somehow left out—and we've opened our third bottle of celebration. Dancing on extra screws and crumbled instructions, Teller spins me as treble and rhythm play from his cell phone, loud enough for just the two of us. Dizzy and laughing out loud, I turn and turn and turn before he catches me in his arms, pressing his chest against my back.

My heart beats with the bass of the song, up-tempo and heavy. Heat reddens my cheeks and softens my skin, and the feel of his form pressed against mine causes every nerve ending in my body to become hyperaware. I'm out of breath and out of a care in the world, and right where I should be.

The song ends, tapering into a slower pulse and softer lyrics, and Teller presses his lips to the top of my shoulder and grips my hips, swaying them lazily back and forth to our melody. I reach back, holding my hand to the back of his head, and close my eyes, melting as the warmth of his kiss raises the temperature.

"Do you know how long I've waited for this?" he whispers. "Despite everything, having you here ... this is the happiest I've been in a while, Ella. This is going to work. We're going to be all right."

"Of course we are. You've always promised to take care of me."

"We'll take care of each other."

He turns me in his arms, ending rationality with the intensity in his bright green stare. I circle my arms around his neck and tilt my neck to the side, opening myself to his assault. Crying out with the touch of his tongue on my pulse point, my skin becomes alive and thrives. Each touch feels hot and cold, electric and vivacious and killing me. Teller pushes me forward, pressing his body flush against my own as lips I don't want to ever leave me come closer to my own.

My back hits the wall.

Then my head.

And we remember the paint is wet and laugh.

"I am so sorry, baby." He laughs, looking at the fresh paint coating his palms. "I'll fix it when we get back from vacation."

Powerless to speak or think or be concerned, I nod.

"We have to be up in a few hours. We should go to bed." Teller takes a step back, running a hand through his hair, coating the ends in lovely lavender. He drops his shoulders and sighs when he realizes what he's done. "And I'm going to take a shower. In my own room."

Pressing my lips together, I smile shyly and say, "Goodnight."

He gets as far as the door when he stops and looks back. "I'm glad you're here, Gabriella."

"Me, too."

After I've scrubbed the day from my skin and paint from my hair, I'm cozy and drifting off under new blankets on top of my new mattress in my new home, with the window open. Under the stars and moon, sleep lures me away with thoughts of vibrant eyes that bound me, a past that scares me, and truth that I've known all along.

Heavy eyelids close when the mattress beside me dips with the weight of fate's body. Lingering tension evaporates in the familiarity of his arms, and I exhale.

"Tell me what this is," I whisper.

"Tell me what this isn't."

The alarm chimes what feels like minutes later, but the sun's up, bright in my sleep-heavy eyes. Teller's sprawled across the bed, forcing me to the very edge with nothing but the corner of my blanket to cover myself with.

I kick him awake. "Get out of my room, Prick."

He falls onto the floor and springs up immediately, puffy-eyed with bedhead. He's shirtless, barefoot in gray boxer briefs, and too hard to look at without blushing.

"You're an asshole," he mumbles, scratching the back of his head. There's still paint in his hair. "Get your ass up so we can leave."

"Shut the door!" I shout as he leaves, tossing my pillow at his back.

We're not morning people, but I still roll onto his side and inhale ginger and soap.

Three hours of sleep before a five-hour drive is bad planning. I don't bother to get dressed. I brush my teeth, wash my face, and throw some clothes into a bag. With a pair of black Ray-Bans covering the purple beneath my eyes, I wait in the G-Wagen for Teller, hoodie up. He follows soon after with a beanie on his head, dressed in a red and black flannel and a pair of dark denim jeans. He looks amazing with no effort at all, and I hate him for it.

We back out of the driveway, ignoring the other's existence, miserable. He turns on the radio, but I shut it off just as fast. I roll down the window for fresh air, but Teller rolls it up. We both scowl.

Exhaustion's a horrifying third wheel.

"Dick," he mumbles, but gives nothing away in his blank expression when I snap my head in his direction.

"Did you say something?" I ask, blinking heavily behind my dark lenses.

A year ago, he would have pulled over and tried to

leave me on the side of the road, and I would have back-handed him across the chest. Today, he's eating his words and driving under the speed limit, and I can appreciate the effort, even behind the haze of my bad mood.

Tolerance skips the gas station where we're meeting his sister and drives straight to Coffee Bean, slamming the door without inviting me in or asking me what I want before he gets out. I ignore the stream of text messages incoming from Maby and crew, asking where we are. I consider following Teller into the shop just to throw sugar packets and recycled paper napkins at him, but I don't get a chance to before he returns with coffee and muffins.

"Good morning," I grumble, taking caffeine straight to the vein.

"Oh, so she does talk," he responds with a smirk.

Maybe it's java or the fact that we are going to Las Vegas, but my outlook on life improves with each sip and mile we put between us and the house. I guzzle my coffee as if it's the last cup of ice water in hell and squeal as Teller pulls onto the freeway.

"That's my girl," beanie-beautiful says. "We need to work on our mornings, Ella. I don't think we'll survive many more like this. I almost regretted asking you to move in."

"I can go back to the apartment with Emerson and Nic."

"Not a fucking chance in hell, babe."

He races down the freeway, and I keep him company long enough to text his sister our whereabouts and ravage my muffin before I surrender to the sandman and snooze. The next time my eyes open, the side of my face is pressed against the glass window, and my neck is stiff.

"You're terrible road trip company, Smella."

Teller's removed his beanie and flannel, lounging behind the wheel in a plain white tee. I follow the artwork from his fingers to his elbow, to the curve of his bicep, strong under shirtsleeves.

"I'm sorry," I say, blinking forgotten dreams from my eyes. Desert and small mountains in every shade of brown surround us on the two-lane highway. "Do you want me to drive for a while?"

He shakes his head, taking my hand in his. Teller nods toward the horizon. "We're already here, baby."

Brilliance suddenly appears at the skyline, a mirage in the middle of nowhere. Sunshine reflects from mirrored glass on high-rise hotels, shining like chrome and glitter. As the highway turns into a freeway, billboards line the side of the road, selling sex, steaks, and Cirque du Soleil. Yellow-orange cabs clog already congested lanes, and Teller has to slam on the brakes more than once to avoid hitting another car. But we don't care, because just being here is an adrenaline rush.

My driver exits the freeway and heads to Las Vegas Boulevard, where our smiles can't get higher and our heartbeats dance inside our chests. The smell of exhaust, chlorine, and sticky drinks welcomes us to this devil's playground, and the blinking lights, seas of people, and the allure of money mesmerize us.

The Skylofts at the MGM offers a private entrance and in-room check in. Teller pulls the G-Wagen to the concierge. Everyone else arrives in a second car minutes later.

"Welcome to the top of the world, Dr. Reddy." Our doorman relieves us of our keys and directs us toward the

Skylobby with a polite smile. "Your rooms are ready. I'll be up with your bags shortly."

Our ambassador, Catrina, a slender thirty-something with a tight bun and practiced grin, greets us at the door. "I'm at your service day and night. Please don't hesitate to ask if you're in need of anything."

Teller drapes his arm over my shoulders and tucks me into his side, thanking the woman and leading us toward the elevators. Four pairs of feet follow closely behind us; our excitement barely contained and slipping in each small laugh and hurried step.

"So, I got two rooms. I figured you can stay with us, Teller, and Ella can stay with Em and Nic. Each loft has two bedrooms, and they're obviously large enough that privacy won't be an issue," Maby says, standing with her back to us in front of the gold-plated elevator doors.

"That's nice since you and Husher will be staying with Em and Nic. Ella and I will take the second loft. Feel free to give us the smaller of the two," the older Reddy child says sarcastically. "I'm not sharing a room with my fucking sister, Maby."

Small but mighty turns to face her brother, tight-lipped and red in the cheeks. "Why would you and Ella need your own room?"

"Teller, I don't mind—" I stop midsentence as I watch Teller's jaw tighten and the muscles in his arms flex. I share a cautious look with Emerson, knowing Teller's temper could send this elevator crashing down.

"Can we not start the week out like this, please?" Nicolette interrupts the family feud, tossing her sandy blonde hair over her shoulder. "It's not a big deal. Give them the damn room, Maby."

"I swear to God, Teller, if you start your shit—" The elevator doors open to the very top floor of the hotel, ending Maby's threat.

Cool, sweet-scented air casts the best kind of spell over us, calming tension from the short ride up and washing away the last few weeks like they never happened. I hold Teller's hand, lacing our fingers together, allowing him to guide me toward our loft. I'm light on my feet and in my heart.

"I reserved a cabana. Meet us at the pool in thirty minutes," Maby calls out.

"Ready to see our room?" he ignores her and asks, looking back at me.

I follow him inside, and my jaw drops. "Holy shit, Tell. This is amazing!"

On top of dark wood floors, white furniture and gold fixtures set off the huge space. Fresh flowers sit inside the vases, and the full kitchen is stocked, complete with a bar. A wall-sized door opens to a private pool and deck, facing the Las Vegas strip, and I can't wait to see what this place looks like lit up tonight.

In the bedroom, a button tufted and quilted leather white lacquer headboard pairs with a custom stiletto light fixture to highlight the custom mahogany sleigh bed. Blackout drapes of raw linen silk with metallic sheers cover another huge window. The connecting bathroom offers an infinity tub and steam shower bigger than the apartment I shared with Emerson.

"Can we stay here forever?" I ask, taking in the beauty of our hotel room.

Stepping out of my shoes, I jump onto the king-sized bed and disappear amongst the soft blankets, sinking into goose feathers and Egyptian cotton. A small-town girl raised on a single parent's income, this luxury is something I've only experienced after meeting Teller Reddy. It's a gift too wonderful to deny.

"Go to the pool without me. I'm not moving from this spot until we leave." I close my eyes, tossing my arms above my head.

"What's on your mind, Ella?" Teller's soothing voice brings a smile to my lips and sends a chill down my spine.

"Nothing, absolutely nothing," I say softly.

He positions himself over me, large and hard and warm, muscular arms perch on each side of my head. My eyes open, wondering for a moment if this is wrong … if this is taking it too far, but I relax. It's only us, and there's absolutely nothing holding us back. I attempt to circle my arms around the back of his neck, but he holds them against the mattress.

"Keep them here." Heavy lids blink over dark green eyes, and he licks his lips. "Don't move."

He slowly lowers himself down my body, and I close my eyes and inhale a sharp breath as his hands slide along my sides and slip under my hoodie. Teller drags his fingertips down my rib cage, tickling and teasing me to the point of madness. Curving my back, I moan and half-laugh, coming undone and softening under his touch.

He lifts my sweater over my head, leaving me in a black lace bra; my chest rises and falls with quick breaths. Teller kisses my stomach, pressing a trail of tenderness from my belly button to my bra-covered breasts.

"Is this okay?" Teller asks, nervous and bold all at once.

"Yes," I whisper to my best friend of seven years, knowing there's no going back from this.

This will change everything.

This can't be undone.

I lift my hips and he draws my pants over them, down my thighs, and off my feet. Covered in lace that matches my bra, I'm exposed in ways I've never been before, under a stare so penetrating I already feel fucked. This is skin he's touched and kissed and fought for; it's the emotion that's new and terrifying.

The willingness.

The openness.

The honesty.

Teller positions himself between my legs, firm amongst my soft thighs, and the reality of what's happening yanks me completely under. I drown in a river of misconnections and avoidance, a history so vicious we shouldn't be here. But we are, because we're nothing if not persistent, and to hell with the consequences.

Releasing bedsheets from my grip, I tug his cotton T-shirt until the neck stretches and thread snaps. I dig my fingernails into his sides, arching again when our bare stomachs touch. The shirt comes over his head and is tossed to the side before he lowers himself completely on top of me, and we both gasp and sigh.

It's been so long. It's been so, so, so long.

"You're beautiful," he says between soft lips I've never kissed.

But this can be it.

This *will* be it.

I hook my legs around the small of his back, trapping him within me. Trapping him, because that's what we do. He open-mouth kisses the fullness of my breasts, along my collarbone, and right under my chin. His hair is thick between my fingers, firm at the roots despite how hard I pull. Teller strokes against my center, and I cry out, frustrated with the clothes keeping us separate.

Pushing my hips into his, I pant his name, combusting from the inside. "Teller, please. Teller, now."

Lowering the straps of my bra, he moves my hands out of the way and says, "Let me do it."

Not bothering with the clasp, greedy hands lower B-sized cups, exposing my tits. My nipples harden and then soften under his tongue, hot and wet and never enough. I use my feet to push his pants down to his knees, unashamed and seeking when his manhood rests against my sex.

"Ella, look at me," Teller demands, clasping my chin in his grip. "This changes everything. You understand that, right?"

"Kiss me," I whisper in response.

"Hey, motherfuckers." A heavy pounding echoes through the loft. The door rattles on its hinges. Emerson's voice booms. "Your bags are out here. I want you guys sleeping in separate bedrooms."

The moment shatters with our privacy, and I hide my face behind my hands. "You have got to be kidding me."

Teller drops his forehead to my shoulder, inhaling and exhaling at an accelerated rate.

"We didn't come all this way so you could hide in your room. Don't make me break down the door, Ella."

MARY ELIZABETH

The Nevada sun's relentless, and the pool brings out the most beautiful people in the city. Drinks flow freely, the music's loud, and my spot under the cabana gives me a perfect view of the bodies filling the swimming pool to capacity. Jersey Shore douchebags with spiked hair and greased muscles fist pump and hump the air in their attempt at dancing, and ladies in nothing more than strings trot around in high heels and gold rings, because they're not here to get wet from the water.

At least they're keeping it real, which is more than I can say for myself. I haven't looked Teller in the eyes since my brother interrupted what could have easily been a huge mistake. We used to mess around all the time, never under the clothes, never sex, but close enough. That ended with Joe.

How could I let it start again so soon after he's died and live with myself?

Because I am living with it. I can't stop thinking about Teller's mouth…

"How's it goin' in here?" Our three-pound cocktail waitress, Amanda, saunters in, swaying bony hips and accentuating ungodly sized tits. She's come by a few times with eyes for my man, and I've let it slide off my back until now.

Because now I've had three gin and tonics.

"We're good. Thanks," I say dismissively, but she doesn't take a hint.

"Are you brother and sister?" she asks, cutting a lime for Teller's beer.

He laughs, but I answer, "No, we're not. Not even close."

"Oh." Amanda giggles. "It's just that you look alike."

"We don't look anything alike. Maybe you need your eyes checked." I consider tossing my empty glass at her, but we just arrived, and I don't want to go to jail. "That's enough lime. Feel free to leave."

"Come here, baby." Teller pats his lap after dumb as rocks leaves with her tail between her legs.

Unsteady on my feet, I walk across the cabana and fall against his chest, resting the back of my head against his shoulder. Sweat pools between our bodies, chilled by misters spraying overhead. He holds his glass to my lips for me to drink, and I finish the whole glass in one shot.

"Were you jealous of that girl?"

"What girl?" I ask, rolling my eyes. "Are you trying to get me drunk?"

"Do I need to try?"

Teller rubs lazily across my stomach, my sides, and my thighs, and kisses my throat, my shoulder, and the top of my hand. I melt to nothingness and surrender to the control he has over my body from the top of my head to the tips of my toes, etched on the surface of my bones. I am his.

"We're not going to fuck this up, Ella," sincerity whispers right above my ear, shooting chills down my arms. "I won't let you go this time."

Instead of losing ourselves to the deep stuff, knowing there's always a chance Teller and I can and will screw this up again, I turn in his arms and straddle his legs. "Can we not talk about that right now? Let's have fun while we're here. Do you want to dance?"

"Down there." Teller's eyes look over my shoulder toward the DJ and the dance floor, where the rest of our party has been for the last hour.

"No, right here is fine." I pull him up by the waist of his board shorts and lead him from the chair to the couch. Imported beer bubbles and spills over his fingers, dripping onto the concrete under our feet.

"What are you up to, Ella?" he asks, half-nervous, half-curious, topped with a crooked grin that makes me weak in the knees.

"Nothing." I let go of paper-thin guilt and surrender to sensation.

"You're a liar."

Large hands settle onto my hips, and he tries to lower me onto his lap again. I close my eyes in concentration, calming nerves with an inner pep talk.

He wants me. He always has. I don't have to be embarrassed with him.

Teller Reddy is my person.

"Open your mouth." I grab the vodka bottle from the small table at the side of the couch, dripping ice-cold condensation onto his chest as I tip it over. Thick liquor swishes in the clear bottle, and I wink as Grey Goose pours down his throat. A small drip streams down his chin, and I lick it off.

"That was fucking hot, baby." Teller pulls me forward with his hands on my ass. "I thought you wanted to dance."

"I do." Returning the vodka bottle back to the ice bucket, I get up and close the curtain around the cabana, shutting out the party. "I'm going to dance, and you're going to sit there and watch."

Teller scrubs his hands down his face. "Who are you and what the fuck have you done with my girl?"

"You better enjoy this, Dr. Reddy."

"Are you drunk? You don't have to do this, Gabriella."

"I'm a little tipsy," I reply, walking with one foot in front of the other like a runway model. "And I want to, but don't laugh at me, okay?"

"Never," he says, sitting back for the show.

Standing in front of my audience of one, I sway my hips to the beat of the DJ's song and bend over at the waist, dragging my hands from my right ankle up to my thigh. Teller adjusts his shorts, watching the swing of my hips with a curve in his lips. I tease him by pulling the ties of my bikini bottoms, but stop before they come free.

Turning around, I shake my bottom and laugh out loud, never taking myself too seriously. Placing my hands on his knees, I lower myself where he's hard for me and circle my hips against his manhood, popping my bottom like the girls do in music videos.

"Is it okay if I touch you?" Teller asks in a rough voice.

"Not with your hands," I say, turning to straddle his lap. Snatching the vodka bottle for the second time, I pour a shot into my mouth, grasp Teller by his face, and squeeze his cheeks until his lips part. When his mouth opens, I lower mine right above his and let the tasteless liquor pour from my mouth to his.

"Fuck, babe," he lets out, licking Grey Goose from his lips before sucking it from my chest.

Stepping away from his eager mouth, I kick the table in front of him, knocking over the ice bucket and spilling water everywhere. Something I should consider when climbing onto the metal surface, but tipsy's advanced to utterly shit-faced, and there's no going back now.

I don't get both feet on the table before I fly off, slipping on an ice cube. My legs come up from underneath me, and I fall headfirst onto Teller's lap, skinning my knees and busting my nose on his pelvis.

"Ouch," I groan, slowly lifting my face from Teller's crotch. I'm not bleeding, but it's definitely sore.

"Holy shit, Smella. Are you okay?" He shakes from laughter, caught between helping me and doubling over.

He doubles over, and I'm not surprised.

CHAPTER TEN

Before

Ella

"I don't want to impose on your family for the holidays, Teller. And I can't leave my brother. We're fine here. Go home, Prick."

Christmas in Southern California is nothing like it is in the North. I've traded snowflakes for sunshine and sand in my sheets. Venice Beach Santa wears sunglasses and Hawaiian printed button-up shirts. He also plays drumbeats on buckets for money, and Mrs. Clause is a chain-smoker.

As is the boy at my door.

"You don't even have a Christmas tree, Ella." Teller blows white smoke into the night sky, dropping the butt of his cigarette into an empty coffee can I left by the bushes for him. "It's fucking depressing. Pack a bag and come home with me."

"We have a tree," I say, pointing toward the two-footer

on the kitchen table. "I even decorated it."

Teller walks past me into the quiet apartment, leaving the scent of nicotine and ginger behind.

"That's a shrub with a star on it, Smella. It's depressing." He flicks the top-heavy tree topper and it falls over, flickering before it burns out.

My home intruder looks around, scoping out the bowl of popcorn on the coffee table and the cheesy Lifetime Christmas movie on the television. Besides the dim light above the stove and the glow from the TV, the rest of the apartment is dark.

"Where are Emerson and Nicolette?" Teller opens my brother's bedroom door to find an empty, lightless space. "Are you here alone? On Christmas fucking Eve?"

Flopping onto the sofa, I cover myself in an old quilt my mom made before she lost her mind and disappeared and bring the popcorn back to my lap. "He's having dinner with Nic's family. He promised to be back sometime tonight."

"He didn't invite you?"

"Yes, he invited me. But I didn't want to impose," I repeat, shoving a handful of extra butter movie theater popcorn into my mouth. "Teller, honestly, I'm fine. Christmas hasn't been a big deal for me in a long time. Go home and spend some time with your people."

"You are my people. I'm not leaving, Gabriella." He shuffles out of his zip up sweater and hangs it on the back of a chair at the Christmas tree table. "Scoot over."

"No," I say, unwilling to budge. "This is normal for me, Tell. I promise. But you have a family to spend the night with. You need to be with them."

Diligence squeezes himself between the arm of the couch and me, dipping his hand into my buttery dinner. "If you don't want to leave, I'm staying. There's not a chance in hell I'm leaving you alone tonight."

Confiscating the large plastic bowl, I turn my gaze toward the made-for-TV movie before Teller can see my eyes gloss over. Since my dad died, nothing has been easy, but the holidays are excruciating. An invitation to Thanksgiving dinner is simple enough to accept or plan with friends, but there's something intimate about Christmas. Something special and private and gut-wrenching. It's the magic in the air and the scent of peppermint and chocolate that resurrects memories I'd rather forget than relive at the sound of sleigh bells.

Memories of a family that no longer exists.

A reminder of how alone I truly am.

"Thank you," I whisper a few minutes later, falling against his side. My Christmas miracle rests his arm around my body, holding me tight, and I absorb the affection, not realizing until this very moment how badly I need human contact from someone other than Emerson.

I blame my tears on the movie about faith and recognizing devotion when it's right in front of our faces. In this case, it's Tori Spelling's secret Santa from work, a man who stalks her until he realizes she returns his feelings and then changes his psychotic ways. They confess their adoration under the Rockefeller Christmas tree in New York City and live happily ever after until the sequel, when she dies from a rare disease, leaving the ex-stalker turned lover with the kids and farm.

He finds love again.

"Don't tell me you actually like this shit?" Teller asks, looking down on me with judgy eyes. "She falls in love with the man who used to break into her apartment and steal her underwear? He wrote creepy messages on her mirror in lipstick, and she's okay with it because he kisses her under the mistletoe?"

"He did buy her an excellent Secret Santa gift," I remind him, wiping away sadness from my cheeks.

"You're joking, right? That shit isn't romantic, Ella. It's insane."

"They're unconventional," I defend women's television. "I appreciate it."

"We're not doing this all night." Teller uses the remote to turn off the TV and stands up. Popcorn falls from his lap to the carpet, and I laugh, shoving another handful into my mouth when he looks at me with straight lips, unamused. "Where's the booze?"

"In the cabinet above the stove. I think there's scotch."

"Put the fucking popcorn down and get your ass in here."

He pours Johnnie Walker over ice and holds a glass out for me as I saunter toward his direction, barefoot and braless under an oversized band tee. Watching him over the rim of my glass as I sip dark liquid that warms me from the inside out, it dawns on me that this is the ninth Christmas without my mom and the fourth Christmas without my dad.

But it's also the second Christmas spent with Teller.

Over the last year and a half, the Reddys have become family to my brother and me. Theo's fatherly advice and Mili's motherly touch help fill a hole Emerson and I have in our hearts. They've made it apparent that we're welcome in their home and their lives, and more times than not we accept their dinner invitations and generous support in everything from school to birthdays. I answered Mili's multiple phone calls about spending Christmas with them this week, but I politely declined, knowing I needed to grieve my family on my own for one night.

I'm not surprised Teller showed up at my door.

He's never been the type to accept a *no* from me.

"What's going on with you?" he asks, filling my empty glass. Liquor goes straight to his eyes—or mine—scotch-heavy lids open and close slowly, and his lashes look longer than they ever have. Teller's green irises change from light to dark right in front of me, speckled with flakes of blue and gold.

I can't look away, but he wouldn't want me to, anyway.

"I've been thinking about my mom a lot," I admit, unable to recapture the words the liquor uncages and lets past my lips. Once the truth escapes, it hangs between Teller and me, clouding judgment and ruining vibes. Not that we haven't spent dozens of nights drinking until lies are impossible—not that future Dr. Reddy and I have never been anything less than disturbingly transparent.

"She doesn't deserve your thoughts, babe," he replies, leaning against the counter beside me.

"The thing is," I say, turning my body toward him. Crumbs and dust stick to the bottom of my bare feet, and the shitty florescent kitchen light hurts my eyes. "My dad didn't choose to leave me. He died. Cancer killed him. And I'm not okay with it, but I can accept that shitty things happen to good people. But my mom ... she chose drugs over her family. She made the conscious decision to be a heroin addict instead of a wife and mother. I can't accept that."

"You don't have to," Teller offers. He moves a lock of my hair over my shoulder, sending a wave of goose bumps down my arms. "You don't even need to understand it, Ella. She's not your responsibility."

"I know that, but it doesn't make it any easier. Most of the memories I have of her are good ones … normal ones. One day I had a mom, and the next day I didn't. After she left, I'd ride my board around town trying to find her. My dad told me she moved away, but I found her once, about a year after she left us."

Teller drops his head back and closes his eyes.

"It would have been a lot easier to find her in the suburbs with a new husband and baby than it was to actually see my mother in the gutter of some dirty backstreet downtown. She was sleeping or passed out or dead, so I didn't get closer. I rode home, dropped my skateboard on the front lawn, and locked myself in my room until my dad threatened to take the door down. And then he told me the truth. My mom had been addicted to pills for years, and when the doctors cut her off, she turned to something stronger, something so greedy it didn't let her love anything else."

"He said that to you?" Teller asks.

I shake my head. "No, but I was old enough to figure it out."

Dropping my eyes to my turquoise painted toes, I remember the rich sadness in my father's dark brown eyes, paleness in his lips, and the quiver in his chin. He hadn't shaved his face in a week, so black and gray stubble freckled the lower half of his face. His hair, three shades darker than my own, was overgrown, scratching the tops of his ears and the back of his neck; he looked like Em, who was going through a phase and growing his hair out.

Abraham Mason was a simple man, proud and compelling, but in that moment, looking into the crying eyes of his only little girl, he was lost.

"Come here, baby." Teller grabs me by the shoulder and lures me closer, circling his strong arm around my body. He kisses the top of my head, and I turn my nose into his neck, inhaling the mixed scents of nicotine, vanilla, and dark chocolate scotch leave on his breath. "You can call me Daddy now, if it'll make you feel better."

I shove him away and smack his arm, leaving the impression of four fingers across a skull tattooed across his bicep. "Idiot!"

"Ouch." He rubs his arm, smiling the most deliciously drunk smirk. "I was just trying to make you laugh."

"I'm so glad my heartbreak amuses you." I hit him again, holding back a smile. "Jerk."

"Okay, okay, okay." Teller reaches out for my wrists to keep me from beating him to death. "I'm sorry. Your heartbreak doesn't amuse me, Smella. I was only trying to lighten the mood before you ruin Christmas."

Fighting against his hold, not able to keep the grin from my lips, I stomp on his foot, but my bare feet stand no chance against his shoes and he laughs at my struggle. And I love the way his laugh starts in his stomach and ends in his eyes, brightening everything from the color in his tattoos to the barely-there freckles on his cheeks.

"I'll always take care of you," he says, kissing the inside

of my wrist. "Always."

We drink the entire bottle of Johnnie, burn two batches of chocolate chip cookies, and spit out the dozen we manage to salvage. We don't realize we used too much salt and not enough sugar in the batter until we have undercooked cookie in our mouths.

We open a bottle of champagne to wash the bad taste away.

After midnight, with no sign of Emerson and Nic, Teller kicks off his shoes and borrows a pair of my brother's sweatpants and settles in, with no intentions of leaving. He turns on the stereo, and we slow dance on the linoleum floor. We suck on miniature candy canes and drop them into our flutes when the ends get pointed. Teller left my gifts at his house, so he slips me a hundred-dollar bill from his wallet instead. I decline and watch him open the concert tickets he mentioned months ago.

He shoves two hundred dollars down my shirt after that.

Cheap champagne makes us sleepy and we collapse onto the couch in a mix of limbs and sighs and hiccups. He lies on top of me with his ear to my heart, and I run my fingers through his hair over and over and over, thinking about nothing but the texture of his curls between my knuckles, until his eyes close and his breathing evens out.

I'm nearly asleep when Teller's phone chimes once, twice, three, and four times from the coffee table. It vibrates harshly against the wood surface, spinning in circles each time a new text comes in, scratching at the hint of a hangover I'm sure to wake up with.

"Tell," I say, shaking him awake. "It might be an

emergency."

He groans, reaching for his phone, searching the table before his hand finally grazes the top of his cell and knocks it to the floor. Teller lifts himself onto his elbow, fishing for the nuisance and finally opening the home screen with squinted eyes. I can't see what the messages say, but I can see who they're from in bold black letters.

Maddy.

Prick sits up and angles his phone enough to make it impossible for me to see the response he types. He doesn't wait for *Maddy* to respond, turns the power off, and pockets his cell.

"Who's Maddy?" I shuffle to an upright position before he traps me beneath him.

Madness instantly crowds the apartment, making the space too small for the both of us, and we can't sit far enough apart. I see the shift in Teller's eyes, as I'm sure he sees it in mine, too drunk, too lonely, and too tired to simply let this go. My blood pressure rises, and my heartbeat can't keep up with anger.

"This chick from school. She had a question about an assignment," he says defensively, sitting forward with his knees apart and his hands in his hair.

"Really?" I reply. "She had a question about school-work during winter break at two in the morning on Christmas?"

"Yeah, I guess." Teller stands up to fetch a cigarette from his sweater still hanging on the back of the chair at the kitchen table. He slips it in the corner of his mouth and heads to the front door before he lights it.

I throw a pillow at his head.

"What the fuck, Ella?" The broken Marlboro hangs from his lips.

"This is why I won't commit to you, Teller. Everything you say to me comes across as bullshit because of things like this. Who is she? Are you sleeping with her?" The thought of it turns my stomach, and I grab the remote, prepared to use it. "Who the hell is Maddy?"

"You're crazy." Caught red-handed points his finger in my direction, continuing his walk to the door. "She's a girl from school. I'm not fucking her. I'm not fucking anyone because you're a prude bitch."

I throw the remote and it shatters against the door-jamb, spraying plastic and rubber numbers across the living room.

"You make me this way," I accuse, scotch-brave and blinded by my insecurities. "I was so fucking normal before I met you."

He smirks. "I doubt it."

The walls are thin, and Emerson's not here to break this up, so the neighbors might hear and call the cops, significantly upping our chances of spending Christmas in a holding cell. These are things I should consider before knocking his teeth out, but consequence is far from my mind as Teller lights his broken cigarette in my apartment and exhales smoke in my path.

"Go outside before I put it out in your eyes," I growl. My hands are fisted at my sides, and my feet are ready to launch me across the room.

Chain-smoker takes a second hit, blowing smoke over his shoulder. "I'd like to see you try."

A half hour later, Em and Nic come home with an

armful of presents and leftovers from dinner, only to find Teller standing under my doorjamb, refusing to move.

"Let me explain," he insists. His shirt's stretched out at the neck, but all his teeth are still in his mouth.

"Move your hands before I break them," I say, ready to swing the door shut on his fingers. "I'm not having this conversation with you. Go home like I asked you to when you showed up uninvited. Leave me alone."

"Ella, she has my number because we had to work on a lab together. Nothing more." He tries to step into my room, but the look on my face sends him back. "I'm not sleeping with her. I don't even remember what she looks like."

"Because that makes a difference with you?" I scoff.

Nicolette doesn't bother to act offended by our argument. She grabs the broom and sweeps up the broken pieces of our only remote control. "You're both lucky I recorded *Real Housewives* in my room."

My brother drops the plate of food onto the kitchen counter, along with the gifts, and steps behind the only person who doesn't live or belong here.

"Teller, let's go, man." Emerson keeps his tone low, but he's had to physically remove this boy from the apartment on more than one occasion, and we're not fooled by the passivity of his voice. "Can we not do this on Christmas? Sleep on the couch, but let her close the door."

A mischievous smile spreads across Teller's mouth, and he turns to face Em. "I wouldn't be here if you hadn't left your sister alone, dick. It's cool that you want to do shit with Nic's family, but your *only* family was drowning her fucking sorrow in popcorn and shit movies. By herself.

On motherfucking Christmas Eve."

Emerson's eyes narrow, but Nicolette couldn't care less. She goes into her bedroom and shuts the door.

"I asked you to come. We all wanted you there." His self-control snaps and he yells, holding his hand out to me. "You said no."

"And that's when you should have stayed home," Teller replies sharply.

Em scrubs his hands down his face and exhales loudly, losing his patience. "I'm not doing this, Gabriella. I can't come home to a warzone every time you're together. Get it figured out—now."

I throw a shoe at his back.

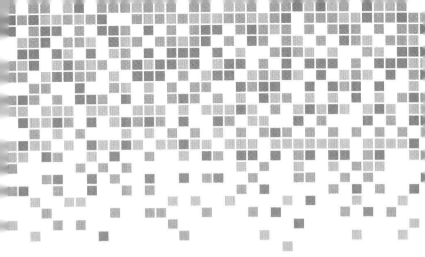

CHAPTER ELEVEN

Now

Ella

"**D**o it again." Teller buries his face between my neck and shoulder, kissing the sensitive skin right below my pulse. "Your landing will be softer this time, and I won't laugh when you fall."

With a towel in my wet hair and my skin just-washed soft, I'm wrapped in the silkiest robe ever made, licking my wounds and my pride. I drank too much yesterday, and my knee hurts from the dance-gone-wrong, so I took a shower and climbed back into bed with my favorite troublemaker, because I'm not getting up until he does.

"Come on, baby," Teller whispers with an undertone of laughter. He slips his hand under my robe and sweeps it across my bare stomach. "It'll be so much sexier in here."

I unsuccessfully push his arm away, wondering what it would be like if he went a little lower, a little slower. "Not a chance, Reddy."

Cradled in the softest bedspread money can buy, on a mattress big enough to fit ten people, Teller smells like yesterday's vodka, and I don't remember much after I fell off the table. The pounding in my head and the knot in my stomach guarantee it was a good time.

"I had to carry you back to the room over my shoulder," Teller replies when I ask him to fill in the hazy spots. He's shirtless, covered from the waist down with blankets. Ab muscles contract with every word he utters, and the artwork across his chest and stomach glows, backdropped by white sheets. "Our cocktail waitress came to take away the empty bottles and you threw a tray of limes at her. And missed, which is why we didn't get kicked out."

"My mom was a thrower," I say matter-of-factly, unsurprised by my choice of violence. "There are worse qualities I could have inherited from her."

"*Amanda,*" Teller emphasizes her name. His smirk is easy, and his eyelids are swollen from sleep and bottle green brilliant. "Wasn't mad. She said it happens all the time."

The memories I do have of her scoping out my man resurrect an irritation I can only imagine was ten times worse after a day of drinking. We had more than enough limes, but that didn't stop her from moseying in every thirty minutes to cut more. She smelled like coconuts and chewed pink gum with her mouth open, smiling with it jammed between her back teeth.

"She was doing her job, babe." Teller laughs, tucking his hands under his head.

"I don't think her job description includes hitting on customers," I answer, wishing I had thrown a fist instead of citrus.

"I guarantee it does." He turns his head, hitting me with the full force of his crooked grin. "Those girls get paid to flirt. They survive off their tips."

"Whatever," I say, sitting up. The towel falls from my head, and locks of wet hair tumble down my back. Lavender and mint-scented drops of water soak through my robe. "We had enough limes."

Teller towers behind me, pushing the silk from my shoulder and pressing his lips to my sun-kissed skin. I tilt my neck, opening the space for his mouth, melting under his persistent caress. We haven't had a conversation about what this is, but admitting we're going down this road again might ruin how amazing it feels to have him against me, and I'm okay with negligence. We can't label our relationship without acknowledging why it never worked in the first place.

Confessions come with consequences. As wrong as it may be, it takes no effort to start right where we ended things.

Our affection never lacked passion. We're deficient in self-control.

"What do you want to do today?" He lowers the robe until it falls free from my right arm and pools around my waist, revealing my naked chest. Cool air puckers my nipples, and my lips part as he cups my breast in his large hand. "We can stay here. In bed."

My chest rises and falls with every slow inhale and exhale passing through my lungs. Teller's breath is warm against the back of my neck, the bend of my ear, across my cheek, and I sink into his body, gasping when our skin touches, closing my eyes when his thumb brushes across my nipple.

"Keep your eyes open, baby," he whispers, lowering his hand from my chest to my stomach.

I follow blueish veins from his elbow to his wrist, not at all upset that some of the scars on his knuckles were put there fighting for me, and watch his fingertips sink lower and lower, past my belly button, past the waistband of my white panties, and down more … and more … and more.

"We have to stop," I gasp, reaching back and grabbing onto his hair.

"We don't *have* to do anything." Teller circles my clit, biting my earlobe between his front teeth. "We can stay in this room for the next three days and fuck the entire time."

"Oh my God," I whisper, opening my legs for him.

"Do you have any idea how long I've thought about being inside of you?" His fingers slide between my folds, and a jolt of electricity shoots through my body. "I lost you once, baby. I won't let it happen again."

When the phone rings, we break apart like we're caught kissing behind the bleachers in gym class. Teller falls back against the mattress with a hand to his forehead, and I jump off the bed, correcting and retying my robe.

"If that's one of those motherfuckers—" Teller warns, covering his face with a pillow.

I run to the telephone on unsteady feet, brushing damp hair away from my overheated face and answer breathlessly, praying it's not Emerson. "Hello?"

"Hey," Husher replies in a low, even tone. He's not a man of many words, but when he does speak, I listen closely. His voice eases my anxiety, and the one small word calms my erratic heart. "I know we had plans to meet up for lunch, but Maby's not up for it today."

"Is everything okay? Is she hungover?" I ask, looking out the window toward the strip. Making plans with them must be in the *forgotten file* with Liming Amanda.

"No, just the normal stuff," he answers. "You know how it goes."

"Let us know if you need anything," I answer, keeping my voice low as if it might disturb Maby from here. "Does she have her medication?"

"She has it. I think everything that's happened finally hit her, and her mind's dealing with it like it does whenever she's overwhelmed. We'll let her sleep it off today and see what happens tomorrow."

"Sounds good." I look toward the bedroom. Teller's resurfaced from under the pillow, catching bits and pieces of my conversation. "Is my brother with you?"

"They took off this morning. Said something about traveling down to Fremont."

"Okay, Husher. I'll check in later."

Teller watches me walk past the bed toward the bathroom, where I grab my brush and battle tangles in my hair from letting it air-dry. Clear bulbs above the mirror expose every sunspot and freckle on my face and reflect light off my dark irises. My complexion holds a pinkish tint, lasting excitement from having my best friend's hand between my thighs.

"What's going on with Maby?" disorder asks. He turns on the shower, and the small space fills with steam.

"Bed bound," I say, plugging in the blow dryer, spying on him through the mirror.

"Do we need to go over there?" He turns away from

me, showcasing a piece of art that marks the entirety of his back. From shoulder to shoulder, to the base of his neck to his waist, bold color and elaborate design transform typical to extraordinary, and I'm spellbound.

He drops his boxers and steps into the shower.

"Husher said he'll give us a call tomorrow, but I don't think we should worry about her too much right now. It's only been a day. She took her meds."

His sister's mental state of mind seems like the wrong topic of conversation to have when I can't take my eyes away from his naked form. Clouded glass keeps it PG, but I can distinguish the shape of his body and what parts are where.

He's still hard.

We need to leave this hotel before I take him up on his offer.

"I'm not sure why we're here. My idea sounded a lot better." Teller smiles, kissing the top of my head while we wait for the hostess to escort us to our table.

I lean against his arm, lacing my fingers with his, and blush at the thought of what we'd be doing if we'd stayed at the loft like he suggested. Now that we're amongst other people, head heavy from a hangover that won't be ignored, I'm second-guessing my decision to leave. The smell of tobacco is only appeasing when it comes from Teller, not the hundreds of people at blackjack tables, flicking ash into gold-plated ashtrays.

And why isn't there a mute button on slot machines?

"Can we have a table somewhere quiet?" Teller slips

our escort a twenty-dollar bill, and she gladly accepts it, leading us to a corner booth furthest away from the casino.

Teller thanks the woman, sending her away with a smile that reddens her cheeks and lightens her steps. Not noticing the effect he has on the girl, he steps aside for me to slide into the booth, and instead of sitting across from me, he slips in at my side.

He's brushing my hair away from my shoulder and kissing the spot below my ear when our waiter arrives to take our drink order. Teller doesn't bother to look up, so I order a couple of beers and thank the man.

"No limes." Possessiveness smirks with eyes for no one but me.

"Afraid you're going to throw them at him?" I look through the menu, trying my hardest to pretend the way he kisses me doesn't weaken my bones.

"I'll shove them down his fucking throat if he so much as looks at you for too long. You look gorgeous in this dress, baby."

"Don't be embarrassing," I whisper, swallowing a gasp when his teeth pinch the soft place where my neck and shoulder meet. "People can see us."

"No one can see us, Ella." He fingers the thins straps crossing my upper back, tickling my exposed skin, touching every part of me he can get his hands on. "Are you wearing a bra?"

I drop the menu, deciding on enchiladas, and shake my head. "No, I don't need one with this dress."

Lie.

It's a typical linen summer dress, suitable for any strapless bra. Despite having three in my bag, I didn't wear one on purpose, because I wanted him to notice.

I want to be the only one he ever notices.

"Why the fuck are we here?" he groans, dropping his forehead to my shoulder. "Please, let me take you back to the room. Aren't we past this shit, Gabriella? It's you and me, right? You can't tell me you don't feel this. You can't do this back and forth shit with me again, not after Joe. I won't live through that again."

Leo, our server, places two frosted glasses and our beers in front of us, drops off a basket of chips and salsa, and walks away to grab napkins before he takes our order.

"Can we save this topic for later, Tell?" I drink my brew straight from the bottle. "Until we're alone."

The scent of his cologne and the natural trace of ginger and vanilla on his skin make it hard to form a coherent thought. My brain's a jumbled mess of chaos and avoidance, and it *would* be easier to go back, not speak a single word to each other, and have sex for the next three days like we are the only two people in the universe. I have no doubt we could easily lock ourselves in that thousand dollar a night loft and consume ourselves with a very real need we've been consumed with since the very first day we met.

But I'm scared.

Joe and Kristi haven't been gone a month, and we're already falling into each other's arms. What does that say about our character? What does that say about the two years I spent with Joe? What does it say about Teller for letting it happen and choosing to be with Kristi instead?

"We're alone, Ella," Teller replies, waving his hand at the empty section of the restaurant.

Sometime later, our food arrives and we dine with

tension, emphasizing every scratch our forks and knives make across our plates, every move one of us makes, and every word that's not being said. I swallow my sorrows with ice-cold beer, ordering a third before my second is gone.

"Food's good," I say, moving around red sauce and cheese.

"Yeah," he answers nonchalantly, having only eaten half of his burrito.

"Don't be mad at me, Tell."

Green eyes that see me like no other fall upon my face, and my pulse rises with the temperature. Heat flashes through my palms, and my stomach tightens like I did a hundred somersaults. Joe never made me feel this way, and it's something I ignored the entire time, because Joe never made me feel a lot of ways.

Like blind rage.

"I'm not mad at you, baby." Teller rubs his hand up and down the inside of my thigh, sweeping the hem of my yellow dress with his pinkie finger.

Sipping from the glass of water Leo brought with my third beer, I play it cool, scoping out the restaurant to see where the other customers and servers are.

Then I part my knees.

Teller doesn't skip a beat, pressing his finger to his lips, asking me to be quiet and winking as his hand goes higher, and higher, and higher.

"Is this okay?" he asks quietly, casually like we're a normal twosome on a normal lunch date.

"Yes," I hum, gripping the edge of the table. The knot in my stomach comes undone, releasing butterflies in dozens.

Gripping the thickness in my thighs, he pulls them

apart. The back of my legs sticks to the leather seats, and I whimper at the force of his parting, the strength in his touch.

"Quiet, girl," bound and determined whispers through a smirk I'd love to smack from his face.

With a trembling hand, I reach for my beer bottle and bring the cool glass to my warm lips. Teller teases the seams of my lace underwear, slipping his finger beneath the elastic, caressing my folds before sweeping his hand down to my knee and back up.

"Stop messing with me," I say, pressing his palm against my warmest spot with one hand and drinking my beer with the other.

Before I can swallow, Teller moves my panties to the side and plunges two fingers inside of me so roughly, my bottom scoots to the back of the booth. I slam my glass bottle to the table before dropping it completely and slump my head back, biting my lip with a smile. As if nothing's out of the ordinary, thrusting in and out of me at the slowest pace, he looks around the room and swigs his Corona with no lime.

His movement's gentle and exact, hitting my clit with the palm of his hand as he fucks me with his fingers, soaking his hand and my underwear in desire.

A small moan escapes my lips.

He smiles at the mouth of his bottled beer.

All of a sudden he stops, but doesn't pull his fingers out.

"Another round?" Leo asks, collecting our empties from the table.

I close my thighs on Teller's hand and pull my dress down to hide what's going on under the table. My face warms, and my stomach drops, but nothing can stop the tingling between my legs.

"What do you think, babe? Should we order another round, or are we ready to go?" Teller curves his fingers, brushing against the place inside of me that tosses caution to the wind and reduces me to nothing but sensation, utterly shameless.

"Yeah, whatever," I force out, trying to smile.

"We'll take two more, my man."

"No problem. I'll be right back with those."

He walks away, and Teller waits until our waiter is around the corner before he thrusts his fingers fully into me, unapologetic and rough, over and over and over. Tingles explode to full-on inferno, and I catch on fire, rolling my hips as I become engulfed.

"You have to be quiet, Ella," Teller whispers against my ear, kissing the side of my hot face.

I clasp onto his arm, gathering his T-shirt in my fisted hand, pulling as pressure between my legs becomes uncontainable. I feel myself tighten around his fingers, and he leans over, coaxing me, guiding me, urging me to come for him.

"Just like that. You look so beautiful, baby. You're so fucking sexy, Ella." Beer-scented breath tickles my skin, and I pull him closer. "You have no fucking clue how stunning you are."

Coming apart, I bury my face in his shirt and bite my bottom lip until the taste of copper coats my tongue.

"That's it, babe. Open your eyes and look at me. Let me see all of you."

It takes every stitch of restraint I have not to jump his

cock and scream his name loud enough for the entire hotel to hear as I ride out the last of this orgasm. It's been years since it was this good, since this drunk pleasure was taken from me so unabashedly, since I was this brazen about never wanting it to end. Since the days he used to thrust and press and rub over my clothes until I was gripping the bedsheets and forgetting that anything existed outside of Teller and those moments.

One last wave of fever and shivers stretches through my body before it slows, leaving me breathless and reset, unmoving in his arms.

"Here you go." Leo places our refills on the table. "Is there anything else I can get you?"

"Just the check," Teller replies, kissing my forehead, my nose, and my cheeks. He holds me in his arms, as if he's trying to hide me from the rest of the world and keep me to himself.

"Yes, sir. My pleasure," Leo responds before he turns and leaves, shuffling away so that coins in his apron jingle.

"I shouldn't have done that to you," Teller straightens my dress, making sure I'm decent the next time our server comes around.

"Don't apologize to me," I say, smiling, feeling lighter than I have in a long time. "I knew what I was doing when I wore this dress."

CHAPTER TWELVE

Now

Ella

"What do you mean you got married?"

I sit up from the chaise lounge, glistening in suntan oil, and lift my sunglasses to the top of my head. Emerson sits across from me with his forearms resting on his knees and his hands laced together, blinking thoughtfully under long lashes I wasn't blessed with. My heart hammers inside my chest, beating so hard my hands tremble, and my eyes immediately burn with tears.

Teller woke up early this morning to play a round of golf with Husher. My plans were to tag along since we had an early night, electing movies in bed over booze and a hangover, but I woke up this morning knowing I needed time to unwind. With a stomach full of pins that gradually spread through my limbs, I changed into my bikini, ordered food, and haven't left our private pool in the sky all day, decompressing.

"We didn't plan it, Gabriella. We were there, and it seemed like a good idea at the time." Em drops his head between his shoulders, and my heart falls with it.

"And it doesn't now?" I ask, wiping my eyes dry. "I don't understand."

"I wanted to marry her," he answers in a low tone, lifting his dark eyes to mine. In times like these, when his expression is void of anything but the struggle, he looks so much like our father it takes my breath away. "I want to be married to her. It's something I've thought about for a while, but I can't give her the wedding she deserves. Her family…"

He doesn't need to finish the sentence for me to understand. Nicolette's family is wealthy, and we're not.

"Sell the house," I reply without hesitation.

I've watched this person give up his entire life to shoulder my burden and his. Dreams, hopes, and his future went cold on the backburner in order to guarantee I was taken care of, happy, and more than a girl with no parents. To watch him sacrifice something so momentous turns pins to rusty nails, and it's killing me.

My brother shakes his head with the hint of happiness at the corner of his mouth. "I'm not selling the house to pay for a wedding, Ella. We should give Nic more credit than that. She's not that kind of girl."

Bullshit.

"It's just sitting there, and you deserve it, Em. After everything you've given up—"

"No," he replies, sitting straight. "I never did anything I didn't want to. You're my baby sister, and taking care of you has been a gift."

"A gift that keeps on giving." I scoff, licking salty tears from my lips.

"Like herpes," Em mumbles playfully. I threaten him with a knuckle sandwich, and he holds his hands up defensively.

I toss Emerson a beer, and we toast and take a long, much needed swig that eases regret and burns our eyes. The sun reflects from the gold band around his ring finger, and I recognize the scratched surface right away: my dad's wedding ring.

"I didn't even know you had that," I cry, unable to stop the flood of emotion that jumps me like ninjas in a street fight. "You didn't even invite me to your wedding."

Big brother laughs, closing the space between us to embrace me in his reassuring hug. I cling to him, not with the urgency I do with Teller, but with honest regard, unashamed of the tears that soak into his shirt, happy, and terrified, and unsure of what's to come for either one of us. For the first time since we lost our parents, Emerson and I are at a point in our lives where we don't need each other to survive. We have our own lives to live now.

"There wasn't time to call anyone, sissy. It wasn't planned, and when she said yes, I knew we had to hurry before she changed her mind."

"She wouldn't have changed her mind, Em," I say with a small smile, holding my hand to the side of his face. "She's lucky to have you."

The light in his eyes fades, and his grin wavers. A look of concern that creases the skin between his brows and stops my heart from beating veils his face, and I know exactly what's on his mind.

It's on mine, too.

"What's going on with you and Teller?" he asks in his I-am-your-guardian-you-will-respect-my-authority voice, reading my mind.

Exhaling, I drop my sunglasses over my eyes and lie back. "The last thing I need is a lecture."

He shakes his head, spinning the ring on his finger. "That's not what I'm here for, Gabriella. You're twenty-five years old and can make your own decisions, but I know better than anyone what it's like when things get bad between the two of you. I want you to think about it before you jump back into a relationship with him."

"We were never in a relationship, Em. We're not in one now." Weak but not entirely a lie, it's second nature to excuse dysfunction with semantics. Our behavior should be dismissed because it's without a label, nothing permanent, nothing lasting.

But here we are, seven years later, at square one.

"You and I know better than anyone how hard it is to lose someone, and I hate that it's happened to you again. I wish I could bring him back, Ella. I wish I could bring them back, because then maybe you wouldn't feel the need to hold on to Teller like he's going to leave you one day."

"That's ridiculous," I whisper, knowing it's the absolute truth.

"He's the only person you talk to. He's the only person you *ever* talk to. You haven't said two words about Joe since he passed, and now we're in Las Vegas, in these absurd rooms, acting like none of it happened. Don't let vulnerability cloud your judgment. Remember what you said after Teller was arrested. Remember why you ended it with him."

Emerson places his hand on top of mine, but I shake it off.

"Don't judge me. I'm doing the best I can, Emerson," I say defensively. "Despite what you think, I'm not totally messed up, and Teller lost someone, too."

"I know that." He rubs the back of his neck, avoiding eye contact. "But you don't see what I see when you're with him. It's like you disappear."

"Stop," I say before I push him over the side of the MGM Grand. "Why are we talking about this when you just told me you got married? Shouldn't we be celebrating?"

The groom smacks his hands on the top of his thighs and stands up. He stretches his arms above his head, and the ring once again gleams in the Nevada sun. "Yes. VIP at Hakkasan. Some DJ's spinning tonight."

"The DJ whose face is on the side of the hotel? The *entire* side?" I ask, laughing.

"Yeah, apparently he's a big deal, but I've never heard of him."

"He's only the biggest DJ in the world, Em. You can't be that out of touch."

My brother shrugs, walking toward the door back into the loft. "Hey, I'm only here for the booze."

"**D**o you want a drink?" Teller appears behind me with a bottle of champagne and a flute hanging between his tattooed fingers. He drops his hands and lowers his eyes to my bottom, smirking. "Please tell me that's what you're wearing."

On tiptoes in front of the bathroom mirror, I lean over the counter and straighten my eyelid, applying liquid eyeliner in one smooth, practiced motion. "I didn't plan on wearing just my underwear, but we are in Vegas."

He places a glass of stars beside my makeup bag and leans against the wall. Black denim hangs low on his hips, loosely held up by a spiked belt, and ink shows through his thin undershirt. Teller's clean-shaven, kissed by the right amount of sun, and staring at me like he's never seen a woman's body before.

"Those aren't underwear, baby. Those are a dream come true. You're stunning."

I don't know why I packed the sheer lace panty and bra set, but I'm wearing it because I'm tired of other people trying to dictate what I do with my life. After my conversation with Emerson, the truth has never been more apparent: Joe never made me disappear.

I never talked to him. I never let him truly know me. What I did was give him yes and no answers when questioned, filled silence with what I thought he wanted to hear, and avoided deep conversation whenever it came up. And he let me.

Joseph didn't push when I said I didn't want to talk about my mom or why she left. He knew my father died of cancer, but not that I was the one who found him in his bed after he passed during the night. Joe never dug deeper or demanded my undivided attention. We made generic plans, and expressed generic feelings, fueled by a generic need for normalcy.

Our relationship was a thing of convenience, and I wish he were here so I could apologize for not needing him like he deserved.

"Thank you," I say shyly, extending my lashes with

expensive mascara. "But my dress is on the bed."

"Wear the red lipstick," he says, standing back with the green bottle of champagne in his hand. The steady rise and fall of his chest and easy grin on his lips go right to the spot between my legs, and I pick up the tube of red rouge. Teller watches me apply it to my bottom lip, advancing my backside as I fill in the top and press them together. "Every time you wear that color on your lips I think about how they'll look around my cock."

Our eyes meet in the mirror, and he drops the champagne bottle, releasing a chorus of hisses and pops as it coats the bathroom floor. Cool liquid touches my bare foot as Teller presses his chest against my back, trapping my curled hair between us. He moves the dark brown tresses over my shoulder at the same time the aroma of wine and roses assaults my senses.

"What's bothering you?" he asks, dragging down the cup of my bra on his way lower. "What's on your pretty mind, baby?"

His hand sinks into my panties.

Teller cups my heat, slipping four fingers between my folds.

"Joseph," I breathe, holding on to the counter. I can't breathe. I can hardly stand on my own two feet. "Do you wonder about Kristi?"

"Yes," he answers easily, gripping me harder. "But she's not you. She never was. We didn't know them like we thought we did."

It would be so easy to drop to my knees and show him exactly what it'll look like to have these red lips around his dick. Our absence wouldn't surprise anyone. They expect it.

We're supposed to meet in ten minutes, so they might have written us off already—counted us out. But I want them to see what we see. They should know, so far, it's different between Teller and me.

We're not moving too fast.

We're right on pace.

"You're going to make us leave again, aren't you?" disappointed asks, removing his hand from the lace to correct my bra.

"We can't miss this, Tell. My brother and Nic would never forgive us."

Teller drops his head and groans playfully, conceding to my commands. He carries me away from the champagne puddle, setting me on my feet at the end of the bed where my dress awaits. The black mini dress hugs my bust, squeezes my waist, supports my full bottom, and highlights every curve in my body. Cut out at the side, it shows enough skin while leaving some to the imagination.

"You're killing me, girl." Teller buttons his light denim shirt to the very top button and cuffs the sleeves.

"Ditto," I say, loving the color against his eyes.

While I strap on my shoes, magnificence pulls up his pants, tightens his belt, and puts on a pair of brown boots. I respray my hair, wipe smeared lipstick from the corner of my mouth, and reemerge as Teller's straightening the gold watch around his wrist.

Our family's catching the elevator when we step out of our room, and they do a terrible job at hiding their surprise at the sight of us. We say our hellos, offer congratulations to the newlyweds, and share a concerned look with Maby.

"I'm fine," she says, wrapping her arms around my

waist. "I needed to catch up on some sleep. That's all."

Teller leans against the rail in the elevator, holding me against his lap between his legs on the ride to the fourth floor. Maby talks a million miles a minute, asking Nicolette about the impromptu wedding.

"What did you wear? What did you say? Have you told your parents?"

Included in our insanely price-per-night rooms is VIP service at the club, complete with private entrance, bottle service, and prime view of the stage over the sea of bodies moving to the beat on the dance floor, broken by strobe lights, topped by misters, and screaming when confetti rains from the ceiling as the entertainment approaches the turntables.

Emerson didn't give Nic the wedding he thinks she deserves, but he gives her a night she'll never forget. They cut a three-tier cake shooting sparklers from the top while the entire dance club watches, cheering from below. He's polite, careful not to ruin her makeup, but Nicolette shoves vanilla buttercream into her husband's mouth and smears it across his face.

"I need to use the ladies' room," I say into Teller's ear. His skin is warm, intensifying the spice in his cologne.

We haven't left each other's side since we arrived. While watching the show, taking shots, and dancing, uncertainty dissolves when I'm safely in his arms, and the past is easy to forget when it's this good. I watch the lights reflect from his eyes and like the way his lips curve when he looks at me, and I'm sure this is what I want.

I'm sure we'll be okay.

He holds his palm to my lower back and bends at the

knee to place his lips right over my ear. "Do you want me to come with you?"

Shaking my head, I point in the direction of the restrooms. They're not far from the VIP area, and there's not a line as if we were downstairs with the masses. Lifting to the tips of my heels, I press my lips to his jaw and turn to walk away. I haven't traveled three steps when Teller, with my lip print on his skin, reaches for my wrist and pulls me against him.

His breath smells like spearmint and vodka, and his eyes are on my mouth.

"Come with me." Maby pulls my arm, and Teller lets me slip from his grasp. "I need some air. It's so hot in here."

"I'll be right back," I mouth to my man, following Maby toward the exit.

It takes a moment for my senses to adjust to the normal lighting and lower volume in the restroom. Stepping in front of the mirror to freshen my makeup, my ears rings, and I feel like I'm speaking too loudly when I ask, "How are you feeling, Maby?"

"Better," she answers right away. Not that I expected her to admit differently. She pushes open a stall door, lowering her underwear to her ankles when she says, "It was just one of those days. I know Husher called you, but it wasn't that serious this time. I'm good."

She emerges a minute later, tugging her blue dress down her short legs and coercing an unconvincing smile for my benefit. As strong and as bossy as she normally is, her pale complexion and the dark circles under her green-like-his eyes are a dead giveaway to the madness that plagues her mind.

"So, you and my brother." She meddles in true Maby form, washing her small, trembling hands. "I want it to work out this time, Ella. But if it doesn't—"

"It will," I say, opening the door back to the nightclub. Decibels move in immediately, drowning out any sort of response she has.

The last thing I want is to upset her during an episode, but if she's well enough to impose, she's well enough to handle my indifference. Two years ago I might have overreacted and argued, ruining everyone's night. But right now, I want to get back to Teller. This is my life, my choice, and I'm the one who has to live with the consequences if it goes bad, so I hope brushing her concern under the rug is one more move in the right direction.

Maby takes my hand, and I tighten my grip, settling depression's quiver. The sister I never had works hard to put on a brave face for our sake, having missed important events before because of the unexplainable sadness that lingers within her, a true Jekyll and Hyde story.

But when we exit the hallway, swallowed by lights, noise, and heat from thousands of moving bodies, Maby tightens her grip on me … with both hands. Not that she can or has to hold me back, because I'm stuck, unable to comprehend the scene playing out in front of us. My heart doesn't drop, tears don't burn my eyes, and I don't get angry.

I just stop.

I stop.

Amanda, the cocktail waitress from the pool, has Teller pushed against the wall with her hands on his chest and her body pressed to his. I can't make out what they're saying to each other, but the smile on her face is telling enough.

My brother and Nicolette are nowhere in sight, and Husher's sitting at our booth with his face in his cell phone, oblivious to the avalanche of emotion I'm about to wreck this place with. Disappointment breaks my heart into a million little pieces that cut veins from the inside, flooding my lungs with misery. Resentment tap, tap, taps on my bones, looking for soft spots bitterness can splinter and stab my soul with. And a tiny little voice inside my head whispers, *it was too good to be true,* as deceit breaks the light inside me.

"Gabriella, don't!" Maby shrieks as I brush past her, loud enough to catch everyone's attention, unsuccessfully holding me back. It's advice I almost consider until Amanda lifts her finger to Teller's mouth and places a white tablet on his tongue.

He's smart enough to step in front of the girl before I'm able to grab a fistful of her stringy blonde hair, but stupid enough to put himself within my reach.

"Spit it out," I say, squeezing his cheeks between my fingers and thumb. "Spit it out or I swear, Teller, you'll never see me again."

Green eyes glow, staring intently at my face. He doesn't break my grip or move away; he just stares as everything I was certain of dissolves to nothing.

"Sissy, let him go." Emerson's soothing voice lessens the ache in my chest. He places a large hand on my shoulder, standing at my back where he's always been.

Tears fall from my eyes, and I release Teller's face. "You're disgusting."

He spits the tablet at my feet.

When I turn around, Maby, Husher, and Nicolette don't say a word, but their expressions say it all: we told you so.

Checking their shoulders on the way out, no one stops me from leaving, and besides the five people I'm here with, and one skinny drink server who's lucky she still has all her teeth in her mouth, no one knows my world imploded.

I exit the first door I stumble upon, steering me to a florescent-lit hallway with white tile floors and dirty walls. Music from the club is reduced to a muffled hum, and the air is cold enough to form goose bumps on my exposed flesh. Heading toward the service elevator, my heels tap on the glossy floor beneath my feet, and I suddenly feel exposed in this ridiculous dress.

Just like our time here has exposed what an idiot I am.

"Ella, stop." Teller's voice carries through the white space, but I keep walking. The door slams heavily behind him.

"Get your hands off of me," I say, yanking my elbow free from his clutch. Shoving my palms into his chest, I send him five paces back. "I don't even want to look at you."

"Dammit, Gabriella, let me explain." He holds his hands to the back of his head before dropping them and taking a step toward me. "Please, baby."

"You didn't have anything to say to me out there." I nod toward the door, tears flowing freely down my cheeks.

Teller drops his eyes and licks his lips. "I didn't want to argue with you in front of everyone. I didn't want us to end up like that again."

I scoff, turning away from dysfunction. My heart's too broken to hurt any more than it does, and I can't stomach his bullshit a moment longer. I've listened to it long enough. I've listened to it for seven years. "That's something you should have thought about when you let that girl all over you the second I wasn't around."

He shakes his head, eyes red-rimmed and glossy in the fractured light. "I'm sorry. I—I don't know what I was thinking, Ella. She came out of nowhere and asked if I wanted to feel good, and—"

"You're pathetic," I say, backing away toward the elevator. "Stay away from me, Teller. I'm done."

My back's against the wall, and I'm caged between his arms before the words leave my mouth. Teller takes my face in his hand, forcing me to look into bright eyes gone dark, and I want to claw them out. Fueled by adrenaline coursing through my bloodstream, I grab his wrist and pierce my nails into his marked skin until beads of blood appear. We smile, dosed on the imbalance in our brains that makes this exciting.

This is what they warned us about.

This is what I was afraid of.

And now it's too late.

"How does it feel to know you'll never fuck me, Teller? We'll never get this right. We never had a chance." I want him to hurt like I hurt, and suffer like I'm suffering. I want him to drop to his knees and beg for my forgiveness so I can spit on his face like he spit on mine the second that girl put her finger in his mouth.

"You *are* mine," he seethes with anger, tightening his hold on my chin.

A single tear streams from the corner of my eye into my hair, but excitement numbs heartbreak and intensifies the rush. I'm lit, high, stoned on breaking him, and we're just getting started.

"Prove it," I say, grinning like a maniac.

He drops his forehead to mine, breathing in and out of his nose. Teller vibrates with pent-up aggression, slumbering since the last time we found ourselves ready to kill each other. "Watch what you say to me, Gabriella."

"I said prove it." Craving pools between my legs, and my chest heaves with quick breathing. My lips tingle, and the tips of my fingers and toes lose feeling. "If you want me, Teller, take me."

"You don't know what you're asking for." His mouth is at my throat, hovering over an erratic pulse, and he presses his body flush against mine.

This is us, crazy out of our minds, obsessed with the thrill, and willing to break each other just to lick madness.

"Stop being a fucking pussy and do it already." The warmth from his body is enticing, mouthwatering, and so within reach I can sink my teeth into it. I lick blood from his wrist and watch his pupils expand.

"I won't be able to stop." His harsh words skim my face but affect nothing but the ache in my sex.

"Like you couldn't stop Amanda from riding your dick?" I laugh, dropping my head against the wall so I can see his entire face.

My laughter only becomes more uncontrollable when his fist whooshes past my head, splitting drywall and old scars. Paint chips and powder sprinkles my shoulder and dusts my hair, but I don't so much as flinch. It's another syringe filled with my favorite type of drug: Teller Reddy.

Does he think he's the only one hurting? My heart's bleeding out.

Grabbing a handful of his dark hair, I lower his head until we're face-to-face. Black painted fingernails dig into his scalp, and my arm is numb from lack of circulation, but I don't let go of control. Teller consumes me. Teller devours me. Teller demolishes me. Every fiber of my being screams for me to never let him out of my sight. It's an animalistic need neither one of us controls, even after all these years, even after everything we've been through. I want to hurt him as much as I want to savor him.

I jerk and shove and scream, pushing his face away from me, only to grab his shirt and pull him back. Buttons fly off under my hands, and thread stretches and snaps. Teller takes every slap, every dig, every word I don't mean, so I keep hitting and scratching, filtering frustration on a body that's taken it before, like a mad person, a psychopath.

Until he breaks.

"You better be sure you want it, baby, because I'm about to make sure you can never belong to anyone else again." The smirk curving his lips is to die for. Literally. "That's a mistake I won't make twice."

"You don't have the balls." I spit, begging with my eyes for him to just do it.

I reach under my skirt and pull down my panties, kicking them to the side in a dare. Teller's smirk bends into a full-blown smile, and he circles his hand around my throat, shoving me against the wall, knocking half a breath from me. His free hand swoops down my thigh, curving under my knee to hitch it over his waist.

"Last chance to change your mind," he warns, unbuckling his belt.

Spike studs brush against my skin with sharp tips, scratching my delicate skin. Biting my bottom lip, I welcome the simple ache, rocking my hips to feel a little more.

It takes focus away from my heart that beats so erratically, I'm certain it's going to burst inside of my chest.

"I'm not yours until you make me." At the sound of his zipper going down, I wrap my other leg around his waist, hooking it on my ankle.

Teller releases my throat, placing his hand on the busted wall beside my head for leverage, and I feel hardness slip between my folds. Before either one of us can say another word, seven years of anticipation disappear, and he pushes into me.

I cry out in pain and pleasure.

Pain, because the spikes on his belt dig into my inner thighs every time he thrusts forward. Pain, because his hands bruise my skin, holding me harder. Pain, because this is not how it's supposed to be.

Pleasure, because somewhere in the back of my mind, behind all this bullshit, it feels right.

"Say it, Ella. Tell me you're mine," he demands breathlessly.

"Fuck you," I moan, meeting him stroke for stroke.

Thrusting harder, deeper, and longer, spikes carve into me, breaking skin and bleeding out. Moving bodies, gasps for air, and the struggle to get closer fills the empty hallway where anyone can intrude in any moment. I've never felt so good and so bad at the same time in my life. I both hate and want him, push and pull, right and wrong. It's disgusting, but I wanted him to finally claim me. I wanted this.

"Come on, Teller. You can do better than this." I can't bring myself to meet his eyes, afraid of what I'll find. My head falls forward against his shoulder, overcome with fire licking passion. His grip on my hips tightens as he crashes where we're connected, and I feel every inch of him sliding in and out of me. Tingles envelop my body, and pain from his belt dragging up and down my thighs disappears, leaving only the feeling of him.

The sound of my skin slapping on his, the warmth of his breath on my neck, and his words, *mine, my girl,* over and over only make me want more. Teller fills me up, and we're complete, even in this fucked-up situation—he sees the crazy in me and likes it.

My body's on fire, and I can't get enough…

Ripping his shirt open, what buttons he has left scatter, hitting walls and rolling down the dirty tile. I lift his undershirt and scratch my nails down his chest and stomach, over designs that took hours and skill to complete, hoping it hurts. Hoping they're ruined.

With his skin under my nails, I grab the collar of his white undershirt and pull. Cotton stretches and misshapes, but despite how hard I yank it won't rip, but it doesn't stop me from trying hard enough to leave a mark on the back of his neck.

Exposing his collarbone, I put my mouth on him, slowly at first, careful in spite of the wreckage we're inflicting on our bodies. The taste of him on my tongue resurrects a flicker of affection, a softness, a reminder that he's the most important person in my life and we shouldn't be doing this.

Then his fingers dig into my bottom, and my back crashes into the wall. I cry out in pain, but give it back tenfold, sinking my teeth into the top of his shoulder.

His thrusts become faster, his moaning louder, and I bite harder. The taste of blood does nothing to stop the assault I inflict on his skin. It only makes me sink deeper.

"Fuck," he groans into my neck. His cock hardens inside of me.

He pulls my head back by my hair, ripping my teeth from his skin. Blood and saliva drip down my chin, and he licks it away.

"You don't scare me," he says, smirking before he returns the onslaught on my neck.

I dig the heels of my shoes into the back of his legs, and circle my arms around his neck, holding him closer, wanting him to suck harder. Blood vessels break, bruising skin, turning it purple and blue. Screaming only makes him kiss harder, moving across my neck until there's no question who I belong to.

After a while the pain fades, like everything else.

CHAPTER THIRTEEN

Now

Teller

S he's mine, and everyone's going to know it after this.

From the soft spot below her ear to her thin collarbone, I suck, and suck, and suck, forcing blood to the surface of Ella's skin. Mouth-sized bruises discolor her throat, like graffiti on porcelain, a work of art only I can appreciate.

"Harder," she begs breathlessly, sliding up and down my cock. "Harder, harder, harder."

Delicate skin will easily tear if I bite too hard, kiss too hard, need too hard, but it doesn't stop me from marring every spot my lips touch. There's not a rational brainwave in my head, flooded by indulgence and the need to stake my claim. I'll fuck her until she gets the point. I'll fuck her until the words leave her mouth. We've pushed each other too far, and this was a long time coming.

Hurting, marking, and fucking her all at the same time are more powerful than anything I've ever experienced.

Ella's arms are wrapped around my neck, and her nails spear my shoulders, like the stiletto heels digging into my calves. She's dripping wet around me, tight like I knew she would be, warm like I imagined time and time again. The smell of her sex is in every breath I manage, and I can taste fear on my tongue, mixed with sweat and perfume, throwing me over the deep end.

Anger courses through my veins, laced with legitimate terror. She wanted to leave me again, like not belonging to me has ever been a choice, like I would once again sit back and watch her fall for someone else. As if it wouldn't kill me. As if she could actually do it. She'll have bruises on her thighs from how hard I'm grabbing them, her neck will take weeks to heal, and her head will be sore from how hard I'm pulling her hair, and I should care, but I don't.

I'm consumed.

"Come on, Teller. I'm so close. I'm almost there…"

I pull almost all the way out before plummeting back inside, driving my hips into her as hard as I can. As the pressure where we're connected becomes stronger and stronger, I lose complete sense of reality, and we're the only two people on the face of the Earth, seeking answers, looking for refuge.

Arrogance diminishes to whimpers, a slow and quiet begging that shifts bitterness to gentleness. Ella kisses the side of my face, panting as she starts to contract around my cock, draining brutality from her body.

She throws her head back and closes her eyes, breathing in and out of her mouth. "Don't stop. Don't stop."

"Say it, Gabriella. You better fucking say it." I need to hear the words before I finish. I'm right fucking there, and by the way she's pulsating around me, so is she. "Now, baby."

"I'm yours. I'm yours, Teller," she whispers.

We hold tight as indescribable pleasure rocks our cores, stealing breath from our lungs and sight from our eyes. I bury my face in her neck, kissing her softly, listening to every moan that leaves her lips because of me. Thrusting in as deep as our bodies will allow, pressing her into the wall, I fill her to the brim, rocking my hips. It might never end.

It does.

And when it happens, I'm devastated.

Everything stops but the rush of our breathing and the hammering of our hearts as recklessness subsides and reality files in, stacking on top of us. Ella's legs fall from my waist, stepping unsteadily to the floor, but she keeps her arms circled around my neck to keep from collapsing.

"Are you okay?" I ask, breathless. My still-hard dick rests against her stomach between us, and I hurry to put myself back into my jeans.

Ella shakes her head, letting go of my shoulders to grasp the front of my shirt with bleeding fingers and hands that shake. I follow her wrists to her elbows, then to her shoulders and neck. Six large red and purple bruises stain her normally pale skin—a line of spite from her throat to the fullness of her breasts. Sickened by my ability to ruin beauty, my stomach turns at what I've done.

"I'm sorry," she whispers, sadness falling from her dark brown eyes. "I'm so sorry, Teller."

Wrenching her hands from my shirt, I hold her wrists and take a step back to inspect the damage I've done. Starting from the top of her head, down her face, past her neck, down, down, down to her thighs.

There's no air.

No mercy to this suffocation.

No way out.

The harm I inflicted on her throat is nothing compared to what my belt did to her legs. Gashes from her knees to skin hidden under her dress bleeds, inflamed and torn, like a savage attack on someone threatening your life. My back hits the wall across from her, and I'd give anything for it to open up and swallow me whole.

"Please, don't leave me," devastation says, sliding down the wall to her bottom.

I fall to my hands and knees, dropping my head between my shoulders and cry out, "What the fuck have I done?"

She's there, wrapping her arms around my neck, kissing the top of my head and apologizing. "I'm so sorry. I'm so sorry."

Cradling her hands in my face, I kiss the tears away and say, "I did this, baby. It was me. It was me."

I blanket my button-up around her shoulders and lift the key to my broken heart into my arms, carrying her down the hallway to the service elevator that thankfully takes us to the top floor. She keeps her eyes closed for the entire ride, with her lashes wet from crying and a flushed complexion.

The loft smells like hairspray and spilled champagne, dimly lit by the lamp we left on and the lights shining in from the hotel across the street. I take her into the bathroom and set her on the counter, prying her fingers from my undershirt when she won't let me go.

"I'm not going anywhere," I say, unsure if it's a lie or

not.

Streaks of blood from the wounds on her thighs have dried down to her ankles, and the bruises on her neck are more purple and blue than red, deepening in color as seconds pass. She's a pathetic sight, fatigued and broken, with mascara under her eyes and red lipstick smeared outside the lines of her lips.

Ella dips her face to her hands and cries, "God, Teller, we really fucked up this time."

Running a towel under warm water, I clean ruined makeup and sticky tears from her face, careful around her eyes and making it worse around her mouth. Shimmering blush and thick foundation rub away, exposing a clutter of freckles across her straight nose.

"Have you even seen what I've done to you?" she asks. "Look in the mirror."

I purposely keep my gaze from the reflection, unconcerned with my own wellbeing, and unable to come face-to-face with the person I've become—the kind of man who does harm to the people he cares about for his own sick satisfaction.

Rinsing the towel under scalding water, I burn my hands wringing it out and carefully pat the scratches on her inner thighs, turning the white cloth pink. Ella hisses, but as the dry blood comes clean, I get a better look at the wounds the spikes in my belt caused. Most are superficial, slight scratches and red marks that will fade by the end of the night, but a few are deep and bleeding even as I hold the towel over them.

"This shouldn't have happened like this, Ella. That wasn't how it was supposed to be." I drop the bloodstained towel to the champagne coated floor and unbuckle her shoes, slipping them from her feet.

I press my kiss to every lesion, mixing blood with tears, coating my lips in her life source. There's no way we can hide this from our family. Emerson will take one look at his sister and know I'm guilty, and he'll do everything in his power to keep us apart—as he should. While I still have her within reach, each kiss becomes a promise to stay away if that's what's best for her. Each tear is my pledge to disappear if that's what makes her happy.

I would die for her.

All she has to do is ask.

Ella gently places her hand on the side of my face, urging me to look up. I kiss the inside of her palm and stand to my feet, setting my hands on each side of her against the counter.

"Are you going to leave me?" she asks.

"I shouldn't be anywhere near you," I reply, licking my lips. "But first I'm going to draw you a bath."

I lift her dress over her head, discarding it with the bloody towels. Unclasping her bra, I'm not honorable enough to look away when it falls down her arms, baring her naked chest, and she's not ashamed enough to ask me to look away, letting sheer and lace drop with her clothes, leaving her utterly bare. Ella sweeps her hair over her shoulders, brushing it out of her face, displaying a perfect view of her body. She's small, exposed in front of me, injured and perfect all at once.

I wrap her in a clean towel until the tub is full, and she holds it together with unsteady fingers. I stare into the running water while flashing memories from the hallway turn my stomach inside out, and I want nothing more than to crawl from my own skin.

"I shouldn't have pushed you, Tell," Ella says in a quiet voice, thick with devastation. "This is my fault as much as it is yours."

"No, it's not." I turn off the water and sweep my fingertips through the surface to test the temperature. "It's not the same, because I'm a man and … I shouldn't have touched you."

"I wanted it!" she shouts. Her voice echoes off the walls. "I wanted you to do it. I wanted you to finally fucking do it."

Cutting my gaze from the bruises on her throat, my eyes brim with defeat. My heart's rickety, barely beating, nothing without her.

"Let's get you in the water," I say, helping her from the counter and into the bathtub. "I'll be outside. Call me know when you're ready to get out."

"No." She grabs my wrist and pulls me down. "Don't leave me alone."

"You want me to wait here with you?"

"I want you to come in with me." Persistence brings her knees to her chest. The ends of her hair float in the warm water, and steam ribbons around her frame.

I clear my throat to keep from crying out. "Are you sure?"

"Of course. I want you, Teller."

Too tired to argue, I draw the belt from my pants and toss it into the trash bin. It hits the metal can with a clink, but I don't give it a second thought. I go to remove my undershirt, but it snags on my back, stinging when I pull. Ella looks at me from the tub, wide-eyed and guilty, with her bottom lip between her teeth.

Checking it out in the mirror, the shirt's stuck to raw scratches on my back, blood-soaked. I give it one hard pull, ignoring the pain, and throw the shirt into the trash, too. Giving my back a quick glance, there are a dozen or so long red scratches, carved in no order. They start to bleed again, burning against the cool air.

"I told you," Ella whispers.

After taking my pants off, I get into the tub behind my girl. She leans against my chest, and I drape my arms around her. I admire her naked body, appreciating the feel of her skin against mine. She places her feet right on top of mine, and I place my cheek on the top of her head. Every single part of us is completely touching the other, and I don't deserve it.

CHAPTER FOURTEEN

Before

Ella

"**D**on't look, but Teller just walked in the door and he doesn't look too happy." Nicolette stirs a tiny black straw in her drink, swirling ice in liquor and something sour. "What the fuck is his problem now?"

Ignoring her advice, I turn my head toward the bar entrance where tatted and pissed scopes the tables, no doubt looking for me. The corner of my mouth twitches, not entirely unhappy to see him. He's gorgeous in dark denim and red, unshaved and rough around the edges. His first year of medical school and lack of time to shave every week have done amazing things.

I dig the scruffy look.

But he can kiss my ass.

"Should we get out of here? I'm sure there's a back door we can sneak out of." My brother's girlfriend reaches for her purse, but I place my hand over hers, ending the retreat. "I don't feel like dealing with his shitty mood tonight."

"No," I say. "Let him come over. It's a free country, after all."

Nic smiles, but it doesn't reach her eyes. "Nice, Ella. The *free country* argument, because we're in middle school. What's he pissed about, anyway?"

I sip my cocktail, too sugary and sweet. "Dad stuff. School stuff."

"You stuff." Nicolette rolls her hazel eyes.

"Me stuff," I confirm, setting my drink down onto a wet paper coaster. "I overheard Kimberly Evans mention hooking up with him at some party. I was in the bathroom at school and she didn't know I was there."

"You realize Kim's a slut, right?" Nic blows her sandy blonde bangs from her eyes, tapping her acrylic nails against the wooden table. "She's a med student groupie. Teller's a dick, but I don't think he'd sink that low. And besides, he obsessed with you. He has been for the last three years. It's weird."

Disappointment and mistrust are bitter in my mouth, but I know the blame's partly my own. For the last few years, Teller and I've played *tug-a-war* with our hearts, constantly heaving in different directions, never on the same team. It's complicated, but it's ours, and I assumed we had a silent agreement about exclusivity.

You don't, and I won't, and we'll figure out the rest along the way.

I assumed wrong.

"Not sure if I agree, Nic. Kim sounded pretty convincing." Tension hardens my backbone, packing my chest with fiery pressure.

"What did he say when you asked him about it?"

I shrug, sliding my finger around the rim of my glass. "Not much. I sent him a message that I knew what happened and blocked his number."

Nicolette purses her perfectly glossed lips, and I can see she's holding back a few choice words. At this point, she's the only one who stays tight-lipped. Unless we break something, or disturb her television schedule. Teller and I know to keep our issues to a minimum during *The Bachelor*.

"Well, my guess is you're about to have an overdue conversation, because here he comes." She nods over my shoulder, sitting back to enjoy the show. A few drinks in, who's not going to enjoy the entertainment?

My counterpart pulls out the chair beside me, dropping his car keys and cell phone onto the table, knocking over the drink specials stand-up menu. I pretend he's not there, ignoring ginger and soap and the electric current that ups my heartbeat when he's near.

Husher and Maby come back from the bar, hands full of shots for the table. My brother follows not far behind, ready to partake. They all look like deer in headlights when they realize our party is one person bigger than it was when we arrived.

"Nice," Teller says in a clipped tone. "All you motherfuckers are here and no one called me."

Four sets of eyes fall on me, but I ignore them like I do my favorite green ones. If he's messing around with some med school groupie like Kim Evans, it's no longer my responsibility to make sure Teller gets an invitation to anything.

"Sorry, Tell. We assumed Ella—" Maby stops, taking in the angry expression from her older brother.

"You assumed wrong," Tell grumbles. He leaves the table and heads toward the bar, pushing himself between the crowd.

I hold my hands up in surrender, refusing to take the heat for Teller's bad attitude. It's something I've done for long enough, and I choose now not to give a shit anymore.

"Handle it, Ella. I don't want this to get out of hand tonight. I work here," Emerson warns, deepening his voice to mimic our father. As if his security job here a couple days a week is some dream prospect. "I'm not in the mood to babysit."

Flipping him the bird, I take my shot, pretend it doesn't catch my esophagus on fire, and head toward the restrooms on the far side of the bar. No one calls me back—not that it matters. I'm twenty-two years old, able to make my own decisions, and not in need of four care-takers who have their own issues to figure out.

After a week of midterms, this place is full of exhaust-ed college kids looking to take a load off on a Friday night, drinking their worries and stresses away. Conversation carries as frat boys talk over each other, and jocks arm wrestle while girls in short skirts swoon and fight over who's going home with whom. Then there are the groups who are just here to get drunk, cheering over games of pool, gathering darts to hit the bull's-eye over pitchers of beer.

The line for the ladies' room spills out into the hall, crowding an ancient pay phone and a corkboard advertising tutoring and minimum wage jobs. I'm scoping out employment options when someone reaches over my arm, tearing a number tab from a dog walking opportunity.

"I fucking love dogs," tall and dark says, pocketing the inquiry. "There's something about the hairballs that makes me feel so complete."

"It's probably because they can't talk back," I say, smiling shyly.

"You'd be surprised," he answers. Gray eyes scope out my chest, then my face. "Can I buy you a drink? To say thanks for leading me toward a promising career prospect? It's the least I can do."

Looking toward my table, I relax when I see Teller's back in his seat.

"Not sure how I did that. I'm just waiting in line." I nod toward the five girls in front of me, all looking at their phones. Tiny screens glow yellow, blue, and neon green across their zombie-like expressions.

Animal lover smiles, and it's not enough to weaken my knees, but it's enough to keep my interest.

"Well, I was over there with my friends." He points toward a pool table directly across the room. "And when I saw how beautiful you are, I had to come over and ask your name or regret it for life. The job's a bonus. Right place at the right time."

I move up with the line, expecting the dog walker to take off the closer I get to the restroom, but he follows like a puppy. Which makes me laugh.

"Gabriella Mason. Science," I say, shaking his hand.

"Phillip Graves. Business."

Of course, I think to myself. *You and everybody else.*

Business is one of those failsafe, go-to majors one chooses when they have no idea what they want to do after college and don't want to spend too much time thinking about it. Not when there are toga parties to attend and bitches to fuck. He's smug now, big bad college guy, but in a year he'll work IT at a warehouse selling replacement parts on copy machines, in debt up to those chilling gray eyes.

"Science?" Phillip shoves his hands into his back pockets. "Environmental?"

Typical.

"No, actually I'm working toward a BSN. I can be a registered nurse with an associates, but I'll get paid a hell of a lot more with a bachelors degree. I just need to finish the year before I go to nursing school. Technically, I can get my RN license and earn a bachelors while I'm working, but I may as well get it over with all at once, right?" I smile condescendingly. "Because what are we here for?"

It goes in one ear and out the other, and I can practically see him chanting, *toga, toga, toga,* in his head.

"Yeah, that's cool," he says, plastering a rehearsed smile on his face. "How about that drink?"

I'm one person closer to the door, and he follows me deeper into the hallway that's beginning to smell like powdered soap and Lysol.

"I would, Phil. Can I call you Phil?" I jab my thumb over my shoulder. "But nature calls."

He runs a large hand through his chocolate brown hair, and it's apparent I was wrong about Phillip. He won't just be IT at a warehouse selling replacement parts for copy machines. He'll be a *bald* IT at a warehouse selling replacement part for copy machines. Male pattern baldness strikes some at such a young age.

"Oh, no problem. I can wait."

Awkward silence rains on our heads, but I don't mind much. I'm more worried about my bladder exploding before I reach a toilet. Phillip joins the two girls left standing in front of me, losing himself in technology wonderland, like everyone he's friends with isn't here, so there's no pressure to make any kind of small talk.

And true to his word, he waits patiently until I've had my turn and resurface from the hell that is a bar restroom.

I have to give credit where credit's due. Phillip Graves is nothing less than dedicated when he sees a piece of ass he wants, but Teller's here, and I'm not walking out there with another man. Not even I'll be able to stop him once his possessive wrath is unleashed, and good ol' Phil doesn't deserve it.

"Actually, I'm going to call it a night, but thanks for waiting for me." I pat his shoulder, leaving a hand-shaped water spot on his blue shirt. They were out of paper towels.

"What? Really?" he asks, thickening the charm. He doesn't notice I've wiped bathroom water all over him. "One drink. No strings."

I think about it for a second. Between midterms and Kim Evans, I've earned a free drink after the week I've had. "Do you have beer at your table?"

"Yes," he replies right away, broadening his smile.

"Fine, I'll have one of those, but then I really need to get going."

Following Phillip out to the main barroom, my hair

falls over my shoulder, providing a curtain between my face and Teller's eyes. The only problem is, I can't tell whether or not he can see me, but I assume the coast is clear when my escort isn't hit on the back of the head with a chair.

The beer's warm, but his friends are cool—all business majors—and one glass turns into two, and I'm not having a terrible time. I stay tucked away in the corner, praying I'm out of sight behind linebackers and silicone breasts. Maybe Teller will think I've left, and he'll leave, too.

A lot of roid rage and testosterone are over here—not that Teller Reddy would ever back down from a fight—but it would be in everybody's best interest if he doesn't see me.

"So, are you going to give me your number? I want to see you again." Phillip leans on the table across from me. Illuminated by the yellow-orange light from the exposed light bulb above our heads, he's not as cute as I thought in the dark hallway, and his hair is really thinning on top. He should intervene before there's no going back.

"You don't even know me," I say, pushing my empty beer mug away and scooting my chair back. "Maybe I'll see you around, though."

Phillip straightens his posture to follow me, disappointment written across his features, but I don't get entirely around the table before a Hulk-sized meathead moves to the right and my worst nightmare and I make eye contact.

"I didn't fuck Kim Evans," Teller says, like he's been chewing on the words for a week.

Crossing my arms over my chest, I have to keep myself

from smiling at the rush of relief flooding my nervous system. It's like jumping into a pool on a hot summer's day. Or realizing disturbia hasn't noticed the dog walker practically sniffing my ass yet.

"She's just making things up? It's not like she even knew I was listening." I should lead him back toward the other side of the bar, but I don't want to be too transparent.

He doesn't flinch, narrowing his eyebrows and pinching the bridge of his nose in frustration. "Do I look like a motherfucking mind reader?"

I laugh, a little bit drunk, a whole lot irritated. "She must have been talking about another Teller Reddy then, right? Or maybe I imagined the entire thing."

Teller lifts the hat from his head and runs his hand through his hair, ruffling soft curls gone flat. With the intensity of green eyes that keep me up at night in the best way focused entirely on me, I want nothing more than to wrap my arms around his back and press my ear to his chest to listen to his steady heartbeat.

I believe him.

I believed him the second he said it wasn't true.

"Is there anything I can say to make this better, Ella? Do you want me to get on my knees and beg? Because I will."

His sideways smirk lets loose butterflies in my stomach, and I say, "Take me home."

Teller exhales audibly and holds his hand out for me, but as soon as I reach for it, the dog whisperer speaks up. It's as if all the lights turn off and a blistering spotlight's shining on me. I close my eyes, drop my hand, and say a quick prayer to the big guy up above, hoping He can save us all.

"Who's this guy?" Phillip asks, pressing his hand to my lower back.

"This is my best friend, Teller." Stepping away from his touch, I straighten my shirt and keep the easy grin on my lips, turning my attention to the person in question. "Teller, this is Phillip Graves. He's a business major."

Satisfied with my explanation, Phillip doesn't give Teller's presence much thought, supposing he's not a threat and happy he might still have a chance to get in my pants. It's an assumption Teller corrects by hitting the mug from his hands, shattering the thick glass and spilling its contents across the sticky floor.

"No!" I shout, holding my hand to Teller's chest. I can feel him vibrating through the tips of my fingers. "Don't, Tell. Take me home—now."

The commotion doesn't gain much attention, muted by high dialogue and loud music, but it'll only be a matter of time before this place's turned upside down if it keeps on. Phillip shakes beer from his fingers, jumping away from the puddle at his feet.

"Whoa," he exclaims, finally … *finally* losing the charm.

I'm not naïve enough to believe this is all about me. Teller's possessive and jealous, and he's gotten himself in a few fights on my behalf, but the anger darkening his eyes and fisting his hands results from being backed into a corner. He lives a life his father chose for him, rebelling with ink and his relationship with me. The pressure to be as great as the man who gave him life suffocates him, but he doesn't want to be a disappointment.

But they constantly treat him like he is.

His parents. Maby. Em and Nic.

Even myself.

"He bought me a drink, Teller," I explain calmly. "But we can leave now. It's not a big deal."

Social distortion slowly nods, eyes locked on Phillip, waiting for him to make the wrong move so he can strike. My heart dislodges from my throat and falls to its normal spot in my anxiety-riddled chest, hammering so hard I can feel it in my teeth.

"Sure," Teller replies. He beckons me forward. "Let's go, baby."

I step away from Phillip Graves without a second thought, relieved to slip my hand in Teller's. Our family's still at our table with drinks in front of them, chatting without a clue as to what almost went down.

I'm envious of their oblivion, and then fearful when the dog walker suddenly says, "You better get the fuck out of here."

It's so childish, so after school special bully edition that it takes me a split second to register it as a threat. Teller figures it out right away, gladly jumping at the chance to relieve his pent-up anger and frustration. He yanks me back and stands in front of me protectively, keeping his hand in mine.

"Please don't," I beg, tugging on his fingers. "Teller, please don't do anything."

People start to notice the rise in tension spoiling the atmosphere, and the fellas Phillip's here with lower their pool sticks and finish their beers, gearing up for a brawl. Teller doesn't need an entourage to get his point across; the tone of his voice and the look on his face are frightening enough.

"Say something?" he asks.

Phillip looks over his shoulder to double-check with his friends that he's not in this alone, boosting confidence and arrogance. "You spilled my beer, buddy."

"Fuck your beer, and fuck you. Come near my girl again and I'll break your motherfucking neck." Teller walks away, but we don't get very far.

"Your girl approached me. Maybe you need to teach her a lesson instead of starting shit you can't back up." Phillip and his friends laugh, and now the entire bar is watching.

Teller lifts my knuckles to his lips and then nods his head toward my brother. "Go over there with him. I'm going to have a talk with this guy."

Before I can protest, Teller grabs Phillip by the front of his shirt and shoves him back into the table, knocking it and everything on its surface over. Wood splinters and breaks, glass shatters, and girls scream, scattering out of the line of impact. The bitter scent of cheap beer mixes with fear, and everything goes perfectly still for a second when we pause to let the damage sink in and figure out who's on what side.

Then all hell breaks loose.

I'm rammed against the bar by a crowd of people running to the exit as more tables flip and stools are thrown from one side of the room to the other, trapped and unable to get closer to Teller. Security in bright yellow shirts shove their way through, and the bartender behind the counter's on the phone with police.

"Get the fuck out of here, Ella." My brother, not in

uniform, grabs ahold of my shoulders and pushes me toward the door as Husher bolts past us, right into the thick of things. I stumble forward, tripping over my feet before catching myself on some redhead's arm. "Go outside with Nicolette."

I can only see bits and pieces of the brawl, but it's not a one-on-one fight anymore. Fists and kicks are thrown at random, drawing blood and bruising ribs, turning a minor scuffle into a riot. As soon as my brother turns his back on me, I chase him, propelling my way through the mob and elbowing anyone who's in my way. Red and blue lights flash through dark tinted windows, and more people flee once they realize the cops are here.

My heart freezes at the sight of Teller on the floor, curled on his side, protecting his head with his arms as Phillip and two of his friends kick him while he's down. His mouth's bleeding, and his left eye's swollen shut, but he's not alone. Emerson grabs Phillip by the throat and slams him to his back, pressing his knee into his chest so he can't get up. And Husher—the most non-confrontational person I know—takes on one of the friends, capturing him in a headlock.

"Get up!" I scream. "Tell, get up!"

Enduring a thrashing until he's upright and steady, Teller knuckles up, swiping blood from the corner of his lip with his thumb. Friend number three's not bold on his own, petrified prey in the eyes of an untouchable predator. Security moves in a minute later, heaving Teller from the guy before he beats his face in, but rage doesn't back down easily.

"No!" I shout, unable to reach him in time.

Beaten but nowhere near broken, Teller lifts a barstool from the floor and swings it around. Anticipating hitting the guy who gave him a bloody lip, he breaks it over the back of a security guard who got in the way. Shock sobers fury, but it's too late. Five armed officers storm the bar, and everyone scatters, leaving behind shards of glass, broken pool sticks, and upturned tables and chairs.

"Get the fuck down!" a police officer shouts, pointing his weapon on Teller. "I want to see your hands."

Teller slowly sinks to his stomach, hands in the air, with his eyes locked on the law. Emerson, Husher, Phillip, and five others are apprehended, cuffed and left on the floor until the scene's under control.

"Emerson, what should I do?" I ask as I'm shuffled away by security. "I don't know what to do."

My brother doesn't hear me, but Teller, with the side of his battered face pressed against the dirty barroom floor, hangs on every word like he might never hear the sound of my voice again.

"Keep moving," a man in yellow orders, driving me out the door. "Party's over."

I'm ushered to the parking lot where the night glows in red and blue, changing faces and reflecting off windshields and windows. Police officers write in notebooks, taking statements from the bar's owner, bartenders, and other witnesses from inside. People laugh, some cry, but most are indifferent, waiting for a cab.

Turning in circles, searching for a familiar face, I can't see past the panic closing in around me. Heat flashes through the palms of my hands, and the hair on the back of my neck stands straight, triggering the deep-set anxiety that creeps through my bones at the flashing image of my brother, Husher, and Teller in handcuffs.

"Gabriella." Nicolette's voice rises above the ringing in my ears.

She darts between the hood and the trunk of two police cruisers, with an oversized purse on her delicate shoulder and lights streaking her blonde hair blue. Recognition doesn't lessen the dread building in my chest, but it does elicit tears from my eyes.

Relieved and horrified in equal amounts, she wraps her arms around my neck and holds me against her small frame with a giant's strength. The idling scent of my brother, cinnamon and citrus, hugs the curve of her throat and hangs on her cotton top, igniting guilt so hot I have to step away before Nic catches fire.

"Where's Em?" she asks, looking over my shoulder. "Wasn't he with you?"

Before I have a chance to tell her, Maby follows Nicolette's footsteps, slipping between cop cars with a cell phone in her hand. Her short dark hair's untidy, in disarray from her restless fingers, and streaks of eyeliner and mascara stream down her face with worry.

"Are they in there?" she asks frantically.

I nod, looking toward the bar entrance. "Yes."

"Wait. Why are they still inside?" Nic looks from me to Maby, who's now heading toward the collection of police officers at the front doors.

Exhaling a large breath from between my lips, I run my hands through my hair and look to Nicolette with tears blurring my vision. "Teller was in that fight."

She rolls her eyes, unsurprised. "What does that have

to do with Emerson and Husher?"

"They were in the fight, too," I say, watching her eyes widen. "I think the cops are holding everyone involved."

"Are you fucking serious, Ella? Emerson's being arrested? Why didn't you say something to me?" She storms away, running across the parking lot to catch up with Maby.

It's over an hour later when my brother and Husher are let go, escorted out of the bar with a few others who were involved in the brawl. I've kept my distance from Nic and Maby, afraid of how angry they are with me, and ashamed of my part in this. But when I see Emerson's face, I run to him, overcome with relief and unable to stop my feet from moving.

He takes me in his arms, squeezing me tightly against his chest until he's not anymore. He holds me at arm's length while everyone watches, disappointment etched in his expression.

"I lost my job thanks to this shit, Gabriella," he says, shaking me like a child.

Sobbing, I can't take my eyes off him. He looks just like Dad. "I'm sorry. I didn't mean—"

"They've placed Teller under arrest. He's going to jail. Probably for the whole fucking weekend."

"What?" Maby shrieks. "What did you say?"

He doesn't need to repeat himself, because before Emerson opens his mouth to speak, the front doors come open. With his hands cuffed behind his back, two police officers lead Teller toward an awaiting cruiser.

"Where are you taking him?" Maby asks, her hysteria barely contained.

"Miss, you'll be able to call the station in the morning for more information," a third officer explains, holding his arm out to keep her from chasing after her older brother.

Tugging my arms free from Emerson's tight hold, I sprint from his reach, past Maby and the cop, after Teller. He's lowered into the police cruiser, staring at me through the one eye that's not swollen shut.

"Please don't take him," I beg. "Please, this was my fault. He can't go to jail because of me."

"Step back," cop number one says, holding the door open. "Unless you want to go with him."

"But he didn't do anything." I make the mistake of grabbing the officer's wrist.

Cop number two places his hands over the cuffs at his waist.

"Gabriella!" my brother shouts, coming after me.

I'm miniscule under the law's dark glare, an afterthought and an inconvenience, preventing them from completing their job safely and going home. There's nothing stopping the law from placing me under arrest for intervening, but I only want everyone to understand.

"Please," I whisper, wiping sadness from my face.

"Step away from the vehicle or you'll be the next one going in," number one warns, leaving no room in his tone for misinterpretation.

"Baby," Teller suddenly says. His voice muffled through the closed door. "Go home, Ella. I'll be okay."

My brother pulls me away by the back of my shirt. "Are you that fucking stupid?"

"I'm sorry, Tell!" I yell, unable to fight Emerson off. "I'm so sorry."

CLOSER

We watch the cruiser drive away with Teller in the back seat, speechless and unsure of what to do next. Four pairs of eyes glare at me, frustration and deserved judgment coming from all angles, and I'm not brave enough to stare back.

"Dad," Maby cries into her cell phone. "We need your help. Teller's been arrested."

CHAPTER FIFTEEN

Now

Teller

A heavy pounding at the door wakes me up after it feels like I've just closed my eyes. Pre-dawn light fills the loft with gray shadows and silence even the city that never sleeps has at this time in the morning. Dressed in the pants I wore the night before, having put them back on after the bath with Ella, I step barefoot and shirtless to the hammering.

"Where the fuck is my sister, Teller?" Emerson brushes past me, shoving me out of the doorway. Nicolette steps in behind him, avoiding my eyes, following Em to the room as he shouts, "Gabriella!"

I close the door quietly, already knowing exactly where this is about to go, and follow the couple into the master bedroom where I left Ella alone after she fell asleep on the bed. She wanted me to stay with her, but guilt tapped my heart with her in my arms like nothing happened. It was a normalcy I couldn't stomach with the bruises on her neck and the scratches between her thighs.

Ella sits up as I walk in, letting the thick white comforter fall around her waist. Her hair's still wet, unbrushed and tangled, and nothing's hidden under the old concert T-shirt she's in. A lesser man would look away, but I can't take my eyes off of her.

"What's going on?" she asks. Her tone is thick with sleep and scratchy from hours of crying.

Emerson pulls the blanket off her body, tossing it to the floor. Ella curls her legs against her chest, wrapping her arms around her knees, tiny in the massive bed.

"What the fuck, Em," I say, moving forward as rage re-sparks, ready to burn.

"Emerson, don't," Nicolette says, stepping to him before I can.

He ignores us all, turning on the lamp to get a better look at his sister in the light. Ella squints against the brilliance, holding her arm up to block it from her eyes, but it does nothing to block her from us. Reds are redder, blues are bluer, and purple has gone black, from her throat, down her arms and legs and knees.

"Oh my God," Ella whispers, lowering her arm to stare at me. She asks, "I did that to you?"

I still haven't taken a very good look at myself, but if it's as bad as I feel, it's not much different than her.

"Don't worry about me, baby—"

"You son of a bitch," Em snarls, possessed with a father-like rage. "What did you do to her?"

Deserving his anger—wanting his wrath—I don't avoid being hit. His large fist connects with my jaw, but it doesn't hurt as bad as the sight of Ella does. The girls scream, and I stumble back, catching myself before I fall.

"I'll fucking kill you." Emerson hits me again, this time in the stomach. Oxygen leaves my lungs in a quick whoosh, leaving me breathless but nowhere hurt enough.

"Stop." Ella throws herself in front of me, holding her hands out defensively. "Don't hurt him, Em. It's not what you think. It's okay."

His eyes widen, shaking his head in disbelief. "This is not okay, Gabriella. This is nowhere close to okay."

Coughing, catching my breath one small gasp at a time, I move bravery out of the way with tears in my eyes and face consequence.

"Nicolette saw you," he says, spitting the words in my face. "She went looking for Ella when you guys didn't come back, and she fucking saw what you did to her. I had to pry it from her, because I knew something was wrong. I knew I couldn't trust you."

"What we did to each other," Ella says boldly, standing by my side. "He didn't do anything to me I didn't want him to."

Emerson's booming laugh fills the entire loft, echoing off the walls. He takes a quick step toward me, but Ella places her hand on his chest.

"Do you realize how ridiculous you sound? Have you seen yourself?" he asks his sister, softening his tone. "I tried to give you the benefit of the doubt, but this isn't healthy. It's abusive, and I wouldn't be doing my job if I sat back and let it happen."

Ella straightens her shoulders, covered in bruises the size of my fingertips. "I'm not a job."

Her bottom lip trembles, and her hands shake in the face of outcome, unwavering and sure. It would be so fucking easy to let her fight this out and win, smarter than the rest and cunning beyond belief. We could keep on keeping on, doing what we've done for the last seven years, destroying everyone and everything in our way until there's nothing left but wreckage left in our wake.

But I have to give her a chance to change her mind.

"He's right." I feel my face pale.

"What?" Ella asks in a small voice.

"Baby, you can't act like this is normal. You've had normal." I swallow bitterness at the mention of Joseph West because it's not entirely true, but he might have been better than me. "And this can't be what you want."

Dark brown eyes overflow with grief, spilling down her tear-soaked cheeks. "Shouldn't that be my decision?"

I look up at the ceiling, incapable of facing her when I say, "Not this time."

"Don't do this to me again, Teller," she says through clenched teeth. Rage comes off of her in waves. "I know you don't mean it."

"Ella, maybe you should come stay with Em and me in our room," Nicolette chimes in. "I can help get your things together."

"No," Ella says right away. "I'm not going anywhere."

Shoving my hands into my pockets to keep myself from reaching out for her, I stare at her mouth instead of her eyes and say, "You should go."

When she comes after me, hitting me harder than her brother ever can, I don't stop her either. I take every small strike proudly, honored to be a target of emotion so overwhelming, only I can stir it from her.

"I'm sorry, baby," I whisper, wrapping my arms around her body, crying into her hair.

Emerson yanks devastation from me a moment later, taking an elbow to the face as he drags her away kicking and screaming. I help Nic gather Ella's belongings, finally taking in my reflection when I go into the bathroom for her toothbrush and makeup bag.

"You need to keep her away from me, Nicolette," I say, tracing the deep scratches across my chest with the hint of a smile on my lips. "I won't be able to tell her no again."

I don't leave the room or talk to anyone until the next day when we're scheduled to leave, in need of the time alone and not trusting myself if I found my way back to Ella. But the knocking on the door was unavoidable today, and I can't wait to get out of here.

"I took care of the rooms," I say, packing the last of my things. "They're going to call us when the cars are ready."

"Thanks," Maby says, standing in the doorway. There's no sign of the girl who couldn't get out of bed when we first arrived. She's been replaced with the headstrong version of my sister, in search of answers to her questions so she can find a way to fix everything. "Any chance you want to talk about what happened?"

"Which part?" I ask, folding a pair of jeans before placing them inside my bag.

"How about you start with why it looks like you and Ella we're in a cage match." She comes closer and sits on the edge of the bed. "She's not saying a word to anyone."

Zipping my suitcase closed, I close my eyes and take a deep breath. The sound of her name sends a chill down my spine, and I don't know how we're supposed to make it through the rest of this trip in one piece.

"Maybe I should get a car and head home," I say, placing a hat over my head.

"Or maybe you should tell me your side of the story, Teller. You don't look any better than she does, so I know there's more to it than what Em's saying." She picks at a feather sticking out from the comforter. "After Joe and Kristi, I thought you guys might have gotten it together this time."

"Thought wrong," I reply.

Yearning crushes my chest like a stack of cement bricks, blocking my lungs from expanding and pressing down on my heart as it struggles to beat. It's heavy on my shoulders, bending bones and straining my back, tearing muscles and tendons. Truth's burden is more weight than I can carry alone, but I don't think it's something I can let Ella suffer because of me anymore.

The phone rings, shattering the quiet moment between my sister and me.

"Mind getting that?" I say, lifting my bag from the bed to carry it toward the door.

"The cars are ready," my sister calls out.

I ride the elevator down with my sister and Husher, where Catrina waits for us with three bottles of cold water, a gift basket for our long stay in their most expensive rooms, and a plastic smile on her easy-to-forget face.

"I hope you enjoyed your stay," she says robotically. "We look forward to seeing you in the future."

211

The thought makes me want to throw up.

Lacking energy to spare to return her enthusiasm, we walk by, offering nothing more than slight nods and exhausted expressions.

"Ride with us," Maby says, squeezing my hand when we approach the vehicles. Ella's G-Wagen is parked in front of Maby's Cadillac Coupe. Both engines are running, ready to take us out of town.

I'm tipping the concierge with a cigarette between my lips when Emerson, Nicolette, and Ella arrive. My heart drops into my stomach at the sight of her, mostly hidden under an oversized hoodie, hugging a blanket to her chest. The marks on her throat are concealed under the thick cotton, but the circles under her makeup-free eyes and sight of her pale lips kill. Deluded doesn't look at me, slipping right into the back seat of her car, and I want nothing more than to save her from this pain.

"Come on, Tell. We're going to the next stop together, and we'll figure out the rest when we get there." Husher clasps his hand on my arm, offering me the front seat.

I climb into the back.

The four-hour drive to the Grand Canyon is torturous, and listening to Maby go on and on about how unfair Emerson and Nicolette are only makes it harder to endure. Husher's mastered lowering her voice to a hum, nodding at the right time and smiling when he needs to, but it's talent I've yet to learn despite growing up with the chatterbox.

"They wanted to take her home, like she's a twelve year old," she says, looking back from the passenger seat to gauge my reaction. "There has to be a point when we back off and let the two of you figure this out, right?"

"Right, honey," Husher says, mechanically agreeing with everything she says.

Miles and miles of dry shrubs, dirt, and rock-strewn mountains roll past us as we race forward. I watch them pass, finding it hard not to crawl out of my own skin and take my chances with the sun and snakes as I sit here instead of with my girl.

"You and Ella have always had your own ways of doing things, and something like that's going to take time to correct," she says, sitting straight in her seat. "It could be worse. At least you're successful and mostly have your lives together. Lord knows it wasn't easy for either one of you to get where you are today. How long do you have until your residency is over, Tell?"

"A little over a year," I mumble, hoping she doesn't do the math. Cutting my residency short isn't a conversation I want to have.

Not that the current topic is awakening.

"You may not have done things Dad's way, but you should be proud of your accomplishments. Husher and I are proud of you, right, Hush?"

"Yeah, real proud," he replies with a little more emotion in his tone.

"What I'm trying to say is, if you want to be with Gabriella, then I support you. Oh, this is where we need to get off!" She points to the exit, and Husher crosses two lanes to make it in time. The G-Wagen follows closely behind. "And toning down the rough sex until everyone's on board might not be a bad idea. Are those teeth marks on your neck?"

"I'd let you bite me, babe," Husher says, reaching over

to squeeze Maby's knee.

I close my eyes and groan.

"We have a couple of hours before we can check-in at the hotel. Should we head straight to the canyon? We can grab something to eat or hike a trail," Maby ponders, typing in the GPS on the dash of the car.

"Or jump off the edge," I say, dropping my head back.

She scoffs. "Don't say that, Teller."

The navigation system directs Husher to the entrance of the Grand Canyon National Park, where we idle in a short line to pay the thirty-dollar permit fee to park the car. Desert tapered off to lush trees and greenery along the way, and I feel a million miles away from the lights in Las Vegas. But my problems followed me here.

Literally.

After the ranger gives us a map of the park, she directs us down the road. "You'll run right into a parking lot where you can leave the car. Welcome to the Grand Canyon, where it'll make your *hole* vacation."

"That was cute." Maby rolls down the window to let in the Arizonian air. "I like this place already."

Neither car has come to a complete stop once we reach the parking lot and visitor center when Ella opens her door and jumps out, running toward the edge of the Grand Canyon. We watch her in disbelief as she brushes past other visitors, like she can't get away from us fast enough.

"Where the hell is she going?" Maby asks.

"Probably to jump. That's how I feel after long trips with Nicolette, too." Husher shrugs.

"Let me out," I say, tapping the side of Maby's headrest. My heartbeat surges, propelling a dose of anxiety through my veins as my chest swells with heavy pressure. She can't get out of the two-door car fast enough, and I'm not above kicking a hole through the fucking side.

Once my feet hit pavement, I bolt after the one who always gets away, determined to fix my sorry behavior. Tourists and employees watch us curiously, not daring to come nearer as crazy chases crazier to the edge of the world.

If she goes over, I'm going with her.

She reaches the brink of the canyon and stops, kicking up dust and lowering her hood to let the sun warm her pale face. The enormity of the crevice swallows Ella whole, framing her in quartz and clay, highlighted by shades of oranges, reds, and browns I've never envisioned. It's incredible, and she's more beautiful than all of it.

"Are you here to tell me how to live my life, too?" she says without turning to face me. "Because if you are, I've been given enough unwanted advice in the last twenty-four hours to last a lifetime. Save your breath."

I come to a standstill with five feet between us, not above lighting a cigarette at the Grand Canyon to stop the nerves wreaking havoc on my insides. I'll set this whole motherfucker on fire.

"Or did you follow me to say it's over again? Because I've heard it before, so don't bother reciting the whole speech twice." Ella looks over her shoulder, wiping tears on her sleeve. "I don't even know why I'm here. I wanted to go home."

"I'm sorry, baby." My insides collapse at the look of suffering in her brown eyes.

She brushes a lock of hair behind her ear, pressing her chapped lips together. "For what?"

Taking a step forward, I pocket my hands to keep them from her. "For it all."

Golden sunlight tints soft cheeks pink and glistens from the tears clumping misery's long eyelashes. The tip of her straight nose is red from crying, and the marks across her throat match my own. The bond that links us together swells, stretched out and fucked up, but used to the wear and tear.

"Why am I unlovable?" Ella looks down at her shoes, unlaced and dusty. "What did I do to deserve being left repeatedly?"

Tears fall from her eyes, and I reach out and catch one in the palm of my hand. It runs along my heart line, coating the deep stripe in sadness from the only person I've let this close.

"I'm right here," I say, swiping more sadness from the roundness of her cheekbone.

She shakes her head, and my whole world shudders with it. We've been here before, and I know what words are going to leave her lips next.

"We can't," Ella whispers.

With my heart in my throat, I reach for her and say, "We have to."

Pressing my mouth to hers before she can say another word, everything around us dissolves to stardust, and nobody exists beyond this. Our hearts beat the same, too swift and pounding, driving fever-laced blood through veins and arteries. We're dizzy and frantic, forgetting to breathe, because who needs air when we have lips and tongues and small cries that send chills up our arms?

Ella reaches on the tips of her toes, and I bend at the

knees so she can wrap her arms around the back of my neck. Her bottom lip fits perfectly between mine, warm and supple, as if it were made for only me. My heart, my lungs, my soul feel like they're going to burst at the taste of her mouth, sweet like strawberry candy with a hint of spearmint.

We needed this.

I *needed* this.

Holding Ella's face between my hands, I tilt her head back and make it deeper, because I never want to stop kissing her. I never want another day to pass where I'm not kissing her. I don't want to kiss anyone but Gabriella Mason for the rest of my life. A heated sensation seven years in the making floods my chest cavity, balloons through my torso, and warms my skin. It's destiny, hardening around my bones, and destiny whispering, *you're fucked now.*

Pressing wet lips to the corner of her mouth, to her chin, to her forehead, I whisper, "Ella, open your eyes, baby."

"Don't make me," she replies.

Resting my forehead against her, I say, "Trust me."

She opens them slowly, blinking tears from her lashes, hesitant to show me the need radiating from my favorite brown irises. Dotted with copper and gold in the sunlight, they're glossy with emotion that won't stop, triggering it from myself.

How am I supposed to say anything if I can't man the fuck up and do this?

"I've been lying to you," I say with a smirk on my lips.

Panic crosses her face, but she doesn't look away; she holds tighter.

"I've known exactly how I felt about you since the day we met." I let out a small laugh thinking back to that day. "And I've allowed this back and forth shit to go on, when I knew what I wanted all along."

"I don't understand, Teller."

This is it—now or never.

"I want you so fucking much it hurts, baby. It causes me physical pain to think about a life without you. It's always been this way, but after you met Joe—"

She cries, looking away from me, "I'm as guilty as you are."

"No, you're not. I pushed you into that relationship with him. I knew how I felt about you, and instead of making it work, I ignored what my heart was telling me and drove us insane. Things could have been so different, but I was scared. I'm still scared."

"What are you so afraid of?"

"That I'm a fuck up. I'm afraid that you'll wake up one day and realize that I've ruined your whole life. I don't want you to feel like you've wasted this much time on someone who'll never make you as happy as he did." My voice shakes. Ella doesn't know the truth, but that doesn't change the facts: he was good for her, and I'm wrecked.

She smiles, brushing my hair away from my forehead. "Not possible."

"You saved me from myself, Ella, and I took advantage of you. I used you."

"What do you mean?"

"I wanted you around because you made me happy, and you made me feel important, and all I gave you in return was stress. I made your life hell to keep you in mine and made sure that I could be around you whenever I needed."

I fucking hate myself for letting our friendship get so screwed.

Ella shakes her head and exhales. "Why don't you understand that *you* make me happy, and *you* make me feel important, too? The shit we stirred, Teller, we did that together. I don't regret Joe and Kristi, but do you ever think that maybe I didn't really give you a chance to love me?"

"No."

"My life was as fucked up as yours. I just did a better job at hiding it. I'm messed up, Tell. I'm damaged."

CHAPTER SIXTEEN

Now

Teller

"**G**et the fuck out." I open the G-Wagen's driver's side door and stand to the side. Ella waits behind me, holding on to my hand, pressing her face to my arm.

Emerson looks from his sister to me with wary eyes and says, "So, you're going to do this, sissy? This is going to happen?"

My grip on the door tightens, and I exhale slowly through my nose and talk myself out of grabbing this motherfucker by the throat and pulling him out of the car. He's worried about his sister, and I'm not mad at him, but if he doesn't remove himself from behind the wheel in three fucking seconds...

"Get out, Em," Nicolette says. She unbuckles her seatbelt and lifts her purse from the floorboard. "We're not doing this at the Grand Canyon, for fuck's sake."

Ella crawls over the center console, and I climb in

behind her, slamming the door in her brother's face and starting the engine. Reversing out of the parking spot, I roll down the window, looking past Emerson as if he's invisible.

"We're at the hotel we passed on the way in, right?" I ask my sister. She nods, and I drive away, putting space between them and us.

Massive trees lining the pavement throw shadows across her face as we cruise by, only allowing sporadic breaks of sunshine through their thin branches, enhancing the craving alive in her eyes. I rest my palm on the back of her neck, looking away from the empty road to watch her watching me. Ella turns her head and kisses the inside of my wrist, sending a rush of warmth through my arm.

I lick my lips, scarcely keeping an eye on the traffic ahead when she releases her seatbelt and comes out of her sweater. Static electricity from the worn cotton sizzles and snaps, standing her wavy strands of hair on end. She shakes her head, laughing as unruly tresses sweep across her exposed shoulders, releasing the scent of vanilla shampoo into the cab. Ella moves onto my lap, lying across my thighs with her feet in the passenger seat. Wind outside the open window captures her waves, and she laughs, placing her right arm around my neck.

"Drive faster," she says, pressing her lips where my jaw meets my throat.

With my left hand on the steering wheel, I slip my other under the waist of her leggings, low, low, lower to the warmest spot between her legs. Ella curves her back and parts her knees, rocking her center against my fingers. A web of blueish veins is visible under her closed eyelids, and she has a freckle in the arch of her brow, totally exposed for me to see everything.

"We're here," I say, dipping two fingers inside of her just to hear her gasp.

We check-in to the hotel in a fog of small touches and shy looks, unable to make eye contact with anyone other than each other. She holds on to the fingers that were just inside of her, and I brush my thumb across lips I can't believe I waited this long to kiss.

"Your keys, Dr. Reddy. Enjoy your stay." The clerk passes our keycards, and I take them, whispering a soft thank you.

Ella and I stand on opposite sides of the elevator going up, luggage-less, wordless, breathless, facing each other the entire way. Everything we said and left unsaid is stacked between us, years of half-truths and half-commitments coming down to this.

We finally make it to our room, and my hand shakes, giving irresistible a good laugh when I can't get the card in.

"Shut up." I chuckle, swallowing my heartbeat.

She bites her bottom lip, pressing her forehead against my arm, sighing, "You're killing me. You're killing me."

The suite overlooking the Grand Canyon is ours for the next two days, but I don't give a fuck about the amenities or the out-of-this-world view. I slip the *Do Not Disturb* sign on the door handle and shut it, securing the deadbolt and chain.

"Last chance to change your mind." I linger at the door in case she does. "Do it now if you're going to, because if I take one more step in this room, you're stuck with me."

Ella ignores my warning, lifting her tank top over her head and dropping it to the floor. "Take me to bed, Teller."

I come up from behind her. Holding her back against my chest, I slip my hand into her bra. Ella and I are completely wrong for each other, but we're too far in to ever back out now. We'll kill each other trying to make this work.

She's officially mine, but I've always, in all ways, belonged to her.

There's nothing fast about this. There's no pulling, or scratching, or biting, or crying. We're hasty breaths and easy touches. We're trying to find the room, but unwilling to stop to do so. We're making up for lost time, and trying to stop it altogether.

I pick her up, wrap her legs around my waist, and carry her to the room, never breaking our kiss for anything more than a quick breath. Laying her on the bed, I come up only long enough to remove my shirt.

The room's pitch-black behind thick curtains, glowing orange and yellow with the pre-lit fireplace, and it's hot, stifling, airless. Ella curves her back, reaching under to unclasp her bra. A thin sheen of sweat covers her bare skin, glistening in the low light. Seeing her naked, body flushed from the heat, is almost too much for me to handle.

We take the rest of our clothes of in a rush, kissing messily, bumping heads and laughing in the heat. I climb onto the bed and hover above her, between her legs. She places one hand behind my neck and the other on the small of my back. Fate's beautiful in the fire's burn. This moment's intimate and precious, and I plan on making her feel just that way.

"Tell me what this is," she whispers.

A single tear runs down the side of her face, and I kiss it away, smirking against her skin because I finally have an answer.

"This is falling in love."

I have one hand on the side of her head supporting my weight and the other tangled in her hair. My knees are between her legs, and my cock rests against her stomach, hard and throbbing. Electricity flows freely between us, and I feel her everywhere, and I want her in ways I never imagined. Our souls and our hearts are so fucking close, and they're just going to get closer.

Seven years of blood, sweat, and tears got us where we are now: desperate, devoted, and irrevocably in this.

Softly kissing her mouth, I dart my tongue along her bottom lip, pulling it between my teeth. She tilts her head back, opening her throat for me. I press my kiss to bruises I inflicted, drawing her pulse to my lips, feeling the stream of blood under her thin skin. Dampness pools between our bodies, making us slick and sticky and warm in bends and curves. I lick the spot between her breasts, and Ella inhales a sharp breath. Her nipples harden between my lips.

I'm taken off guard when she stops me from going lower, and a sinking feeling raids my stomach, like I knew she could still tell me no. She urges me back with hands that tremble on my arms, and the small smile on her lips sets me at ease.

"None of that tonight, Tell. I need you." She slides her palm to her sex. "I need you here."

I know what she means, and I feel the same way. We have a lifetime for the rest, but right now we need to be connected.

"We don't have a condom," I say, pushing her to the top of the bed. I lace our fingers together, sliding her hands above her head and holding them there as I thrust my knees up, spreading her thighs.

I hate the idea of having something between us, but I don't want to do anything that makes her uncomfortable. Especially when it wasn't a consideration in Vegas.

"No. I need you, only you."

Her eyes are wide, pooling in love we're experiencing for the very first time. I may not be able to put into words how much I love her, but I have every intention of showing it.

Lifting my hips to position myself at her entrance, the sensation of having the tip there is mind-numbing. I slowly push myself inside, watching her eyelids slowly lower and dropping my forehead to her chest at the initial pant that comes from between her lips.

We're one person.

Literally.

Finally.

Our bodies are connected, but she's tapped into my very being. Her touch alone screams that it was all worth it. I'll take on all the pain in the world for her. I'll fight to make her happy, and kill to keep her that way. After everything— the obsession, desperation, jealousy, spite—we have pure, unadulterated love.

Just love.

Gently lifting out of her, I rock back inside, rolling my hips at the slowest pace to feel all of her—every inch of what I've been missing, touching every spot, memorizing the way her mouth parts and eyelids flutter.

She's beyond hot and soaking wet, luring me back every time I pull out. Her thighs tremble at my sides, and I release her hands so she can hold on. Not quite capable of kissing her anymore, our lips lazily touch, sharing breath and brushing lips. She lets her hand fall from my neck to my lower back, guiding the pace of my strokes. Always slow, never too quick, relishing in the feeling of being inside of her, where I belong. She wraps her legs around me, opening wider, letting me in deeper.

"Oh, fuck, baby." I sigh, gripping the pillow under her head.

Closing my eyes, I thrust deeper and more profoundly, incapable of pulling out. She kisses the side of my face, holding on to my sides, locking her ankles around the back of my thighs. Passion takes over, and our moans get louder, our breathing more erratic, and there's nothing more than Gabriella.

She places her hand on the side of my face, asking me to look at her as pressure builds between us. Ella pushes my hair away from my forehead, drags her fingers across my mouth, and hooks her elbow around my neck. Beautifully tragic, beautifully crazy, beautifully mine rocks her hips, meeting me stroke for stroke, digging as deeply as I am.

Ella's back curves away from the mattress, and she goes completely still, begging, "Harder. Harder. Harder."

"I love you," I say as she contracts around me. "I love you, baby. I love you."

Dropping her arms to the bed, she grips the bedsheets and whispers, "I love you, Teller."

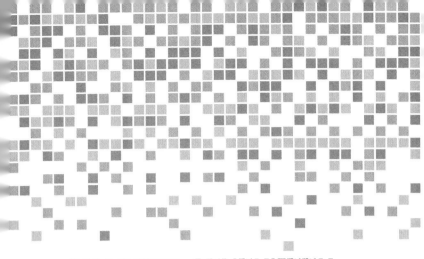

CHAPTER SEVENTEEN

Now

Ella

"**W**hat's on your mind, babe?" Teller asks, kissing the back of my bare shoulder. He smells like hotel soap—part fragrance, part plastic, all skin drying.

After an entire day and night in bed, exploring parts of each other we didn't get to dry humping in our early twenties and fucking in a dirty hotel hallway a couple of days ago, the bed's stripped and my muscles are sore. We fell asleep in a sweaty, sweltering heap of limbs and bared souls, waking up in the early morning to shower.

Early enough for me to drag him onto the balcony to watch the sun rise over the Grand Canyon. Settled on a chaise lounge, I'm between his legs, resting against his chest, wrapped in a blanket Teller grabbed from the floor to cover us in the cool pre-dawn air.

"Our family. Work. Joe and Kristi," I say. His heartbeat pounds against my back.

Teller goes rigid. "What about them?"

I shrug, bringing his hand to my mouth and kissing his scarred knuckles. "We wouldn't be here if they hadn't died, Tell. But I can't imagine a life where they're alive anymore."

"You said you wouldn't have accepted his proposal," he replies in a tight voice. "We probably wouldn't be in Arizona, but where the fuck would you be if not with me?"

Smiling at the edge in his tone, there's comfort in routine, and unease dissipates with jealousy's predictable reaction. I half-expect him to pat his pockets for his pack of smokes, but the only clothes we have are thrown across the room, and he left his cigarettes in the G-Wagen.

"Who knows what I would have done in that situation. You saw what he had planned. Any girl would have been thrilled to be proposed to that way," I admit, even if the thought makes me feel trapped in a small room with the walls closing in. "And what difference would it have made between you and Kristi? Would you have left her because I didn't want to marry Joe?"

"Yes," he answers immediately.

I sit up and turn to face him, expecting to see the lie etched in a smirk across his lips, but his expression is blank and his green eyes glow sincerity. It's another dose of reality: we are anything but normal; we're addicted, defeated, and obsessed, and I can't lose him, because without him, there is no me.

"It doesn't matter, Smella," he says to himself as much as he says it to me. "They're not here. But we are."

Returning to my position against his body, we're quiet as tangerine light radiates over the horizon, shooting beams of color across the dark blue sky. The temperature seems to drop, and Teller tightens his arm around my naked body. Three-day old cuts and scrapes between my legs have scabbed, itching as they heal, and the bruises spotting my body have mostly disappeared.

This new ache is the best kind.

The loving kind.

Violet chases orange past dots of gray clouds, streaked with pinks and yellows as the sun kisses the new day. The entire canyon is tinted rose-gold, peppered with dark green from bushes and trees scaling the massive split in the earth. Jagged edges cast dark shadows on rock faces, and the sound of flowing water tempts me with sleep.

Blanketed in love and brand new sunlight, I blink moisture from my eyes and sink into the be-all and end-all, knowing this is the only place I belong.

Disturbingly in love.

The next time I open my eyes, the sun's shed shades of sunrise in exchange for glaring light, and the sky's crisp blue. Maby's standing beside the lounge chair Teller and I dozed off in, with our suitcases in each one of her hands. I've turned in her brother's arms, and the blanket's fallen to our waist.

"Don't worry," she says, unashamed. "The important parts are covered."

I blink against sleep's haze, incapable of coming up with a single thing to say. I'm so used to discounting the reason why Teller and I have been caught in a compromising position, excusing inappropriateness with a lie, that the truth sticks to the roof of my mouth.

"I thought you'd like to have your things. The maid let me in," Maby says. She sits in the chair across from us. "I might have torn up the *Do Not Disturb* sign first."

Teller groans, scrubbing his hands down his face before realizing we're almost naked in front of his younger sister. He pulls the blanket to my shoulders, tucking it around our bodies so it won't fall twice.

"Long day?" Maby asks. "We hiked some amazing trails yesterday. You guys really missed out."

I hide my smile beneath the comforter, not deeming the activities Teller and I spent the last twenty-four hours engaging in as "missing out."

"Thanks for dropping our things off. Feel free to kick rocks before I call the front desk and tell them someone broke into my room," Teller says, leaning his head back.

"No need for the drama, jerk." Maby stands, light in a pair of hiking boots I don't see her wearing after this trip. "A few things came up while you two were holed up in here. Can we meet for dinner downstairs tonight around eight? Everyone will be on their best behavior. And by everyone, I mean Emerson."

"Is he mad at me?" I ask. The four-hour drive from Las Vegas was loaded with conflict and words we wish we could take back, ending with me jumping from a moving car. I didn't expect him to want to spend any amount of time with me so soon.

"Not at all," the younger Reddy child answers. The tip of her nose is sunburned, and she smells like banana carrot sunblock. "He's concerned, but that's got to be expected from your brother-slash-father, you know?"

Maby leaves us with an easy smile, almost through the French doors when Teller calls her back.

"How are you feeling?" he asks, turning his head to see

her face.

She smiles from ear-to-ear, effortlessly, naturally, promisingly. "Good. I'm doing good."

Tension should have its own place setting. It's our uninvited guest, sucking all the joy from the table, intensifying inelegance and discontent. No one's bothered to order a meal, and our drinks drip condensation onto the starched tablecloth, untouched. The waiter gave up and hasn't come by in twenty minutes, focusing on customers who are here to eat.

Teller scoots my chair beside his and drapes his arm across the back of my seat, chewing a toothpick as he browbeats my brother. Disorder lounges with his legs parted, unbothered and unashamed of what put us in this situation. He twirls the saliva-soaked wood between his teeth, flipping it with the tip of his tongue, wearing a throat of hickies arrogantly.

"If we're just going to sit here all night, Ella and I are going to excuse ourselves. It's been a long fucking month. I hope you understand, and if you don't, I don't give a shit." He spits the toothpick onto the table.

Unamused and cool, Emerson rolls his brown eyes the same color as mine, picking the label from his green bottled beer.

Nicolette's indifferent, scrolling through her phone, tapping the screen with her acrylic nails. Maby and Husher, on the other hand, do their part and pretend we're not being eaten alive by awkwardness, breaking bread from the basket of rolls our server dropped off when we arrived forty minutes ago.

"Pass the margarine, honey," Maby says, eating her third dinner roll.

"I'll butter it for you, sweetheart," Husher replies, incapable of stomaching another piece of cold bread himself.

I sip water, leaning into Teller's side. It's all I can do to keep from climbing onto his lap to hide my face between his neck and shoulder. Em's gaze swoops across my throat when he's not murdering my boyfriend with his razor-sharp glare, stewing. Someone should take the knives off the table before they're used as weapons.

"Say the word and we're out of here," Teller whispers. His lips tickle my earlobe, and a wave of desire rolls through my nervous system.

Crossing, uncrossing, and crossing my legs again, I squeeze my thighs together and try not to blush, ineffectively. The echo of his touch on my body reheats my skin, and I don't need to close my eyes to recall his hands spreading my knees apart, his cock gliding inside of me, or his words changing everything.

I love you, baby. I love you.

Charmer watches my cheeks redden, and he grins, rubbing his thumb in circles on the back of my neck. We only showed up to dinner because I wanted to come, hoping that when they saw us together, they'd somehow feel what we feel and understand there's no choice in the matter.

We're written in the stars.

Nic drops her cell to the table and sighs. "I hate to admit it, but I'm with Teller on this one. If we're not going to get to the point, I have a bag to pack, and we have a long drive home tomorrow. I'd like to get some decent sleep tonight."

Sitting straight, my heart plunges to my stomach, and I ask, "What do you mean you have a long drive home? I thought we were going up north first?"

Driving through St. Helena with Emerson was a huge deciding factor when I agreed to this road trip in the first place. He made it seem like it was important to him, so returning to the house we grew up in suddenly became important to me, too. What could have happened to change his mind?

"This is what we wanted to talk to you about, Ella," Maby reveals. She chews on her last bite of bread like it's a mouthful of sawdust, rubbernecking my brother.

Sincerity diffuses bitterness, easing Emerson's defensive posture. He clears his throat, softening his gaze until it's almost bashful, unable to keep his mouth from bending up. Nicolette projects admiration by his side, smiling shyly and squeezing his hand.

"I wanted this to be a surprise, but nothing seems to go as planned lately." Em's tilted grin falters, but he recovers right away, running his hands through his hair. "We're going home early because I was accepted into the police academy, sissy. I got the call yesterday."

"What?" I choke on overwhelming thrill. Genuine shock and happiness spring tears in my eyes, and resentment melts away. "When did you even apply?"

Tension leaves the table, and we all sigh in relief, able to breathe again. With heaviness' exit, the mood noticeably changes, and it's as if nothing happened at all. That's the wonderful thing about a family like ours. Unconventional and downright erratic, when the going gets tough, we trash entire vacations with irrational arrogances, but we come together in the end to support one another regardless of what was said and done.

"A while ago," Emerson replies. "There's a lot of paperwork, and I didn't want to get my hopes up until I passed the background check. When the accident happened, I put it on the backburner, but the call came yesterday afternoon. I can't pass up this opportunity, Gabriella."

For as long as I can remember, Em wanted to serve and protect, aspiring to be a police officer as soon as he was old enough for the police academy. When we were kids, I didn't play with dolls like normal girls did; I played cops and robbers with my older brother. He was always the cop, and my role as the bad guy changed depending on the crime. Sometimes I was a bank robber, other times a car thief, but most of the time, I was under arrest for being annoying.

His dreams of a future in law enforcement disappeared with his independence when our father died. He knew he couldn't take care of me and go through the academy at the same time. It was Emerson's first sacrifice as my legal guardian, and one a career in security and bodyguarding never fulfilled.

"I … I don't know what to say." Reaching across the table, I take his large hand between my small ones. "I'm so proud of you. Dad would be really proud, too."

A sign of a boy who was forced to grow up too fast, Emerson's self-conscious, unaccustomed to putting himself and his needs first. I feel him pull back, and I recognize the look of unease on his face. It's the same expression that swiped gentleness from his features when his younger sister became his responsibility and he didn't know how to care for her.

"I wanted to make the trip home—" insecurity starts.

"The house isn't going anywhere, Em." I smile reassuringly, smoothing the lines between his eyebrows. "We'll plan something after you graduate. I don't mind going back to California early. There are three more Ikea boxes that need to be put together."

I look to Teller for confirmation, and he nods hesitantly, resting his hand on my lower back. "For sure, babe. Whatever you want to do."

"Actually, Ella," Maby interrupts. "We're going to drive back with them. Husher should get to his classroom next week, and I need to be on a normal routine before I return to work, too. But you guys should go on without us. The hotel room in San Francisco is already paid for, and you'll still able to check on things at your house."

"I'm going back to work, too," I reply. "We all came here together. We can leave together."

"We're not scheduled to go back to the hospital for another two weeks," Teller says. "And I'm not ready to go home. If the room's paid for, we should go."

"If it's the money you're worried about, Tell, I'll reimburse you for your troubles." I sit back in my chair, feeling defensive, shrugging his arm away.

The truth is, I'm terrified to return to St. Helena without my brother as a barrier between the hurt that town represents and me. Occasionally, it feels like another life, as if a different girl went through the heartache I experienced as a child. Coming face-to-face with my past isn't something I'm ready to tackle, not when I'm scarcely holding it together as it is.

"Look, Gabriella," Emerson says, letting me down

slowly. "I need you to go up there and check on the house. I won't have a chance myself until after the academy. Enjoy the rest of your time off. Your shitty furniture can wait another week."

"Em," I groan, crossing my arms over my chest. "You know how I feel about that place. I don't want to go there alone."

He ponders what I've said for a moment, and I watch a series of emotions change his posture and the lightness and darkness in his eyes. From doubt, to grief, to almost waving the hypothetical white flag, Emerson finally exhales a large breath and shakes his head. He has a bad habit of interfering when times are tough, buffering so I never carry burden's weight alone, but that ends now.

"You won't be alone, sissy. You'll be with Teller."

I look away from my brother to the man who's promised to love me—the only other person besides Emerson who has held my hand through the crazy and still dedicates his life to making sure I'm the best version of myself.

"If this is what you want, I'm going to support you." Em's eyes shift from me to Teller and back. "I trust you. I mean, I practically raised you, so I know you're not a shitty person and you're capable of making your own decisions."

Laughing, I wipe tears from beneath my eyes. "Thanks."

"I'm serious, Ella. You'll never get rid of me because we're family, and I love you more than you'll ever know. There's nothing about my life I'd change, including taking care of you. It wasn't your fault, and I don't regret you, okay? I don't regret anything."

Dropping my face into the palms of my hands, I cry out as heartache fills me to the top.

"Take care of my little sister, Teller," Emerson says confidently. "Because if you hurt her, I'll snap your fucking neck."

The next morning, dark gray clouds blanket the sky, and the scent of rain carries with the cold breeze. I'm emotionally beat, having dealt with more heartbreak and self-realization in the last few weeks than I have in my entire twenty-five years. But my conversation with Emerson and my commitment to Teller have given me perspective, and I'm confident everything is how it's supposed to be.

I never loved Joe, but he came into my life when I needed him the most. He taught me things about myself I wouldn't have known otherwise, such as my capability to care for another person without constant conflict, tolerance, and compromise.

Losing him led me back to Teller, so I must trust fate, and trust everything happens for a reason.

"Call me when you get to the house." Em clutches me in his arms, holding me tightly against his warm chest. He kisses the top of my head. "I take that back. Call me every day, twice a day. Or call me every few hours. Actually, just call me when you get in the car and I'll put you on speakerphone and it'll be like we're still together."

"I'll be home in a week," I mumble with my face pressed against his sweater.

"But we've never been apart for this long," he replies like a father with empty nest syndrome.

"You'll be fine," I say, shoving him away, gasping for air. He pulls me back, more gently. "I promised Nic I wouldn't say anything, but you're welcome to come home any time. We have an open-door policy, so don't lose your key. I can make you a few spares, or I'll leave the front door unlocked all the time. If you ever want to spend the night, I can blow up an air mattress, or maybe I'll go ahead and buy a new bed for your old room. Whatever's easier."

"Emerson." I sigh, amused. "I'll call you when we get to where we're going. But you have to let me go."

"Never," he replies. "I'll miss you too much."

After we say our goodbyes to everyone, Teller and I get into the G-Wagen, bubbling with excitement. We've gone on vacations with his family—Mexico for Thanksgiving, Florida for spring break, and Hawaii when his cousin got married—but this will be the first time we've done anything like this alone. Together. In love.

"Do you know how to get there?" I ask, pulling my seatbelt across my chest and buckling it in.

"No, but we will in a second." Teller programs the navigation, typing in the address to the hotel in San Francisco. The fastest route shows up a second later, suggesting we go back in the direction we came from.

"Do we seriously have to drive back through Las Vegas?" I ask, dumbfounded.

"Maby didn't plan this out too well," he says, checking for alternative routes. We soon realize going any other way will add a substantial amount of time to our drive, and we don't have time for that. "I bet we can get the Skyloft for another night."

"No way," I mutter, settling in for the eleven-hour drive. "If I never see the inside of that hotel again, it'll be too soon."

Four hours later, when we drive through Las Vegas, I look over at Teller and smile. What went down in that dingy hallway wasn't the worst thing that ever happened to me, and while I wish our time here would have ended differently and I don't want to come back anytime soon, I wouldn't take it back for the world.

By the time we reach Death Valley, I can't stomach another hour in the Wagen, so we get a room for the night at a ranch style resort. It's an oasis in the middle of the desert, and unlike Vegas, it's low-key and focuses on relaxation. Teller and I explore Dante's View on the north side of Coffin Peak, taking pictures of each other alongside the black mountains before we head back to the hotel and soak up the last of the sun poolside.

After dinner, I show him exactly how my lips look around his cock.

I even wear red lipstick.

"I'll drive this time," I offer the next morning, jumping behind the wheel before he has a chance.

From Death Valley, we planned on driving to Bishop, but I trash those plans and head toward Sequoia National Park. We spend two days amongst the tallest trees in the world and underground streams, bird watching and driving through tree tunnels over and over again, because, *oh my God,* we can drive through an actual tree.

Sex outside is overrated, but when in Rome…

"Give me the fucking keys." Teller snatches them from my hand. "When you drive, we don't end up where we need to go. Now we're two days off schedule."

"You like it," I say, winking.

"I could have gone without the sticks in my ass," he

grumbles, eyeing me playfully.

"All of a sudden," I whisper to myself.

We stop in Fresno for lunch and drive through Palo Alto, where we flip off Stanford University as we pass by. Because fuck their medical; UCLA is just as good. And fuck Theodore Reddy and his expectations; Teller is fantastic, and he's going to be an amazing doctor despite what field he ends up in.

When we reach the Golden Gate Bridge, Teller rolls the windows all the way down and turns the music all the way up. The massive structure doesn't compare to the size of my love for this boy who cusses too much, drinks too much, and smokes too much. I touch him because I can, because he's mine. I lean over the center console to smell his skin, feel his warmth, and whisper, "I see you, Teller. You're all I ever see."

He kisses me with such conviction that night, it feels like it might be the last time. But when he shoves my dress up and my underwear down, and torture pushes himself inside of me, I remind myself this is just the beginning.

We're only getting started.

CHAPTER EIGHTEEN

Now

Ella

When you grow up an hour and a half from San Francisco, it's where your parents take you to get out of town for the day. I remember how excited my mom used to get when we planned a trip to the city. St. Helena would fill up with pretentious vinos, gushing over the small town and vineyards, and she hated it. During the weekend, she'd pack the car with food and blankets, and we'd go to the Golden Gate Park to visit the Japanese Tea House, paddle the lakes, and eat lunch in the botanical gardens.

She also scored pills because junkies are everywhere, but Emerson and I didn't know the difference.

Doing these same exact things with Teller feels like a whole new experience, and as I lie against his chest between his legs, bundled up in a blanket we took from the hotel, under the bright sun, I'm glad to be here again. We're people-watching on the lawn in front of the conservatory of flowers, content in each other's arms. There's no pressure to steal small touches in case someone sees us, or to make every second count because we're going home with someone else. We're together, and we're good.

"What do you want to do tonight?" he asks, brushing my hair away from my neck to place a small kiss over my fading bruises.

"There's a band playing at The Fillmore," I reply, biting my bottom lip as his kiss deepens.

"Sounds fun." His words reverberate against my bones, sending a warm chill down my arms. "But I was thinking we could do something that requires less clothing."

"Don't tease me, Teller," I say, breathless as his tongue presses against my pulse.

"I could fuck you right here, right now, and none of these people would even know." His hand slips under my sweater, cool against my warm body. "Can you be quiet enough?"

"No," I answer honestly. "Not even close."

He groans against the top of my shoulder and falls back, resting his head in his palms. Sunlight intensifies the green in his eyes, tiptoes on his dark lashes, and deepens the scent of ginger on his skin. I lie on my stomach alongside love, soaking up warmth radiating from his body.

"Can I tell you something, Smella?" Teller asks, watching the clouds move through the sky.

"You can tell me anything." I rest the side of my face against his ribs, feeling his heartbeat there.

"I have no interest working in a hospital once my residency's over. I'm not like my dad. That's not where I see myself for the rest of my life." His heart's beat quickens, but

Teller shows no sign of unease on the outside. "For a while, I thought I could do it to make my parents happy and keep them off my back, but I can't. Not with the rest of my life falling into place. It feels too good."

Theodore Reddy's adamant his only son will eventually live up to his full potential, as if the last twenty-seven years are a phase he'll grow out of. He raised a headstrong man who vaguely followed in his footsteps, resenting him every step of the way. A fourth-generation doctor, medicine's in Teller's blood, but he's never had interest in the bureaucracy that comes with it. I have no doubt he'll be an amazing physician, but it'll be on his terms.

"What's your plan?" I ask.

"How many times have you seen patients turned away because they don't have fucking health insurance, or they can't afford their co-payments and deductibles? I've watched people dying from cancer leave the hospital because they can't afford treatment. If I'm going to do this, I want to help those people."

My stomach drops and my eyes immediately well up, because he's right. Medical care's a luxury the less fortunate can't afford. I've watched many families lose hope when money runs dry. It was my family at one point. It was my dad, and it was my brother and I who came undone when we couldn't pay for Dad's medication. People shouldn't have to choose between their homes or their lives, but finances determine what kind of healthcare each individual receives.

"I have money," he replies easily, not like it's a burden, but knowing it's a gift. "And I'll get the rest in a trust when I'm married. It'll be enough to open a community clinic somewhere in need of accessible healthcare. There are a couple other residents at the hospital who are interested, baby, and we can run the fucking thing with med students—"

"Will this clinic need a nurse who's good with kids?" I ask, blushing.

Determination rolls over, supporting himself above me on his hands, smirking the most gorgeous smirk I've ever laid eyes on.

"You don't think it's a bad idea?" he asks.

"I think it's an amazing idea, Teller," I answer honestly. "And if this is what you want to do, I support it."

He looks down at me for a stretched second, from my eyes, to my nose, to my mouth, as if he can't believe I'm real. When his lips touch mine, I second-guess how quiet I can be.

I might be willing to find out.

"He's somewhere in this area," I say, looking out the window to a sea of tombstones in the cemetery my dad's buried in. "I think he's under that tree."

Teller parks the Wagen on the side of the paved road, looking over my head before he turns off the engine. We skipped the show last night, spending the entire evening in bed, connected, forgetting there's a world that exists beyond us.

I woke up this morning knowing St. Helena was the next stop.

The ninety-minute drive felt like ninety seconds, and in the blink of an eye, I was directing my boyfriend around my old stomping grounds. We passed the diner Em and I ate breakfast with our father every Sunday morning until he died, the hardware store Emerson worked at after he graduated high school, and we drove past the side street where I saw my mom for the very last time.

Despite the amount of time that's slipped away, old feelings I left behind welcome me home with bells and whistles, and I'm the same seventeen-year-old girl without parents as I was then.

"Do you want to go alone?" Teller asks. He rests his hands on the back of my seat, patient with my madness today.

Shaking my head, I don't take my eyes off the oak tree I stood under when they lowered my father six feet under. "No, I want you to come with me."

I walk three paces ahead of him, between tombstones and over grave markers, recognizing an old teacher's name, and kicking myself for not bringing flowers. Death doesn't scare me. I've lost enough people I care for, and in my profession, patients pass on regularly, but it's not something I've become immune to. As I come upon my father's final resting place, I decide I've visited too many cemeteries lately. This will be the last time for a while.

"That's it." I point to his headstone, unwilling to take another step closer alone.

ABRAHAM EMERSON MASON
BELOVED FATHER AND HUSBAND

"He insisted we add the second part," I say, remembering the day we hashed it out. Dad planned his own memorial service to relieve us of the burden, but when I saw what he wanted engraved on his headstone, I objected.

Adamantly.

"I'm the one dying, Ella," he insisted. A shadow of the man he was healthy, his headful of dark hair had fallen out, and he'd lost a lot of weight, but he commanded every inch of the room like he always did. *"If I find out you don't follow my wishes, I'm coming back to haunt you."*

"I thought it was utter bullshit to acknowledge that woman at all." I kneel in front of his stone, brushing fallen leaves away. "But he said it was an important part of who he was."

Teller kneels beside me and helps clear away overgrowth, not saying a word, but doing a fantastic job of being present.

"Dad wore a football jersey instead of a suit. His idea, of course. Em might have had something to do with it, too." I laugh, even as my eyes shine with grief. "Guests at the funeral were horrified."

"I won't spend eternity in a penguin suit." He laid his favorite 49ers jersey on the bed. *"I lived for this team, and now I'm going to die for them."*

"But that was my dad," I reminisce joyfully, sitting on my bottom once the leaves and decay are gone. "He was a stubborn son of a bitch."

"That must be where you get it from," Teller replies under his breath. The right side of his mouth bends, and I slap him on the arm before leaning my head on his shoulder.

"Yeah, anger was inherited from my mom, and stubbornness was passed down from my father. I don't even know how I managed to evolve into a responsible adult."

"Whoa," Teller exclaims. He looks down at me with a stellar grin. "I wouldn't go that far. You're an okay adult."

Pinching his side, I collapse deeper into his embrace, tracing each letter of my father's carved-in-stone name with my eyes, reading only parts of the rest.

BELOVED
BELOVED
BELOVED

"You have his eyes, too," Teller says. His voice's even, smooth amongst the silence. "That picture you have of him beside your bed ... they're identical."

"Yeah," I reply thoughtfully. "I do, but Emerson resembles him more than me. I don't think I'd be able to handle it if he grew a mustache."

I miss my brother, but there's something magnificent about having the love of my life and my father in the same place, even if it's in spirit. During the next hour, the sun fractures dense cloud cover overhead, burning the fog away and warming our cold faces. Dry leaves drop from nearly bare branches, gathering around our bodies in heaps. An occasional person strolls by, offering quiet hellos and polite smiles, visiting nearby graves with flowers.

"I can't believe I didn't bring anything," I say as a woman three plots down sets a bouquet of red carnations at a headstone. She leaves a few minutes later.

"Do you think the dead mind sharing?" Teller asks. He stands to his feet, wiping grass from his black denim.

"Don't you dare," I say, watching him walk toward the carnations. "It's sacrilegious!"

Teller lifts his hands in innocence, creeping closer to the plot. He reads the headstone. "Mrs. Schroeder won't mind. Sharing is caring, babe."

He looks from side-to-side for prying eyes, because

who wants to be the human caught stealing flowers from a dead person, especially when he's covered in tattoos and has a cigarette hanging on his ear? Delinquent. Heathen. Thug.

It's despicable and outrageous, but my heart swells watching him grave rob. I don't think there's anything he wouldn't do to make me happy, and it's the thought that counts, not the crime he may or may not be committing.

Up to no good slips a single carnation from the bouquet and runs back, presenting it to me as if the goods aren't stolen.

"We're going to hell for this, you know." I take the flower and place it upon my father's headstone, admiring how beautiful stark red is against granite. The enormity of my grief suddenly throbs, pulsating from deep within consciousness where I store the worst of the worst.

BELOVED FATHER

He is beloved. He is *my* beloved. He is my beloved father, and I miss him today as much as I did the day he passed.

When I turn around, Teller's waiting beside the Wagen, holding the door open. There's one more part of this trip left to do before we can go home and officially start our lives together. So, with a *goodbye for now* to my dad, I stick my hands into my sweater pockets and start toward forever.

*S*tepping into my childhood home is like stepping into a time capsule. Everything's blanketed in a layer of dust, the wallpaper yellowed in the corners, and there's no light with the windows boarded up, but nothing, down to the framed school pictures hanging on the walls is different. My brother's old work schedule is taped to the warm refrigerator, stacks of unopened mail sit beside an old cordless house phone, and a yellow sponge has fallen into the sink, dried-up and shrunken.

We could literally start right where we ended.

"Do we have electricity?" Teller asks. He flips a switch and a dim yellow-orange light flickers on, illuminating the living room.

"Yes," I say, dropping my bag beside the old brown leather couch. "We've managed to keep the crucial utilities on. No cable or Wi-Fi, though."

"But there is a VHS player." He points to the old cassette tape. If I remember correctly, *Armageddon* should still be inside. It might even be rewound to the beginning.

There's not much more to see in the three-bedroom, one-bath, eight hundred square foot home. Nothing seems to need repairs, no one broke in and is secretly living here, and everything is in the same exact place Emerson left it the last time he came to town with Nicolette.

"We don't have to stay here tonight." I lift a pillow from the couch and beat dust from it. "There are a few hotels in town that are nice. Or a bed and breakfast, if you're up for that."

"No." Teller turns on a few more lights. "We'll stay here."

CHAPTER NINETEEN

Now

Teller

"Let's play a game." I lift a slice of pepperoni pizza from the box we had delivered and take a bite. Cheese the temperature of molten fucking lava burns the roof of my mouth, but I play it cool, because I'll be damned if mozzarella ruins this for us.

Ella wipes grease from her lips, crumbling the paper napkin in her hand. Her hair is tied in a knot on top of her head, and she's washed the makeup from her face, but mascara lingers beneath her eyes. Not long after we arrived, I went outside to pry the board from the front window to air out the house and let light in. When I came back to wash my hands, I found her in the master bedroom, clutching her father's clothes that are still hanging in the closet. Her tears have dried since then, but she's heartbroken.

"Okay, which one?" she asks. Ella crosses her legs, sitting on the floor across from me with dinner between us.

"We might have Scrabble in the closet."

"Twenty questions. No rules. No passes."

She arches an eyebrow and curves her lips into a half-smile. "All right, but don't be dumb, Prick. I'm not in the mood for your antics tonight."

"I'll ask the first question." A low-quality version of *Armageddon* plays on the television, scratched and warped during some scenes from age. I lower the volume and move the pizza box before scooting closer to skepticism. She's beautiful like this, homegrown and vulnerable, unlike any version of her I experienced before. Remaining calm, ignoring the hammering inside my chest, I ask, "When did you know you were in love with me?"

Her smile widens, and she lies back, leaning her weight on one elbow. Ella extends her legs and crosses her ankles, looking at me from under her dark eyelashes.

"It wasn't long after we met—a few weeks at the most. Our schedule hadn't left us with a lot of time to spend together during the week, and you're a control freak, so you moved your schedule around to TA of my science class. You'd come over to help me study. We were lying on my bed, and I tried to pretend that I was looking at my computer, but I was staring at you, learning your face. I memorized the shape of your nose, the lines that show in your forehead when you concentrate too hard, and the way your lips curve. Then I noticed your freckles, and I counted them."

"I don't have freckles," I say, vaguely remembering her memory. We had tons of study sessions, and this one doesn't stand out.

Ella's cheeks blush, burning the prettiest pink against her dark eye and hair color. "Yes, you do. They're soft, sprinkled across your cheekbones."

Now my face burns. "Don't embarrass me, Smella."

"In the middle of my count, you looked up from the study sheet to quiz me on the material we went over that afternoon. I wasn't paying attention, and I knew you caught me staring, so I blurted a random answer that had nothing to do with what we were studying." She laughs out loud, turning to hide her face. "I was mortified, and it showed, but you were cool. You didn't make me feel stupid when I totally expected you to, because up to that point, we teased each other about everything. It was just how our friendship was, and that was a prime opportunity to humiliate me."

She presses her lips together, but bashful's unable to keep them from bending into a grin. Ella covers her face in the palms of her hands and groans playfully, before she continues. "That's when I loved you. The way you saved me from myself changed everything. I knew you were special. I knew you were different than the motherfucker you por-trayed yourself to be, and I loved you."

"I remember that now," I say in a low voice. It's all I can do to keep myself from fucking her on the floor of her father's house.

Her smile shifts from shy to knowing. "You have thir-ty-two freckles on the right side of your face, and I love those, too."

Scrubbing my hands down my cheeks, I chuckle. "You're killing me, girl."

Ella sits straight with her shoulders back and her chin up, resembling her normal self. She puts space between us, as if she can see the fever-like tension threatening to end our game early, and hugs her knees to her chest. "Same question."

"When did I know I was in love with you?"

"Yeah."

Licking my lips, I scratch the back of my neck and say, "My dad had been up my ass all morning, bitching about UCLA and how my decision to start another year at a school he didn't approve was disappointing. The only reason I showed up was to drop my classes, but I stopped to have a smoke."

Ella lifts her chin from her arms and meets my eyes. I don't know if she realizes where this is going, but my heartbeat's in my throat, making it hard to breathe.

"So, there I was, minding my own fucking business, ready to wreck my entire future because my dad's a dick, when this girl with the most beautiful brown eyes invaded my personal space, hit my cigarette, and considered death a mercy. And I loved her. At first sight."

"Do you mean that, Teller?" she asks quietly.

"I'd never lie to you, Smella," I reply. A pang of guilt constricts my stomach, but it's overcome by nervousness. "I loved you first."

We take a moment to absorb our confessions, because assuming and hearing the actual words from her mouth feels nothing alike. The truth gives validation to the seven years it took to get where we are now, and the struggle was real, but it wasn't for nothing.

"What do you want from me, Ella? From us?" I ask my second question.

"I want forever," she says boldly, surely, decisively. "I want emotional security, and I want to know you'll never leave me like everyone else."

I'm working on that part.

"What about you, Tell?" insecurity asks.

My answer is immediate. "Contentment."

She pulls her bottom lip between her teeth, stewing on my response before asking, "Are you content with me?"

"That's two questions, babe."

"For my sanity, can you please answer it?"

I inhale a deep breath, filling my lungs with stale air, unsure how to answer. My hesitation isn't with Gabriella; it's all me.

"I'm happy with you, baby, but I'm fucking terrified of us. I can't shake the feeling that we're going to fuck up so bad one of these days and this will be gone. I won't survive it. Not after I've had you. Not after all this time. There's nothing that can keep me away from you, but I'm not confident enough in myself to believe this is the life you deserve. I've never been good enough for anyone, so why would I start now?"

Closing the distance between us, Ella stands on her knees and cradles my face between her hands. "How could you believe something so ridiculous, Teller?"

"It's not your turn to ask a question," I reply, welcoming the way her touch sears my soul. She sits on the back of her legs and waits. Brushing my thumb across her red-stained blush, I ask, "If you could do anything different in our relationship, what would it be?"

Creasing her eyebrows, she says, "Nothing."

"Stop," I demand. "Answer the fucking question. We're almost done."

"If I had to change something in our relationship, I would have told you I loved you every single day. Instead of pounding my fists into you when we fought, I would have hit you with those words instead. You're delusional, and it's my fault. I was a terrible friend, and I'm a worse girlfriend if you can still doubt how much I care."

Is love supposed to feel like this? Is it supposed to hurt?

Ella pulls her hair down, shaking it free between her fingers. She sighs and asks, "What about you? What would you change?"

Smiling at her tactics, I point out, "You're asking the same questions."

"They are good questions. Answer it."

"I would never have allowed Joe to happen," I answer honestly, bitterly. "He's my biggest regret. *That* was my fault."

Meanwhile, a fuzzy Bruce Willis sacrifices his life so his daughter can be with a young Ben Affleck, saving the entire fucking world in the process. He manually detonates a nuclear bomb inside a meteor the size of Texas, which happens to be heading straight for Earth. It explodes across the thirty-two-inch television screen in dull shades of blues and greens, sending a supposed-to-be-neon fireball and Bruce's ashes across the universe. Everyone on the space shuttle propelling home is sad, but they won't ever have to pay taxes again, and they're heroes, and they're not dead, so they're not too broken up about it.

The daughter, played by Liv Tyler, is over the death of her father by the time Ben travels through the atmosphere.

They'll keep Bruce in their memories.

He was a decent man.

The moral of the story: Joe was Bruce Willis, but not as noble, and despite pulling the short straw, I get to keep the girl.

If that makes me Ben Affleck, then so fucking be it.

"Are we done playing?" Ella asks. She yawns and stretches her arms over her head. "We should go to bed."

"Marry me?" I ask.

My brown-eyed girl snaps her head in my direction, suddenly wide-awake. "Shut up!"

"That's my next question. You have to answer. No Rules. No passes."

Reaching into my pocket, I present the two-carat, three stone diamond ring I bought in Las Vegas when she thought I was golfing with Husher. On a whim. On a gut feeling. Never more sure of anything in my entire life.

Covering her mouth with her trembling hands, tears fall from Ella's eyes. She stands, only to sit on the edge of the couch.

"This isn't how I saw this happening, baby. Husher was looking for an engagement ring for Maby when I spotted this one, and I knew it belonged to you. I wanted to make this memorable, but we've waited long enough. I can't risk something else coming between us again, and I'm tired of everything being so fucking hard."

"You're insane. Do you know that?" She shakes her head unbelievably, looking between the ring and me.

Down on one knee, with my chest cut wide open and my heart exposed, I say, "Marry me, Gabriella."

An excited sob escapes her lips, and she nods, "Yes, of course, yes!"

Ella jumps into my arms and we fall back, kissing between yeses. She only breaks away to let me slip the ring onto her slender finger, where it'll stay forever.

"Thank you," I say, admiring contentment.

Teary eyes look from the engagement ring to me, and she whispers, "I love you, Teller Reddy."

I carry her to the room.

I kick the door shut.

I lay her on the bed.

Light pours in from the moon shining through cracks in the old boarded windows, catching the diamond on her ring finger. Branches rustle in the window outside, scratching the paint chipped house. Ancient bedsprings moan under our weight, and the oak headboard hits the wall. Warmth radiates from her touch, soaking bone deep. I hook my fingers under heat's sweater, gently pulling it over her head, dropping it to the dusty wood floor.

I kiss her below her ear.

And her cheek.

I press my lips to her neck.

Her shoulder.

Her wrist.

I kiss her stomach.

Gray sweats slide down her legs easily, and the only thing she's wearing is my ring.

I press my lips to the top of her foot.

To her knee.

On her hipbone.

I undress with haste and climb between her legs.

My hands slide up her thighs.

Her sides.

Over her breasts.

Up her neck.

And into her hair.

I find her left hand and let my fingers brush over the ring that symbolizes everything to come before lacing our fingers together and resting our joined hands beside her head.

My lips travel from her jaw to her ear, and I whisper, "Try to tell me this isn't everything."

I slide inside of her.

I'm slow, and we are quiet, allowing our bodies to say everything our lips can't.

She curves away from the bed, and I thrust harder.

Lowering our hands to where we're connected, Ella pushes the balls of her feet into the old mattress, and I moan into her neck. The sensation of her fingers on me as I stroke in and out hardens my cock and ignites a fire in my soul, and I'm blindsided. Love shifts to raw passion so overwhelming, I feel consumed in the flame and cry out.

She touches my face.

My tears fall to her heaving chest.

Her legs wrap around me.

I push in deep.

Her eyes close.

She whispers my name.

Her back arches.

I kiss her lips.

Her nails dig into my back.

I stroke fuller, harder.

Her skin burns me.

I can't breathe.

She touches me.

She pushes harder.

She loves me.

She is mine.

Forever.

She tells me.

Our mouths meet as she pants my name.

My eyes close as I fill her.

All I can think about is her.

All I can feel is her.

All I can see is her.

All I want is her.

All I need is her.

All I am is her.

My Gabriella.

This is what happens when wrecked and damaged collide.

CHAPTER TWENTY

Before

Ella

I'm transparent under Theodore Reddy's unsettling stare, as if he can see down to my bare bones. Shifting from hip to hip, I lace my fingers together behind my back to keep from biting my nails in front of him and wish I had changed into something nice before I headed over. College girl attire isn't adequate in the presence of such eloquence.

"Thank you for stopping by, Ella, but this isn't a good time," Dr. Reddy says. He steps outside his massive entranceway and shuts the door quietly. His shoes shine in the late afternoon sunlight, and this man's cologne smells so good, I almost drop the pretenses and grab him by the lapels of his blazer to bury my nose in his neck.

But that would be weird, and this isn't the time for games.

"Please," I urge. "There won't be any trouble. I just

want to talk to him."

Time after time, I've listened and watched Teller rage and riot over the relationship he shares with his father. I've never experienced the person he describes—critical, passive-aggressive, firm—until now. He's normally accepting and kind, and I've always been welcome in their home. Judging by Theodore's rigid posture and tight expression, my invitation's withdrawn.

"You do understand my son's entire future was put on the line by his arrest?" he asks, unwavering. "Everything we've worked for could have been stripped away in the blink of an eye."

Everything *he's* worked for. But I don't correct him.

"Luckily, the district attorney is my neighbor and sees the entire incident as a misunderstanding."

Bending my neck to scope out the castle-like house to the right, I bite my bottom lip not to roll my eyes at how predictable this is. Of course, the district attorney lives next door. Next, he'll tell me the mayor is across the street, and he plays croquet with the governor of California.

"The bar owner doesn't feel the same way," he adds.

Remembering the broken tables and chairs, shattered beer mugs, and the security guard writhing in pain after Teller hit him with a barstool, I understand why the bar owner feels differently.

I've spent the entire weekend drowning in guilt over what happened. My brother lost his job, Maby's depression was triggered, and Teller spent the weekend in jail pending a battery charge. I've never been so ashamed of my behavior in my life, but it's how everyone was affected that kills.

Theodore's clear disappointment turns the vise in my chest, constricting my heart between metal jaws. The slow beat makes breathing hard, and I don't want to cry in front of him, but this all-time low is unpredictable at best.

At least he looks at me. It's more than Emerson's willing to do.

"I'm so sorry—"

The massive door behind Mr. Reddy suddenly opens, and I nearly fall to my knees at the sight of Teller. Bruised, busted, and scraped, nothing in his expression gives away any indication on his frame of mind, and the vise squeezes, but to see him in flesh and blood eases some of my anxiety. Green eyes dash across my face before turning to his father and narrowing. He closes the door and steps past the man who gave him life, offering nothing when Theodore asks where he's going.

"Come on," he mumbles, walking past me toward the driveway. "I need to get the fuck out of here."

Dr. Reddy swallows hard, but he's confident in his ability to control his oldest child. Slipping large, important hands into his pockets, he says, "If you leave, don't come back."

It's an empty threat, and Teller knows it.

"Maby locked herself in the bathroom. You should handle that before someone starts to suspect she's not perfect either," Teller responds coldly.

"I know you're disappointed, but please accept my apology," I offer his father, turning my body toward Tell. "Nothing like this will happen again."

Teller starts his car, idling as I rush by the Fastback I

borrowed without asking, slipping into the seat beside my criminal. He reverses out of the driveway, avoiding his dad's deathlike glare, and burns rubber speeding away. Tightening the strap across my chest, I hold on to the door until we exit the gated community and slow down.

My heart doesn't stop racing.

"I hate that motherfucker," Teller says. Scabbed knuckles turn white around the steering wheel, and he clenches his teeth, tightening his jaw.

"You don't mean that," I say.

Apprehension is stifling, and I choke on residuals from the mess we're in. How did it get so out of hand? When did chaos become normal? Where's the stopping point? Teller was arrested, in jail—in fucking jail—and Theodore's right. He could've lost everything he's worked so hard at resenting and loving all at once.

For what?

Because he didn't call me for a few days? Because I didn't invite him to the bar? Because I wanted his undivided attention, so I gave mine to someone else?

I know why.

It's because Teller and I are wrong for each other.

We are poison.

We're a toxicity that spreads to everything and everyone when we break bad, and it's only getting worse.

"What the fuck do you know?" Teller snaps. He slows to a complete stop at a red light and drops his hands onto his lap. "You've seen one side of him, Ella. But you don't have a Goddamn clue what it's like to live with him."

My eyes fill with tears, and my heart completely smashes. Like father, like son. "Is he anything like you?"

Slugging me with the full intensity of his broken expression, Teller finally looks in my direction, and green has never been so devastated. Realization washes away anger, leaving a damaged mess of disorder and humiliation in its place. He drops his head back and closes his eyes, and a single tear falls to his temple.

I've never seen him cry before, and I lose it completely.

"Something needs to change, baby," he says. The edge in his tone is gone, replaced with sorrow. "I can't keep going on like this."

The car behind us honks when the light turns to *Go* and we haven't moved. Teller sits straight, wiping his eyes with the back of his hand, and accelerates. We end up on a bench in front of the lake in Echo Park sitting side-by-side despite feeling a million miles apart. He has his arm over my shoulders, and I lean my head against his chest and listen to the rhythm of his heart's beat.

Joggers run past us, paddleboats make waves in the water, and a man pushing an ice cream cart chimes a bicycle bell as he strolls by. The temperature cools as the sun lowers, painting the sky pink and orange, casting shadows across paradise in the middle of the city. Maybe if we don't say a word, don't move a muscle, and don't breathe, everything will stay exactly like this, and we can pretend nothing happened at all.

"Your dad will let you come home, right?" I ask, crossing and uncrossing my legs.

Teller clears his throat. "Yeah, and if he doesn't, I'll buy a place here."

"No kidding. I don't spend nearly enough time in this part of the city."

Teller leans forward, unconvinced by the normalcy of small talk, and pats his pockets for his pack of Marlboros. There's no smoking in the park, but there's comfort in simply holding his bad habit between his fingers.

"What the fuck happened the other night, Ella?" he asks, flicking his lighter. The small flame ignites and blows out over and over again.

"Did you hook up with Kim?" I ask since that's where the issue stemmed from.

Teller and I have never put a label on our relationship, but it's common sense to everyone we're a duo, and we're supposed to be untouchable. What we have is enough for me, despite the uncertainty, despite the reluctance, and I've never felt the need to seek sex or anything close to it from anyone else. To overhear Kim Evans speak in detail about Teller crushed me.

He won't meet my eyes, and his shoulders drop. "I didn't fuck her."

I refuse to give him my sadness and look away, swallowing bitter regret and hating myself for crying. "What did you do?"

"I was drunk. We talked. She kissed me," he says quietly. "That's it."

I laugh out loud, smacking tears from my cheeks. "That's enough to break my heart, Tell."

"It was a mistake. I wanted to come clean, but you blocked my fucking number. Emerson turned me away when I came over. You wouldn't see me, babe. You didn't give me the chance to explain myself or apologize. Friday was the first opportunity I got, and we know how that ended." He exhales audibly. "What were you doing with that guy? Why were you with him?"

"Because I didn't want to be anywhere around you, Teller," I exclaim, turning to face him regardless of the tears streaming down my face. My traitorous heart swells at the remorse in his expression, but betrayal burns too hot to ignore. "What I needed was space. When you showed up, I went to the restroom to avoid confrontation. That guy followed me, and he offered to buy me a beer. Nothing more."

"You accepted a drink from someone you've never fucking met before?" he asks. Teller spits and scratches the back of his neck, barely containing his anger.

"You fucked a groupie?" I retort.

He captures my chin in his hand, forcing me to look him in the eyes. "I didn't fuck her."

I grip his wrist and cut my fingernails into his tattooed skin until he releases me, bleeding from moon-shaped wounds. Teller stands, dropping the cigarette and holding his hands to the back of his head, exhaling through his cheeks as he looks out to the water. There's nothing I want more than to wrap my arms around him, because that's all it would take to make this better. It would be so easy to brush his arrest and everything that led to it under the rug with the last four years.

"Teller..."

"Don't do this, Ella," he says. His voice breaks.

"You said it yourself. You said we can't go on like this." I place my palm over my heart, searching for signs of life. Surely I won't survive this pain. "We went too far, Teller."

Kneeling in front of me, betrayal cradles my face between his hands, gentle this time. His thumbs sweep across my cheekbones, wiping away damage. "That's not what I meant. I would never mean this. You are the most important person in my life, baby."

"It won't work out." I grasp the concrete bench to keep from clutching on to the front of his shirt.

A couple on rollerblades skates by, whispering between themselves as they spy on us. The odds of this turning into another scene are likely, and that's the last thing we need.

"Let me go." The words are between us before I can reach out and grab them.

He trembles, practically vibrating before me. "I can't."

"You don't have a choice."

Leaning forward, Teller rests his forehead against mine, drowning me in his nearness. I turn my face as his lips press against the corner of my mouth, opening to taste me with his tongue.

"Why won't you kiss me?" he asks, trying again to seize my lips.

I push him away and stand to my feet, holding my hand out so he won't come closer. "Because if I kiss you, I won't be able to stop."

"Did Emerson tell you to do this?" Teller stands six feet away with his hands in his hair and madness in his eyes. "Choose me, if he did, baby. We don't need them. We don't need any of them, Gabriella."

"He's my brother!" I cry out, not surprised he's figured it out. "He's given up his entire life for me."

He drops his hands and lights a cigarette, unconcerned with the rules. I watch his lungs expand with nicotine, and just like the first time I saw him, it stretches to the sky in ribbons when he exhales.

There's no one more stunning than Teller Reddy. He's a sculpture of torment, perfectly chiseled and shaped, from the sharpness in his jawline, to his broad shoulders and long legs. I love the way he holds a cigarette at his lips and lets it hang between his pout. I'm obsessed with the barely-there freckles across his nose; a secret only those he lets close know about. And his eyes, framed by thick eyebrows and long, long lashes, look at me as if I'm the most precious thing in the world.

"Things need to slow down," I say, coming undone. "When the people around us start getting hurt, there's something wrong."

"It's been four motherfucking years, Ella, and we haven't kissed, we haven't had sex, and we haven't committed to shit. We can't go any slower, babe." Teller takes a hit, squinting as he inhales carcinogens. The end of his cigarette glows orange and red before turning to ash.

"I want you in my life," I whisper, holding the back of my wrist to my mouth and sobbing. "But not like this, Teller."

Dropping his half-smoked cigarette to the ground, he snubs it out with the toe of his shoe and chuckles. When he returns his gaze to me, lips I love are turned into a smirk, and his eyes swim with tears. "Just friends?"

"Don't be an asshole."

Teller holds his hands up and walks backward, putting the space I asked for between us. Flipping me off with both middle fingers, he says, "Here's what I think about being *just friends*."

"Where are you going?" I call out, taking a few steps

forward.

"Go home." Teller tosses the car keys. They hit the ground and skid to my feet. "I don't want any more friends."

CHAPTER TWENTY-ONE

Now

Teller

She's different.
        Needy.
I oblige.
The obsession's taken over.
We are never apart.
It hurts to be away.
I am possessed.
She is my possession.
She's mine.

CHAPTER TWENTY-TWO

Now

Teller

"We've been home for two weeks and this is still in front of the door." Ella kicks the cardboard box next to the coffee table and sits on the couch. She shoves her sleeves up to her elbows and breaks the tape sealing it shut. "Do you mind if I open it?"

Sometime during our road trip, Kristi's family flew in to close her apartment. They dropped off my belongings before returning to Alaska with a note stating they'd included a few things they thought I might want to keep for myself. I haven't so much as touched the package, because whatever's inside I haven't missed, and it's from a part of my life I'm ready to leave behind.

"Go ahead," I say, sprinkling flakes of food into the fish tank. "Come over here first. I think Phish is smiling."

Ella sighs, pushing the box away and clapping dust from her hands. She stands beside me, holding her face directly in front of the bigger and badder tank I bought for the little fucker when it became apparent he's here to stay. I completely forgot about him while we were on vacation, but Ella worked out a feeding schedule with my mom. The bastard survived our absence, and he's grown at least an inch since relocating to his new residence.

"He's not smiling, Teller." She laughs, tapping on the glass. I swat her hand away, rolling my eyes when she shoves me back. "What the hell was that for?"

"Don't knock on his tank. Do you have any idea how loud that is for him?" I give him a little more food so he can eat his feelings. "And that's a fucking smile on his lips."

"You love Phish!" She crosses her arms over her chest and smiles. All I see is the ring on her finger, the one our families gaped at the day we returned, and I can forgive her for the attempted-deafening of our pet.

Screwing the cap on the fish food, I scoff. "He's cool. Even cooler because he smiles. But he's had a tough life. Giving him a decent place to swim is the least we can do."

Barefoot, braless under one of my button-ups, and in nothing but a pair of cotton underwear, Ella grins from ear-to-ear. What we should have done in the fourteen days since we returned home is adjusted to a new routine and prepared to go back to the hospital, but all we've done is eat, sleep, and fuck, lovingly. Our bags are still packed, the food in the fridge has gone bad, and our voicemail boxes are full; knocks at the door have gone unanswered, emails are disregarded, and we haven't checked one text message. It's only a matter of time before someone sends a search party.

But she's so … consuming.

"Maybe we should get a puppy since you love the fish

so much," she says, slowly unbuttoning her shirt.

The container of fish food falls to the floor, and my dick twitches. "Maybe you should have my baby."

Ella bites her bottom lip, exposing her left breast and shoulder. "Maybe you should put your baby inside of me."

Pulling my shirt over my head, I smile and say, "I'm going to put something in you."

Ella tilts her head back and laughs, shrieking when I take her in my arms and carry her to the couch. I kick the table over, knocking the box to its side, and hook my fingers under the hem of her panties. Slipping them down her legs, she kicks white cotton and lace from her foot and drapes her ankles over my shoulders.

Pressing the palms of my hands to the insides of her knees, I spread her wide open and moan, "Fuck, baby."

Just-shampooed hair is unruly, cascading over her shoulders, sticking to her lips, and falling between and around her tits. She picks it up, amber and vanilla-scented, and drapes it along the back of the couch, elongating her naked chest and soft neck for me.

"I love you," I say breathlessly, kissing the inside of her thigh, up, up, up.

She nods, pulling her bottom lip between her teeth. A pink blush spreads from her chest to her cheeks. "I love you."

I lick between her folds. Ella buckles, arching her back from the sofa and crying out. I hold her hips down, smirking against her heat before kissing tenderness with my mouth open, watching her come undone above me. She's warm, smooth, and so fucking wet, stretching her arms, reaching for something, anything to hold on to.

"Teller," she moans. Ella knocks a painting from the wall, scratches her nails into the couch trying to get a handful, and hooks her knee around the back of my neck. "Oh my God, Tell."

I slip two fingers inside of her and stop to watch love fuck my hand. She rocks her hips, rubbing her clit against the palm of my hand. With the taste of her in my throat, I climb onto the couch, pull my dick from my shorts, and thrust inside the place my mouth just was. I groan against her shoulder as I'm wrapped in heat, using the back of the couch as leverage to pump harder.

She holds on to my sides, slipping her palms around my lower back, guiding me in and out of her sex. Ella lifts her hips and circles her legs around the back of my thighs until I'm all the way inside of her.

"Go slow. Go so, so, so slow," she whispers, circling against me.

Pressure builds in my chest, spreading through the rest of my body, numbing my lips, my fingertips, and swirling in my stomach. The need for more overwhelms the need for anything else, stripping me of reason, justifying why we've locked ourselves in this house for the last two weeks.

We fuck until my cock can't get hard. We stay connected until her pussy swells, and she can't take me even if I can get it up after being inside of her for hours. I've loved this girl in every position, tasted every inch of her skin, and there isn't one part of Ella I don't know by heart.

It's not enough.

It's not.

But it doesn't stop us from trying to get closer.

It doesn't keep us from forgetting the world and trying

to climb into each other.

Dominate each other.

*M*y first day back at the hospital is a fucking night-mare, and I'm thrown into the thick of things before I have a chance to reacquaint myself with my surroundings. Overworked and understaffed, I'm kept in the emergency room to help with intake, discharge, and treating patients directly.

An eight-hour shift turns into a twelve-hour shift, managing everything from third-degree burns, drug over-doses, repository distress, broken bones, chest pain, and organ trauma caused by a car wreck. A man with a nose-bleed pleads for narcotics to ease his pain, and a woman brought in by the sheriff's department on a fifty-one-fifty hold lunges for my throat when I attempt to assess the lac-eration across her forehead.

I'm puked on, spit on, hit on, and cussed out, and that's before lunch.

When I'm not holding a ten-year-old girl's hand while she gets sutures in her chin from a fall at school, or per-forming CPR on a man in cardiac arrest, I'm dodging sym-pathetic looks and questions from staff. They offer condo-lences and an ear to listen if I feel the need to talk.

"It's so unfortunate," one nurse says, patting my shoulder.

"What a terrible accident. You must be devastated," a phlebotomist states, tilting his head in sympathy.

"Joe was cool," the janitor gushes, replacing the trash bag. "He used to buy me lunch for taking his garbage out."

"Get the fuck out of here, Paul. Pay for your own turkey sandwich," I reply, walking past him.

I buy him lunch.

It's not his fault Joe was thoughtful, and I'm a dick.

Joe was also a liar, but I'm not going there.

Their compassion ends abruptly when Ella shows up dressed in *The Cat in the Hat* scrubs, holding two large coffees and a smile that isn't confused as friendly. Staff is aware of our friendship, but it's common knowledge she was dating Dr. West when he passed. No one hides their looks of bewilderment when I hold her face between my hands and kiss her lips in the middle of the cafeteria for their viewing pleasure. They're stunned stupid and gawking.

"They're loving this," my caffeine dealer whispers against my lips, securing her arm around my neck. "The entire hospital will know by the end of the day."

"Fuck them," I mumble, hiding my face in the crook of her neck. "Are you just getting here?"

"Yeah." She plays with the hair at the nape of my neck, looking at me from under her long lashes. "I'm here all night."

I check my watch and take another gulp of coffee. My shift's almost over, but the thought of returning to an empty house alone after spending the last six weeks with her isn't my idea of a good time. But adrenaline that's pushed me through my first day back is dying down, and I'm exhausted.

"Want me to wait for you?" I ask. There are bunks in the back for staff to sleep on during breaks. I can catch a few hours on one until she's off.

Ella shakes her head, pushing me toward the double doors. "No, but you have to leave before I change my mind.

It's going to be hard enough as it is. I don't need the distraction of knowing you're around."

"Phish needs me, anyway," I say sarcastically, shrugging. "At least someone does."

"Don't flatter yourself, Prick." She smiles, and my heart explodes.

Retreating though the doors to the hallway, reluctant to look away from my dream come true, I'm ready to turn around when I bump into something and stagger. Coffee spills over my fingers, and I drop the entire cup, hopping out of the way before dark roast soaks my pants.

"Dammit," I shout, shaking scalding liquid from my hand. A flash of anger lights me on fire, extinguishing at the sound of a voice I blocked from memory.

"Oh my gosh, I'm so sorry! Let me get you a napk— Teller?" Melanie Garcia, a radiology tech, raises both eyebrows and freezes. "When did you get back? I was going to call you after I heard about Kristi, but…"

"Today's my first day back." I feel my face pale, and I turn my eyes down, pretending to busy myself with cleaning coffee from my wrists and arms when Ella passes me a stack of paper napkins. Clenching and unclenching my hands nervously, the fine hairs on the back of my neck stand up, and the weight of her curiosity compresses my spine.

"Okay?" Melanie replies skeptically, giving me a once-over.

"You know Nurse Mason, right?" I ask before she can say another word. Drilling my eyes into the blonde, I watch her mouth set into a hard line as she looks from me to Ella. "My fiancée."

Melanie's blue eyes widen, but she recovers quickly, forcing her frown into a smile and offering a hand in greeting. "Actually, I don't think we've been formally introduced. I'm Mel."

"Gabriella Mason," Ella offers, mirroring Melanie's uneasy grin as she takes her hand. "Nice to meet you."

The timer on my watch chimes, indicating the end of my lunch hour. It breaks the spell, alleviating awkward panic, giving us a reason to go our separate ways. I circle my arm around Ella's shoulders and kiss the corner of her mouth, feeling my heartbeat pick up as she clutches my sides, eyeing Melanie as we mumble our goodbyes.

I can't get out of the cafeteria fast enough, but regret refuses to be ignored, keeping pace behind me as I follow signs to the ER. My shoes squeak on the high gloss tile floors, and the smell of latex gloves and antiseptics burns my eyes.

"Teller, stop," Melanie demands, running to catch up with me. She grabs my wrist, immediately letting go when I turn to face her. "What's going on? You're going to marry Joe's girlfriend?"

Dipping my head back, I swallow hard and breathe before answering, "Ella isn't his girlfriend anymore."

She draws her eyebrows together and says, "That's because he died. How did she end up with your ring on her finger? I thought … I thought you and I—"

Before I can backtrack to the one time I found myself in a bar with Melanie, my Chief Resident summons me to assist an intern set a broken wrist. It's the out I need, offering Mel a sympathetic glance as I retreat, mouthing *I'm sorry.*

"You do realize how fucked up this is, right?" she calls out, unconcerned with our audience.

"Yes," I say, pressing my palms together in a prayer-like gesture. "Forgive me. I really am sorry."

"Dick," she mumbles, throwing her hands up. "It's always the cute ones."

Three hours later, I'm walking through the Pediatric Intensive Care Unit after my shift. The atmosphere on this side of the hospital compared to the emergency room is as different as hot and cold. At this time of night, the lights are turned down low, and the only noise comes from muffled television sets, the hiss of oxygen passing through oxygen masks, and the steady beep from a heart monitor.

"I'm looking for Ella," I whisper once I approach the nurses' desk. "Is she available?"

"She's in room 202," a man replies in a soft tone, pointing me in the right direction.

I stand in the doorway and listen to her read a book to a little girl hooked up to a ventilator in hushed tones and quiet animation. A bouquet of pink roses beside the patient's bed releases a soothing, floral aroma that outweighs the traces of iodine and rubbing alcohol. Glow in the dark stars are glued to the ceiling, and a nightlight in the wall glows yellow and orange.

She finishes the story, leading the girl to the land of dreams before I enter the room and stand behind Ella's chair. Rubbing her shoulders, I bend down and kiss the top of her head, melting when she reaches for my hand and leans into me. We watch the steady rise and fall of her patient's chest, a stark reminder of how fragile life truly is.

"I told you not to stay," she whispers, squeezing my fingers.

"Like I could leave without you," I reply, helping love to her feet.

Ella pauses for a split second before she asks, "Who's Melanie, Tell?"

My response is instant.

Thoughtless.

A lie.

"No one."

CHAPTER TWENTY-THREE

Now

Ella

"Are you enjoying your day off?" Teller asks. I hear the busy hospital in the background—the rustling of paperwork, patients asking when they're going to be seen, a crying child—never slowing down.

"It would be better if you were here," I say, loading the last plate into the dishwasher. I hold my cell phone between my ear and shoulder, drying my hands on a dishtowel. "But I needed a chance to get this place cleaned up. I'm too embarrassed to hire a maid when it's this gross."

Teller laughs through the receiver, and I can picture the smirk curving his lips perfectly. The image shoots a bolt of excitement between my legs, and I close my eyes, exhaling slowly.

"How long have we been back from St. Helena?" he asks.

"Almost five weeks," I reply breathlessly. I blow loose

strands of hair out of my face and distract myself with the mess that was once our living room before it became a closet. "I don't understand how you managed to keep this place neat when you lived alone. You're a slob."

Gathering discarded hoodies, flannels, and jackets Teller's thrown over the couch, the recliner, and the coffee table, I pile them over my arm to carry the haul upstairs to our room when I see the box Kristi's parents dropped off. It's in the same place I last left it, knocked over on its side, collecting dust.

"My mom used to come over and clean," laziness admits, laughing.

"You're so pathetic." I chuckle, layering the last sweater over my arm. "I can't believe you had your mother pick up your mess."

"I didn't ask her to," he says. His carefree tone sets loose butterflies in my stomach. "But I didn't ask her not to either."

"Do you mind if I go through this box, or do you want me to put it somewhere until you can open it yourself?" I kick it upright and turn toward the stairs with a hundred pounds of cotton in my arms.

"The one from Kristi's apartment?" he asks absentmindedly. Teller talks with someone from the hospital about X-ray results on an eighty-three-year-old woman who took a fall and may have fractured her hip. "Baby, I have to handle this. I'll see you when I get home."

"Wait," I exclaim, dropping his belongings onto our bed. If I don't take care of this now, the damn thing will sit beside the door for another month. "What do you want me to do with the box?"

"Burn it, unpack it, throw it away. Do whatever you want, Smella. Who knows what's even inside of it. I didn't stay at Kristi's a lot."

"Okay, sounds good." I sigh, lifting the basket of dirty laundry under my arm to lug back downstairs. "Hurry home."

The next few hours pass in a blur of glass cleaner and Soft Scrub, and this house is way too big for the two of us. But once I get started, there's no stopping me, and for the first time since Joe passed, an entire afternoon goes by that I don't think of him. I concentrate on the music playing from the surround sound and the way my heart pitter-patters when I see my belongings next to Teller's.

Which leads to me remembering the night before.

My cheeks redden.

My heart rate jump-starts.

My lips turn up.

I can almost feel his breath on my neck, his hand tied in my hair … the way he entered me from behind, all at once.

Those thoughts are swept away once I tackle the refrigerator and open a takeout container. The smell nearly knocks me on my ass, stinging my eyes, and tickling my gag reflex. It's not a mistake I make twice, and instead of checking anything for freshness, if I deem it questionable, it goes right into the garbage can.

By the time I'm done, we have a bottle of ketchup, butter, and a few oranges.

"We can't keep living like this," I mumble to myself, tossing a stack of carryout menus into the trash.

I scrub the showers, dust the ceiling fans, and mop the hardwood floors before opening the sliding glass door to consider the backyard. Teller has a pool boy, but going by the amount of leaves in the water, he hasn't been here in a while. Leaving that for last, I pull weeds from the grass, sweep the porch, and throw away plastic cups and beer bottles, which have been out here since who knows when.

Flopping onto the couch, I rest my feet on the table and exhale a large breath through my lips, admiring the cleanliness. My skin's sticky, my hair's shampoo-needy, and my fingers hurt from the amount of scrubbing I did today, but I'm proud of my accomplishments, and this place feels more like home than it ever has.

Teller should be home within the hour, and we have vague dinner plans, so I sit up to take a shower, only to remember the damn Kristi box.

At first glance, there doesn't seem to be anything of much importance inside of it, but I make a *trash pile* and a *keep pile* instead of tossing the entire thing into the dumpster. Another one of Teller's hoodies goes into the *keep pile* and a birthday card from last year goes into the *trash pile*. I trash an old toothbrush and keep a bottle of cologne and a watch. Setting a heap of photos to the side for Tell to deal with, I keep a set of headphones and trash a pair of Kristi's earrings they must have included on accident.

I roll my eyes, tossing one more pullover into the *keep pile*, wondering how many sweaters one man can own when I see the pile of letters at the bottom of the box. Recognizing the penmanship right away, the sheet of paper falls from my hand a few sentences in.

few of my most vivid memories of Joseph are the letters he wrote. He'd leave long declarations of affection taped to my bathroom mirror or folded on my pillow after a sleepover, and hide small notes in my jacket pockets or between book pages to discover at the most unexpected moments. I left a shoebox full of Joe's messages at the apartment with Emerson, unable to part with his unique gesture completely.

But now I know they weren't as special as I thought they were.

I'm not as extraordinary as he convinced me I was.

Standing at the kitchen counter with Joe's letters to Kristi stacked in a neat pile, letters her parents must have supposed Teller wrote, black ink teases me, retelling their affair one sentence at a time.

"We can never tell them..."

"I don't know if I'm in love with her..."

"I've never met anyone like you..."

Teller walks through the front door as I drop my face to my hands and my elbows to the granite countertop, smearing secrets with my devastation.

"They did this to us. They pushed us together..."

"I can't stop thinking of you..."

"Maybe we should come clean..."

He steps into the kitchen cautiously, stopping where hardwood meets tile. The glow in Teller's eyes dims, and his eyebrows come together. "What's the matter, baby?"

"Why are they dragging us along?"

"Do you see how they look at each other?"

"We have nothing to feel guilty about."

Sucking in a large breath, my chin quivers, and I don't

bother hiding ruin from their unknown accomplice—their secret keeper. "Why didn't you fucking tell me?"

"Say the words, Kristi, and we can be together."

"Nothing compares to being inside of you."

"Not even her."

Caught red-handed licks his lips as guilt immediately glistens in his eyes. "How did you find out?"

Laughing bitterly, I crumple the written skeletons in my hand and throw them at him. Six months of lies sashay in the space between us, gliding from one side of the kitchen to the other before sliding beneath the table, next to the coffeemaker, into the sink, and at his feet.

"How could you do this?" I ask, clutching my broken heart. "You son of a bitch."

"Do you think Teller knows?"

"Melanie Garcia…"

"Has he said anything to you?"

Pinching the bridge of his nose, Teller lowers his hand and looks to me with the corners of his mouth turned down. He approaches me cautiously, reaching with a shaky hand. "I was going to tell you, baby."

What should I do when I'm about to lose the love of my life? When the only person who can fix me can no longer do it?

Scream.

"When?" I shove him away, smacking betrayal across the face, clawing at his throat. "After I fucking married him?"

"We should take it easy."

"Let's slow down."

"I can't lose her. I know that now."

Hammering my fists into his chest, Teller comes back for more, following me around the counter. I chuck him into the kitchen table, and he stumbles into the chairs, only to trail me into the living room. He captures my wrist, ducking when I swing my arm around, aiming for his head.

"This was a mistake."

"A lapse in judgment."

"Nobody has to know."

Stronger and faster than me, determination pulls my back against his chest, circling his arms around mine so I can't get away. I cry out, breaking into a million pieces, incapable of keeping it together. He presses his face against mine, cheek to cheek, whispering apologies and promises.

"Forgive me, baby. Forgive me."

His words ring familiar, sparking a fire that incinerates me from the inside out. The pain's unimaginable, crippling, soul-taking. "I'm done, Teller. I can't do this again. I don't have anything left."

"I'm going to ask her to marry me."

"I love her."

"Forgive me."

Turning me around in his arms, he clutches the front of my shirt in his fist and pushes me into the wall. Teller's hands shake, his arms, his shoulders, his eyes. He strengthens his grip on the worn cotton, like I might disappear if he lets go.

"Please don't do this. I'm begging you, Ella. Please don't leave me again."

Driving his body flush against mine, Teller lifts me from my feet, but I don't wrap my legs around his waist. I clench my teeth shut when his tear-soaked kiss touches my mouth and his tongue sweeps across my bottom lip. Turning my head away as his lips journey down my throat, I ask, "Melanie from the hospital. She's Melanie from his letter?"

"Yes," he admits somberly.

"When you found out Joe was sleeping with Kristi, instead of telling me, you fucked her?"

Teller squeezes his eyes shut, resting his forehead on top of mine. "I didn't have sex with her."

"I don't believe you." I shove him away, burrowing my elbow in his chest, pushing the palm of my hand under his jaw, and pulling his hair. He won't budge. His touch is torturous, his words twisting, and all I want to do is comfort him despite the damage he's done.

It's dangerous.

"I love you. I love you so fucking much," he cries.

Sometimes the bad outweighs the good, and sometimes it's better to let go before it kills you.

"It's not enough. Loving me is not enough anymore, Teller," I say, lowering my arms to my sides and going completely still. Breathing heavily, my chest expands, touching his shirt, so I don't breathe until my face burns and he lets me down.

He falls back, narrowing his eyes, but when I attempt to move past him, Teller cages me between his arms. "What are you saying?"

Studying the face of the only person I have ever loved like this, it's nearly impossible not to run my fingers through his hair and kiss his lips just to dissolve this pain. But he isn't mine anymore, and I take off the ring.

"No." His expression crumbles with his tone. "I made

a mistake, Gabriella. It won't happen again."

"I can't marry you, Teller." Tears distort my vision, and I feel my face fall, my heart fall, the world beneath my feet fall. "We tried to make this work, but we're not good for each other."

"How am I supposed to live without you now?" he asks. The muscle in his jaw tenses, protruding the bluish veins in his neck.

"You should have thought about that before you lied to me." I drop the ring, unmoving as it hits the wooden floor, sliding under the coffee table, and spinning to a halt.

I can't forgive him for this.

He crossed the line.

"There's nothing I can say to you?" Teller finally steps away, patting his pockets for a cigarette. His eyes are rimmed red and bloodshot, and he swallows hard, running a hand through his curly hair. "We're over?"

"Yes."

"Where are you going to go?" He sits on the edge of the coffee table, resting his forearms on his knees, keeping his eyes down.

Speaking over the hammering in my chest, I wipe tears from my chin on the back of my hand and say, "Back to St. Helena for a while. We're going to sell the house, so I may as well go up there and get things ready."

Teller looks up, creasing his forehead. "When did you decide you're going to sell it?"

"Today," I answer. "I told Em I'm going to need the money since I resigned at the hospital."

There's a scratch across Teller's cheekbone, and my fingernails are broken. The red marks around his throat and the rip in the neck of his shirt are my doing. Incapable of controlling my hurt and anger, I lashed out, just like I did in Las Vegas, just like I did a hundred times before that.

Realization hurts like the lies he told.

But not nearly as bad as abandonment.

Loneliness, a constant companion who never goes far, creeps in slowly, hardening my bones, my heart, and my spirit. The light inside of me dims, casting dark shadows on my will to be anything other than bitter. Holding the palm of my hand to my chest, I close my eyes and breathe out as walls are built high, leaving me defensive and untrusting.

Everyone I love leaves eventually.

I'm a curse.

"What the fuck, Ella?" Teller stands, cutting me with his eyes. The muscles in his hands flex, and his face burns. "You quit your job? You're moving nine fucking hours away? When will I see you again?"

Pressing my lips together, I lower my stare to the floor before looking up to say, "You won't."

The color drains from his face, and his expression hardens, shutting me out completely. Teller doesn't prevent me from leaving like I assume he will. Quiet rage proceeds to the front door, opening it with such force the knob punctures the drywall, shaking picture frames and windows. Flinching, I cover my mouth with the palms of my hands and freeze as he walks outside. A long moment later, I recover and gather the small bag I packed to spend the night with Emerson and Nic, slinging it over my shoulder.

Teller's retrieving a wooden bat from the trunk of his Range Rover when I join him in the driveway. A lit cigarette hangs between his teeth, and he squints, pulling nicotine and smoke into his lungs.

"I'll call you when my plane lands," I say numbly, unsure if I mean it or not. "My brother's expecting me."

Flicking his Marlboro into the street, Teller exhales a lungful of dense white smoke over his head and smirks. He strokes the bat in his hand, walking past me, around to the driver side of my G-Wagen.

"Don't fucking bother," he says, swinging the slugger across my windshield. Glass splinters, but it doesn't break completely until he hits it again.

"Stop!" I shriek, dropping my backpack. Panic sends a rush of adrenaline through my veins. "What the hell are you doing?"

Both headlights go next and the passenger side window. "Try leaving me now."

"Teller, please stop." Crying out, I watch in horror as he destroys the first thing I bought myself after I graduated from college and got the job at the hospital. Broken shards of glass rain on the driveway, tapping concrete in a melody of destruction.

"Why would I have told you Joe was fucking Kristi?" he asks, bringing the wood down on the back window. "They're dead, Ella. They're gone. Why did it matter?"

"No!" I shout as he breaks the side mirror.

"I didn't want to hurt you more than you already were, baby," he says, eyes alive with madness. He grins. "But now I don't give a fuck. Good luck leaving me now."

Breaking out the driver's side window, Teller drops

the bat, letting it roll down the driveway to the gutter. He crushes broken shards of glass under his shoes, not bothering to look at me before he takes a walk down the street, leaving me to pick up the pieces.

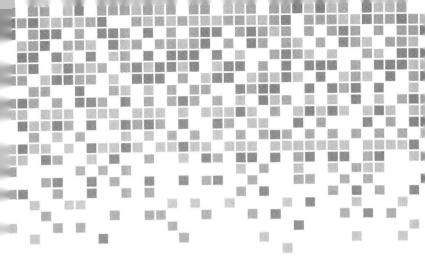

CHAPTER TWENTY-FOUR

Now

Teller

"Hello," she answers the phone.

"Fuck your hello," I say. "Don't say that to me. It's been three weeks, Ella."

She sighs into the receiver. "I'm not ready to come back yet, Tell. I'm still—I'm still thinking about everything."

Cupping my hands over the end of my cigarette in the designated smoking area, I burn paper and tobacco with a match. Sulfur and smoke burn out, and I take a deep drag, needing the chill it gives.

"I got the Wagen fixed," I say, exhaling into the air. An airplane takes off, roaring as it reaches for the night sky. "It's as good as new."

"Do you expect me to thank you?" she answers with an edge to her tone. "Don't hold your breath. Better yet, hold it."

"Please," I reply, unable to keep the corner of my mouth

293

from curving. "Please, come home."

"No."

"Ella?" I say, tossing my cigarette into the street before I go back inside the airport.

"What?"

"Then I'm coming for you."

Sever
(Closer #2)
Early 2017

ABOUT THE AUTHOR

Mary Elizabeth is an up and coming author who finds words in chaos, writing stories about the skeletons hanging in your closets.

Known as The Realist, Mary was born and raised in Southern California. She is a wife, mother of four beautiful children, and dog tamer to one enthusiastic Pit Bull and a prissy Chihuahua. She's a hairstylist by day but contemporary fiction, new adult author by night. Mary can often be found finger twirling her hair and chewing on a stick of licorice while writing and rewriting a sentence over and over until it's perfect. She discovered her talent for tale-telling accidentally, but literature is in her chokehold. And she's not letting go until every story is told.

Follow Mary on Twitter, Facebook, Instagram, and her blog, Mary Elizabeth Literature.

You can also sign up for her newsletter for up-to-date information on her 2017 book releases, including *Sever* (*Closer* #2), and the final installment of the *Closer Trilogy*, *Crawl*.

"The heart is deceitful above all things and beyond cure."—
Jeremiah 17:9

ACKNOWLEDGMENTS

This series is ten years in the making. There's no way to thank every single solitary person who in some way, somehow helped me turn this dream into a reality. But I made a list.

My husband. My children. My family. My animals. As always, thank you for your support and dedication to my craft. Thank you for allowing me to lose myself in these alternate universes I create quietly in my mind. If it were not for you, none of this would be possible.

Catherine Jones. Thank you for taking another ride with me. You are essential to my success. You are the voice of reason.

Amber Sachs. Thank you for helping me bring Teller and Ella to life. I couldn't have done this without you.

Sunny Borek. I wish there was a GIF I can insert here to show my gratitude for EVERYTHING you have done for me. From *Low*, to San Francisco, to Las Vegas, and thousands upon thousands of messages, I literally wouldn't be the author I am today without you. And above all, thank you for being my friend.

EK. Thank you for being the extrovert to my introvert.

Paige Smith. Another one in the bag!

Hang Le. Thank you for making my covers works of art.

Mara White. Thank you for believing in me.

Ellie McLove. #squad

SM: Your words changed my life in ways I never imagined for myself, and in ways you'll never know. Thank you for existing. Thank you for dreaming.

E & B: The originals.

And of course, to my readers. Thank you for wanting this as badly as I do.

64837515R00168

Made in the USA
Charleston, SC
14 December 2016